THE PRODIGAL SON

ROB MACLAINE - BOOK 1

LES HASWELL

1

      ———

ROB MACLAINE SQUEEZED UP TO THE BAR IN THE BUSY RIVERSIDE bar/diner on the Thames embankment and concentrated in attracting the bar staff in an effort to get another round of drinks for him and Joe Harper, who was sitting at a small table in the corner of the busy room. Joe was his business partner and fellow director of Harper MacLaine Security. That day, they'd visited a prospective client to successfully present a final costing for a package of security measures and proposals to them.

On the way back, they'd stopped off to celebrate winning the substantial and very lucrative contract for Harper MacLaine Security and Rob had gone to the bar to get Joe and him another drink. At six foot four in height, Rob rarely had a problem in getting someone's attention when he wanted to and tonight was no exception.

"A Diet Coke and a large Malbec, please" He shouted to a pretty, petite barmaid whose attention he had grabbed.

The Diet Coke for Joe who was driving and the Malbec for himself. He got the drinks and paid or them, then as he was about to turn away from the bar, another customer accidentally nudged him from behind as he reached across Rob to get a wine list from the bar.

"Woah!! Rob warned.

"I beg your pardon, I do apologise, that was entirely my fault" the man said immediately and, seeing the size of the man he had bumped into. He picked up a wine list and with a nervous smile, he hastened down the bar.

"Just as well that was my drink you spilled on me and not your red wine" said a female voice to his left.

ROB SCANNED the woman and her smart mid-blue suit, comprising a short jacket and skirt over a white silk blouse. He noticed liquid had splashed the jacket.

"Sorry, I didn't realise. Will that stain? I'll pay for the cleaning, if necessary," Rob stammered, taken aback.

"Gin & Tonic? No, it will be fine" the woman laughed

Rob stared at the woman. She was beautiful, Rob thought. Even sitting on a bar stool she looked tall and slender. She had long, naturally blond hair pulled back into a ponytail which was set off by large blue/green eyes. Her flawless skin looked tanned and she was smiling at Rob with the most kissable mouth Rob had ever seen. She was looking him in the eye as she said something Rob didn't quite hear.

"Sorry?" he said, as he came back into the room

"I said, its Gin & Tonic it'll be fine" she smiled "just as well it wasn't your drink, or you would have a big cleaning bill"

Rob smiled, "Sorry, yes, red wine does make a bit of a mess when it ends up where it shouldn't be. I must admit to having ruined the odd shirt that way"

He was staring again. The woman was probably a few years younger than Rob, early to mid-thirties Rob would have guessed. His gaze fell to the single-drop pearl necklace that adorned her long slender neck before eyeing the matching earrings. There was no other jewellery. No question, she was stunning.

"Rob, Earth to Rob" a male voice intruded on his thoughts.

"WHAT? Oh, sorry Joe. What did you say?"

Joe Harper was standing beside Rob with his hand on his shoulder

"Going to have to go Rob" he said apologetically "Suzy phoned, she's not feeling too good, so she asked if I would pick up some stuff for her before the pharmacy closes"

"Oh, that's a shame Joe, I hope she feels better soon"

"Wife's pregnant, not having a great time" Joe explained to the woman Rob had engaged in conversation.

"Listen, I'll leave you two children to play. Judging by the looks on your faces, you won't even notice I've gone"

"That's unfair Joe, what am I going to do with a Diet Coke on a Friday night?" Rob chu, motioning the tall ice-filled glass.

"If you're really stuck for ideas, you could always spill it on someone" Joe replied with a wink, "Watch him, he plays dirty" Joe said, touching the woman's shoulder lightly. "Must go, see you Monday bright and early" Joe smiled at Rob with a nod and a wink, and walked off through the crowd to the door

"My partner," Rob explained as they watched Joe amble through the bar.

"Really?" She inclined her head and kept watching.

"Business partner. He's a respectable married man with a very pregnant wife."

"Just teasing. I'd gathered that." She chuckled. "So, what do you guys do when you're not spilling drinks on unsuspecting young ladies?"

"Uh uh!! Friday night, we don't talk about work on a Friday night, sorry. Change the subject!"

SHE MOTIONED the bartender for another gin and tonic, then regarded him intently.

"What does he mean when he says you play dirty, do you spill drinks over all your women?"

"Absolutely, I have it down to a fine art. I never get drunk, just spill most of my drinks over unsuspecting women"

"My name is Rob, as you may have gathered"

"Justine" the blond goddess replied, shaking his hand.

"Look, why don't we grab a table where it's more comfortable, seeing as we both appear to be on our own now. I wouldn't want to risk someone else spilling their drink over you and stealing you away from me" Rod suggested

"OK, I'm wearing your drink now so that makes me yours, is that how it works?" the woman teased Rob

"It's your drink you're wearing and I get the impression you're very much your own woman," he replied with a broad smile and they both chuckled.

They found a table overlooking the Thames embankment and Vauxhall Bridge and spent the next few hours talking animatedly and laughing almost non-stop about all sorts of non-work related things and by late evening they were both quite tipsy when they left the bar and wandered out on to the embankment, Rob's hand resting gently on the back of Justine's neck.

"I love the river at night" Justine said, "My parents have a house on a river and I used to love lying in my bed at night with the window open listening to the river flowing over the rocks"

"You don't live with your parents anymore?"

"No, I live in an apartment in town now. You?"

"No, I don't live with my parents either" Rob teased

"You're being silly now" chided Justine "I meant do you live in town"

"Yes, overlooking the river in fact"

"Really?"

"Yes, just, there" he replied, pointing to the recently completed luxury apartment block on the opposite side of the bridge

"No!"

"Umm, penthouse apartment, top floor"

His companion turned to look at him her big blue/green eyes wide, "No! You're having me on. I don't believe you!" she said

Rob took her hand "All right come on, then"

"What, where are we going? "Justine said, as she followed in Rob's wake along the embankment.

"I'll prove it to you "he said "and, show you the Thames as you have never seen it before."

They stepped out from the living area of Rob's top floor penthouse apartment through the sliding glass doors on to a large curved terrace which overlooked the river Thames, Vauxhall Bridge and the MI6 building directly opposite.

"Wow! Oh wow! You certainly know how to impress a woman, I'll give you that" she said as Rob popped the cork on a bottle of Champagne.

"This is just stunning, absolutely beautiful" she said as she surveyed the view from the terrace.

"Not the only thing of beauty I can see from here" said Rob as he handed her a glass of bubbly

"Umm, flattery will get you everywhere Rob" she said as she snuggled close into him.

"I'm certainly hoping it will" Rob smiled as he kissed her for the first time.

As the evening drew to a close and the early hours of the morning replaced it, the contents of the Champagne bottle disappeared and Rob was vaguely aware of the passage of time as they finally went back into the apartment. They slowly undressed each other, kissing, caressing and exploring until eventually, Rob carried her through to his extra-long king-sized bed and having made love again they fell into a deep sleep in each other's arms

2

Rob woke with a start, his ultra-sensitive inbuilt alarm system telling him that something was wrong. Something moved in the blur that was his" waking up with a hangover world" at that moment. He sat up quickly, his mind focussing instantly and he stared at the blond goddess lying beside him. He had not closed the blinds on the Velux windows in the bedroom ceiling and the dim light from outside illuminated one of her ample breasts as it poked out from under the duvet, reminding him instantly of the magic of the previous night and bringing a smile to his lips. No wonder he felt hungover, God what a night.

Still the alarm bells inside his head were telling him something was not right. A mobile phone was ringing somewhere, wasn't his though, he didn't recognise the ringtone. It must be Justine's, should he wake her and tell her that her mobile was ringing. He glanced at the clock. Five in the morning, they could only have been asleep for a couple of hours. All these thoughts came cascading into his now alert brain in a matter of seconds.

Then suddenly!! The ringtone, "Brown Eyed Girl" from that Van Morrison album, it was *his* mobile. He rolled out of the bed and dashed in the direction of the ringing phone, where the hell was it, this was important, something was wrong. Just after he had left home all these years ago he had given his then new mobile number to Fraser McEwan, his Dad's ghillie. He'd asked that it was only to be used in the event of a dire emergency or crisis and he'd attached "Brown Eyed Girl" as the ringtone for that number only. That was over twenty years ago and he had never heard that ringtone from his mobile, until now.

His pale grey suit jacket lay on the floor by the brown leather corner settee where he had dropped it. It was playing "Brown Eyed Girl" to him. The phone must be in the pocket. As he picked up his jacket, the music stopped before Rob could get the phone out of the pocket.

"Shit! Shit! Shit!" Rob whispered in near panic.

What now! This was new, this had never happened before. Would Fraser leave a voicemail? Should he phone back. What the....?

Rob jumped and almost dropped the phone as "Brown Eyed Girl" started to play again. He stared at the phone for a couple of seconds in sheer disbelieve and then hit the green answer button. He gingerly put the phone to his ear. There was silence at the other end.

"Hello, who is this" Rob enquired tentatively

"Robbie, is that you Robbie?" the woman's voice at the other end asked

Rob hadn't expected a woman's voice. He had given this number to Fraser McEwan, with strict instructions to use it only in an emergency and to give it to no one.

"Robbie, is that you Robbie?" the woman's voice at the other end asked again with added urgency.

"That depends on who's asking?" Rob growled with a touch of anger in his voice.

"Robbie, its Lorna Cameron, Fraser gave me this number, he's in hospital, told me to tell you he needs you here as soon as you can. He needs you right now. I can't talk, it's not safe. I need to go, just get here, Robbie, but be careful. Bruce can't know you're here, Fraser says. Please come Robbie"

"Lorna, Lorna! Are you there? What's the matter? Where's Fraser? What…" Rob suddenly realised that Lorna has ended the call and he was talking to himself. He stared at the phone, what the hell was happening on Achravie.

"Who's Lorna?" Justine's voice from behind Rob asked in a tone that was both curious and petulant at the same time.

"Doesn't matter, another life"

"Matters to me, we've been shagging each other's brains out for the past few hours. Please tell me you're not married Rob" Justine's voice becoming a bit more insistence.

"No, I'm not married…" snapped Rob turning to face the source of the questions. She was standing in the doorway between the lounge and his bedroom wearing a pair of very brief white panties and an "I'm not happy "look. Her arms were folded across her chest to cover her ample breasts.

Rob stared at her for a moment. God she was beautiful, tall, graceful and seemingly intelligent if last night's conversation was anything to go by. They had just instantly clicked last night after Rob had accidentally spilled that small amount of her G&T over her jacket in the bar." sorry" had been the first word Rob had spoken to her, but now he was saying "sorry" again.

"Sorry, I didn't mean to snap. Sorry, sorry, you didn't deserve that" he said with genuine remorse.

"Look, please don't take this the wrong way, but I have an urgent and by the sounds of it" he said holding up the mobile phone," serious family problem that I need to attend to. I know this sounds like a brush off but please believe me it isn't. This has come totally out of the blue. I didn't expect that call, as you may have noticed and please believe me, I would rather go back to bed with you, get up, get showered make us breakfast and then see where the day takes us. Sadly, I need to be in Scotland as of now!"

"OK", she said a little uncertainly," I understand, I think. Can I do anything to help?"

"Probably not, best if you just grab you kit and let me get on with it. I'll get you a minicab."

"Oh, right! Leggy blond, good tits, nice arse, must be thick! Is that where your tiny man brain is taking you" the semi naked blond goddess snapped as she gathered up her clothes, turned and stomped back into the bedroom heading to the en-suite bathroom to get dressed.

Rob followed her back into the bedroom, pulled a robe from a hook behind the bedroom door and shrugged it on.

"Justine, no, I'm sorry, that's not what I meant. God, I seem to be constantly apologising, sorry!"

"Shit! There, I've done it again" Rob said to the bathroom door

"Look, I'd like to make this up to you when I get this "thing" sorted out at home"

"Don't bother, I meet guys like you every other day. Think women like me are just brainless eye candy, only good for one thing!" the door replied.

As Rob turned away from the door, he almost tripped over a small white clutch bag which had fallen on the floor and spilled most of its contents on to the carpet. As he picked it up, a driver's licence fell to the floor, Rob picked it up, his natural curiosity getting the better of him. The photograph on the licence was indeed Justine's. Her name was Justine Fellows. Justine Fellows, how did he know that name Rob wondered? Justine Fellows, Justine....

The bathroom door burst open, banging against the doorstop and Justine Fellows, now fully dressed strode into the room, glowering ay Rob.

"What are you doing? That's my purse, give me it please, I *am* just leaving I'm told"

Rob stared at her in disbelief as a penny dropped somewhere deep in his head.

"Your Andy Savage's PA" he said as she grabbed the purse driver's licence and brushed past him towards the door.

She stopped, turned round and returned his stare. "Sir Andrew, yes. Do you know Andrew Savage?

"Yes, I know him very well. We've actually spoken on the phone, but strangely enough, we've never met" Rob said

Narrowed eyes regarded him closely. "How do you know Sir Andrew? Is he the reason you chatted me up last night?"

"No, no, I didn't realise until just now. I saw your surname on your driver's licence and put two and two together."

"Thank God for that. How do you know Sir Andrew?"

"My company provides all his corporate and close personal security"

Justine Fellows stood transfixed for moment, and then her hand went to her mouth, "Oh God, your Rob MacLaine, Harper MacLaine Security! You had dinner with him on Wednesday. Oh my God, how embarrassing. I had no idea!"

She thought for a minute," The guy with you last night at the bar, was that......?"

"Joe Harper? Yes"

"Oh my God, it gets worse. He's going to know that we..."

"No, no, no, that's cool. Joe left before us. As far as anyone knows we had a few drinks, you went home, I went home on my own. God no, I wouldn't embarrass you like that.

When Rob MacLaine left the SAS five years earlier, he had already done much of the groundwork to utilise his undeniable skills, honed in the darkest corners of twenty first century wars. He had met and worked with Joe Harper a fellow covert operative who left the service a few months ahead of him. Rob had very few friends and was very slow to trust and connect with people but he and Joe had very quickly cemented a relationship of trust and respect which had in time blossomed into a deep, lasting friendship.

Between them they founded and ran Harper MacLaine Security, a company which provided high end corporate security and close personal protection to small number of clients around the western world. Sir Andrew Savage, Chairman and CEO of SGS (Savage Guidance Systems) was one of Harper MacLaine Security's biggest clients to whom they provided both security consultancy and personal protection. SGS manufactures infrared missile guidance systems, passive weapon guidance systems which use the infrared (IR) light emission from a target to track and follow it. He and Rob had developed a personal friendship which on occasions took them outside of business. This was not something either man normally advocated, but Rob wondered if Sir Andrew saw him as a surrogate son to fill a gap created when his own son had been killed in action in Afghanistan. Either way, both were comfortable with the situation.

"Look Justine, I really meant what I said about a serious family problem. I need to get to Achravie"

"Achravie?" Justine asked

"Achravie, its little island off the west coast of Scotland, sits between Arran and the Mull of Kintyre. My family live there, own pretty much the whole island in fact. It's my ancestral home as they say, been in the family for generations. Not the easiest place to get to, as it happens but I need to get there, sharpish.""

Justine frowned at Rob, "How serious, how urgent *is* your "serious" family problem Rob"

Rob sighed, "It's a long story Justine. Suffice to say that I left home twenty odd years ago, when I was just a teenager, in the bad books to put it mildly. I've had no contact with my family since I left, apart from a few letters from a guy called Fraser McEwan, my father's ghillie. I gave Fraser my mobile number not long after I left and told him that if there was ever an emergency or if he ever needed me, he should contact me on that number and never, ever to give the number to anyone else. That call was, Lorna Cameron—she and I were close when we were young and he told her to call me.

That call is the first contact I have had with Achravie in twenty years. Lorna said that Fraser needed me, as in, now, but that my brother Bruce shouldn't know I was there. She said Fraser is in hospital, said it wasn't safe to talk and hung up. Her last words were "*Please come Robbie*"

"Wow, no wonder you wanted me gone. But please, let me help, I *can* help you know, I'm used to making travel arrangements for Sir Andrew and you are going to need to travel quickly. Let me make a couple of calls and you go get your things together"

"OK, thanks, that would be good" said Rob rather than waste time arguing with a very determined sounding Justine and went into the en-suite for a shower. As he cleaned his teeth he contemplated have a quick shave but decided against it.

When Rob left Achravie he left as a tall, skinny, clean-shaven spotty teenager and he resolved to look as little like that boy as he could on his return. At six foot four, Rob was still tall but his years in the military and as a Special Forces operative had seen him transformed from gangly youth to a powerful, athletic man with broad shoulders a deep chest and well developed arm and leg muscles. A petulant teenage had given way to a highly trained, combat hardened ex-soldier—a very dangerous man to cross swords with. He looked at his face in the mirror. His long blond curly hair of boyhood was now cut fashionably short and a white scar which ran diagonally across his left cheek gave a rakish look to his otherwise handsome good looks. Only the vivid, bright blue eyes of the boyish Robbie MacLaine remained in the face that looked back at the thirty four year old Rob MacLaine.

3

HAVING SHOWERED, ROB DRESSED AND WENT THROUGH TO HIS study which the estate agent had described as Bedroom 3 when he had bought the penthouse apartment just over a year ago. This required a four-digit access code to unlock the door and from it, he could view the opposite end of Vauxhall Bridge.

The MI6 building was directly opposite and Rob had almost convinced some of his friends at the bar one night, that he could actually see into James Bond's office from this room. He crossed the study and opened a half height door to the rear of the room to expose a good sized safe which he now opened by inputting another numerical code.

He pulled out a black waxed canvas rucksack which he kept prepacked with essentials for times like this, times when he needed to move quickly, unzipped it and checked its contents, changes of clothes, some toiletries, a passport and drivers licence. His military training had taught him that no matter how sure you are of something, always check. Better to be safe than sorry, better to stay alive than be killed, he had been told.

Rob took out another metal case and again checked the contents, this time a Heckler & Koch SFP9-SF pistol. He quickly disassembled, checked and reassembled the weapon and was in the process of replacing it in the case when Justine swung open the study door and walked in.

"Oh my God, you have a gun?

"Once a Boy Scout, always a Boy Scout. Boy Scout's moto," Be Prepared""

"Don't you need a licence for that? Wow, what am I getting into here"

"Nothing Justine, you just offered to arrange some travel for me and that's all. And, yes, I need a licence to own a gun and I need separate approvals in the UK to take it with me on a commercial flight and I have both."

"You're taking it with you?" she exclaimed

"Yes, I'm sure I'm not going to need it but I've got a bad feeling about this whole thing Lorna said Fraser was in hospital, but not why he was there. She also said it wasn't safe. So just in case, it comes with me"

He shut the case, stuffed the gun case into the rucksack, on top of the leather sheath housing a black KA-BAR, Serrated Edge Tactical knife with a razor sharp seven inch blade, which Justine had not seen. He closed and locked the safe, stood up and turned to faced Justine.

"So tell me about my journey to Achravie, Miss PA, what have you booked in the way of flights? How am getting there and most importantly when will be on the island?"

"Well, actually" Justine replied with a mischievous look, "I spoke to Sir Andrew, told him that I kind of knew you already through your dealings with the company and had bumped into you last night. I said you got a call while I was with you to say that there was a serious family at home problem which you needed to attend to and suggested to him that as Peter Hall, his pilot, had flagged up that he was light on flying hours this quarter he might cement relationships between our two companies by having Peter fly you north. Two birds, one stone.

Andy rather likes you anyway so it wasn't too hard a sell and probably not a bad thing if you're going to tote that thing around with you" Justine said pointing at the rucksack.

"Your joking Justine, you've borrowed Andy's chopper?"

"I WOULDN'T PUT it that way" she said raising an eyebrow, "Lets stick with helicopter, shall we?"

As she walked from the room, she called back to Rob, "Just let me know when you want to leave and I will set things up with Peter, he'll meet you at the Savage building"

Rob followed Justine through to the lounge where she was looking out through the glass doors at the views across the Thames. He stood behind her and put his arms around her slender waist, pulling her back towards him.

"Thank you for doing that, I really appreciate it" he said kissing the back of her neck lightly.

She turned in his arms reaching up to touch the end of his nose with the her finger and said, "You can show your appreciation when you get back big boy, now while Peter is getting organised at his end, how about that breakfast you mentioned earlier. Then, we'll head out."

Joe had been driving the previous day, so Rob's car had been left in the underground garage at his apartment. It was merely a matter of picking up Justine's black Mercedes SLK from the car park at the bar and then driving over to the Savage building to meet up with Sir Andrew's pilot and helicopter. On the way there, Rob had called Joe to fill him in on the morning's events, including Justine's overnight stay, after Justine had reluctantly agreed, having been assured of Joe's discretion.

"There has to be something seriously wrong Joe. I gave Fraser McEwan that number about twenty years ago and he has never called me. Now all of a sudden I get a message to say he needs me, like now, right now. He says my brother can't know that I'm there and that I need to be careful because it's danger-ous" Rob explained to Joe.

"OK, I'll get Eve to clear your diary for a few days, first thing on Monday. Do you need me to do anything else?"

"No, I'm sorted at this end. I've got a bag with me so I have pretty much got everything I need for a few days. Justine has somehow managed to persuade Andy Savage to give me his chopper and pilot for the day, gave him some excuse about making up flying hours she says, but I think there's maybe a bit more to it than that" Rob smiled across at Justine as he said this. "Do you remember "Big Mac", Iain MacDonald, one of the snipers we worked with in Helmand?"

"Yeah, yeah, big guy. About seven foot tall and built like a brick shithouse wall, if I remember rightly"

"Yeah, maybe a bit of an exaggeration, but yeah, big guy. Anyway he kept in touch from time to time and he runs an Adventure Training Camp thing on Arran, about half an hour from the Achravie ferry, would you believe. I gave him a call and he is going to meet us and let me have a vehicle to use for a few days. I thought a helicopter landing on Achravie might just attract attention, so I'm going to his and driving down from there."

"Have you got any hardware with you Rob?"

"Just my Boy Scout stuff"

"I take it that means a handgun and a rather large knife. Boy Scout stuff!" Joe scoffed," Baden Powell would turn in his grave, man. Just remember, you're going to Achravie not Kosovo. Don't go re-enacting the gunfight at the OK Corral, I don't want you getting locked up"

"No, no. I just need to take a look, see what's going down, I'm not going to engage if it seems any way dangerous. I'll talk to Fraser and see what the problem is." Rob assured Joe.

Joe was less than convinced, having seen first-hand Rob's ability to create mayhem in a combat situation "OK, but keep me in the loop. If you drop out of contact for more than twenty four hours, I might have to come looking for you. Text me a number for "Big Mac"

"OK, daddy. I'll be a good boy. I'll text you that number and I'll report back every twenty four hours. See you soon" Rob cut the call then texted "Big Mac's" contacts to Joe.

Justine drove quickly and confidently through the traffic which was now building to it's Saturday morning peak as people headed for offices, shops. As they approached the Savage Building in Chiswick, Justine glanced across at Rob.

"I like you, Rob MacLaine. I don't say that often or lightly."

"I like you too Justine" Rob said, smiling and reaching across to touch her hand which was resting on the gear-lever. "Does that make you my girlfriend?" he teased. "Can't remember when I last had a girlfriend. One night stands, yeah, but not someone that I really liked and wanted to spend more time with." He said smiling

Justine nodded to the security guard at the gate as she presented her pass to the panel on the post beside the main entrance barrier to Savage Guidance Systems. The barrier lifted and she drove to the parking bay beside the main reception, parked her car, threw the gear-lever into park and took out the ignition key.

"Let's go" she said "Pete will be waiting on the roof"

She blipped the remote and the indicators blinked as she led Rob through the automatic doors and over to the elevators. As the doors closed, cutting them off from the rest of the world and the elevator rose smoothly towards the rooftop helipad, Justine looked over at Rob again as she had done in the car with a wistful smile on the lips.

"I don't trust easily Rob, too many broken hearts in the past, please don't play with me"

"I won't Justine, I promise you"

"My friends call me Tina"

"Am I your friend?

"Yes Rob MacLaine, I think you are, which means I can say, "You look after yourself". Don't take any chances up there, do you hear!"

"Oh God, I'm falling for a nagging woman" Rob laughed, pulling her toward him.

"Is that what you're doing, falling for me?"

"Mm, yes, I do believe I am," he smiled as he kissed her lightly on the lips

Justine was about to say something else but suddenly the elevator doors opened and there stood a smiling Peter Hall. The two jumped apart quickly. "Hi Justine. Hello again Mr MacLaine" he said jovially. "All ready to go?"

"If you need anything Rob, give me a call or a text" Justine said, pulling a business card out of her purse and handed it to Rob. "Otherwise, call me when you get a chance, Bye for now". She blew Rob a kiss as Peter Hall turned away.

PETER HALL HAD MET Rob MacLaine on a number of occasions when the later was providing Sir Andrew Savage with personal protection. He was not a talkative man, experience over the years had taught him that the people he flew about the country and into Europe did not normally want to have an ongoing conversation when they were traveling so he did not try to engage Rob in conversation when he saw his eyes flutter then close, soon after the Agusta 109 E Grand Helicopter took-off.

But Rob was not asleep, he was remembering the events of twenty years ago, the events that led to his acrimonious departure from his home and family, sent away in disgrace by his father, blamed by his brother Bruce for accident he did not cause.

4

ACHRAVIE JANUARY 1996

Fifteenth of January, a cold winter's night, but it was Robbie MacLaine's eighteenth birthday party in the library of Hillcrest House where Robbie lived with his father Andrew his mother Elizabeth, his eldest brother Angus and his middle brother Bruce.

Like most boys who were brought up on a large estate like Achravie, or any sizable farm for that matter, Robbie was an accomplished driver before his eighteenth birthday having driven cars, Land Rovers, quadbikes and tractors about the estate from the day his feet reached the pedals. It was therefore no surprise that Robbie was due to sit his driving test the very next week and on the expectation of his passing, his father bought him his first car for his eighteenth birthday. A shiny, if not new Ford Escort sat on the drive outside the house.

The music was loud, the dancing was in full swing and the boys' parents had beaten a discreet retreat for an early night to leave the young ones to enjoy the night. At about ten o'clock someone suggested that they should all go down to the Red

Lion the local hotel which was about a mile or so from the Hill-crest road end. The theory being that this would allow Robbie his first legal pint in a pub, so the party decanted into four cars and set off down the hill.

"We'll take your car," shouted Bruce to Robbie as they raced down the front steps of the big house. "You can drive with your L plates up and I'll sit beside you. I'll not drink a lot and drive you back, which is only fair; it's your birthday."

"OK, sounds good to me" shouted Robbie excitedly diving into the car to drive it for the first time.

FRASER MCEWAN the ghillie watched them, as Robbie who at his age resembled a six foot something skeleton with a skin-graft, racked the driver's seat of the Escort right back to allow his tall frame a comfortable driving position.

"He's needed to do that for a few years now" Fraser McEwan mused and he laughed to himself. Strange how two boys from the same parents could look so different, Robbie six foot odd, lanky, all arms and legs and Bruce, a full head shorter and stocky, more like his father's build he thought.

Robbie felt good driving his own car for the first time. The tractors and Land Rovers were good fun when you're a boy he thought.

"This Escort really motors compared to the stuff on the estate" he shouted to Bruce and the others in the car.

In no time at all they had reach the Red Lion and piled out of the car into the car park.

"Mind out" shouted Lorna Cameron "This car park is getting icy"

Bursting in through the front door into the public bar Robbie was first to the bar

"This rounds on me Hamish" he said loudly to Hamish

Allen, the landlord. The music and chatter seemed unusually loud. "And mine's a pint o' lager"

"Whit's awe this" Hamish shouted back "Wee boys comin' in tae ma pub and wantin' to buy drink?"

"Wee boys my arse Hamish, eighteen today, so as of now you're talking to a man no a wee boy. Anyway, I've been about six inches taller than you for the past three years or so, so we'll have less of the "wee boy"" Robbie laughed.

"Aye, OK, OK. A knew it wis yer birthday, fur yer dad left some money behind the bar fur yer first round, so put yer money away for the time being anyway. Right lads and lasses whit'll it be" he shouted above the others and started pouring drinks for the revellers.

The bar closed at eleven o'clock but as is common in many small village pubs and hotels, Hamish served a few more rounds of drink, including a few more pints of lager for Robbie, behind the closed doors.

By midnight the shutters were down on the bar and as the last of the revellers left the bar to go home, mostly in the village, Bruce and Sheila Stewart whose father worked on the estate poured the by now semi-conscious Robbie into the back of the Escort. Lorna Cameron lived in the village like most of the others and as she started to walk back home shouted to the others "Watch these roads, it's getting really icy now."

A few moments later Robbie's blue Escort shot past her heading for the Hillcrest Estate.

Robbie couldn't remember much of what happened next. In his drunken stupor, he felt a sudden impact and heard the distant crunch of metal against something solid and the sound of glass breaking and falling around him. He then vaguely felt himself being lifted off the floor of the car and lifted outside.

He remembered vomiting over his jacket and trousers and then he blacked out.

He awoke to the sound of voices, shouting. He was aware of flashing blue and red lights. He was being pulled roughly from the car. Now he was sitting in an ambulance, someone was trying to clean vomit and blood from him.

Someone else was asking him, "Can you hear me son? Can you speak? What happened?"

"I don't know what happened", mumbled Robbie, "I was sleeping on the back seat, ask Bruce, he was driving. I don't know what happened. Ask Sheila, she'll tell you what happened. This is crazy, what's going on? What's happening?" I'm going to be sick again." Robbie vomited on to the floor of the ambulance, just before he passed out again.

When Robbie woke up again he was lying in a hospital bed wearing a surgical gown and an oxygen mask. He has tubes coming out of his arms and he was sore all over. He opened his eyes when he felt movement beside him and looked over to see his mother sitting on an upright chair beside his bed.

"Robbie, darling, how do you feel? She said leaning over to touch his arm

"Sore, mum, sore all over" Robbie said pushing the oxygen mask aside. "Where am I?" he asked

"You're in the Cottage Hospital, Robbie. Do you not remember the accident?"

"Accident? What happened? Where's Bruce? Is he all right?" Robbie started to get more agitated as some of the events of the previous night came back to him. The impact, the noise, being lifted from the car, the ambulance. Oh God his new car.

"Is the car OK Mum? Can we get it fixed?" he felt tears coming to his eyes.

"Do you really not remember what happened? Were you really so drunk that you don't remember the accident?" his mother asked through fresh tears, as if she could not believe has son had gotten so drunk.

"MOTHER! I don't remember anything! I was sound asleep in the back seat when it happened. Ask Bruce, he was driving" Robbie pleaded

"Andrew? Andrew! Come here" his mother shouted loudly "Andrew, leave that, come here"

His father appeared at the door "What is it Elizabeth? His father asked impatiently. Elizabeth was his mother's name when his father was angry or upset. Lizzie at any other time but his father was clearly angry.

"Robbie says Bruce was driving, says he was sound asleep in the back of the car, says he doesn't remember a thing about the accident"

His father stared down at the two of them, first Robbie and then his wife "Aye, doesn't remember a thing because he nearly four times over the drink drive limit, drunk as a skunk, that's why he can't remember anything. "He turned back to Robbie "And now he has the cheek to say Bruce was driving"

Robbie looked at his Dad in horror "What! What are you saying? Bruce *was* driving! Did Bruce say I was driving?" he gasped. "No, I wasn't, I was absolutely out of it. I couldn't walk never mind drive. Bruce and Sheila dumped me in the back when we left the pub, Bruce said he would drive back when we were leaving the house. Dad! Ask Sheila, she'll tell you"

"Ask Sheila, ask Sheila, I wish to God I could as Sheila. Sheila's dead Robbie. You've killed her!"

He watched in horror as his Dad fled the room and turned to look at his mother as she sat, her body racked with sobs as she stared at him in disbelief.

. . .

"How could you Robbie? Bad enough to get drunk and kill a wee girl, but to try and blame poor Bruce, I can't believe any son of mine would do that" she sobbed and without another word, rose and walked out of the room. That was the last time Robbie had spoken to his mother.

5

ROB'S THOUGHTS WERE INTERRUPTED BY PETE HALL. "WE'RE almost there Mr MacLaine" he said glancing over at Rob, who had chosen to sit in the second crew seat rather than the separate passenger cabin to the rear of the Agusta 109 E helicopter "The co-ordinates you gave me"

"Sorry Pete, I was miles away. What did you say?"

"We're pretty close to the co-ordinates you gave me. I take it you've never been here before".

"OK, eh, no, I've never been here, but we're being met by an old buddy of mine from the army. He knows we're coming and he gave me the co-ordinates. Said it was the easiest way. He runs one of these survival boot camps for corporate team building and homemade Rambos with too much money. The site has a marked helipad, so we should be OK".

"OK, couple more minutes Mr MacLaine"

Presently, the white Agusta 109 E Grand with its grey and yellow markings, banked to the left and started and started its descent as Pete Hall saw the large white H painted on the tarmac at the end of a largish car park. In close proximity was a long, low stone building with a new grey tiled roof. As he approached the helipad he could see a number of cars and a black 20 seater Mercedes Sprinter minibus parked close to the building. In the middle of the carpark well away from the building and the helipad sat a black 5 door Land Rover Defender 110. A huge man was standing beside it, obviously waiting for the Agusta to land.

"Looks like we've got a welcoming committee, friendly, I hope" said Pete as he eased the Agusta to the ground, "From the size of him, I'd rather have him as friend than an enemy" he added with a laugh.

"Oh, trust me, Pete, you definitely wouldn't want Big Mac as an enemy. Fortunately, he's a friend, a very good friend at that".

Rob jumped down from the Agusta and shoulders hunched against the downdraft from the rotors, strode across the tarmac to meet his friend. They stood looking at each other for a few seconds, shook hands quickly and then both stepped forward. Peter Hall winced as this six foot seven giant of a man enveloped Rob in a tight bear-hug which Rob returned with the same gusto. These were obviously old friends. Pete Hall walked slowly over to the two men carrying Rob's bag which he had collected from the Agusta, giving them time to greet each other. Rob turned round to Pete and made the introductions.

"Pete, this is Iain MacDonald, my old buddy from my days in the forces. His friends call him Big Mac, for obvious reasons. I don't know what his enemies call him, he killed most of them" Rob laughed at the expression of apprehension on Pete's face as Iain "Big Mac" MacDonald stuck out a huge paw of a hand for Pete to shake.

"Joking, Pete" Rob laughed Mac this is Pete Hall. I let Pete drive today" Rob winked.

"Good to meet you Pete" the giant of a man said. His voice was unexpectedly soft and almost lyrical with his west highland accent, his handshake firm but not crushing, much to Pete's relief. "Let's get inside" he said. He swung Rob's bag into the back of the Land Rover, and the trio climbed in, and Big Mac drove off.

HE DROVE PASSED THE LONG, low building at the end of the car park turned right on to well-maintained tarmac road and accelerated quickly away. The Land Rover engine sounded unexpectedly throaty and the vehicle felt very responsive to the throttle Pete noticed, but he said nothing. The man driving, however, noticed his expression.

"6.2 Litre V8, 430BHP or there about is the answer to the question your face is asking" Big Mac smiled back to Pete via the rear view mirror.

"Jeez, it must fly!" Pete answered after a moment's thought

"No, I'll leave the flying to you Pete. But it does motor along fairly rapidly" smiled Big Mac with a note of pride in his voice and the three men laughed.

"What the hell do you want with a beast like this Mac?" said Rob

"Ah well, it's for towing my caravan up Ben Nevis" Big Mac explained

"A caravan, up Ben Nevis, surely that's against the law?" Pete asked with a note of concern.

The two big men in the front of the Land Rover almost exploded with laughter at Pete's obvious concern.

"One thing I should have told you about Big Mac explained Rob, "When he comes away with something as ridiculous as taking a caravan up Ben Nevis, nine times out of ten, he's extracting the urine. Problem is, on the tenth occassion, he's serious!" The two men laughed again and Pete joined in.

As this joke at Pete's expense was playing out, Big Mac had turned off the main road onto a narrower drive which led up to a long, low, stone built house, a professional barn conversion, which provided a main open plan living/dining/kitchen area, three bedrooms and two bathrooms.

HOMEMADE LENTIL SOUP preceded a lamb stew Big Mac had had cooking in a slow cooker. Once sated, they assembled on a long leather sofa situated before a large fireplace. Although high-landers were expected to sit with a "wee dram", the three men shared an excellent bottle of Argentinian Malbec before Pete announced he wanted to get an early start; he excused himself and went to bed.

"Let's go for a wee stroll" suggested Big Mac and he and Rob walked through the small garden to a gazebo at the far end. As the two friends sat down Big Mac looked across at Rob,

"So, what brings you to see me in such a hurry? Sounded serious Rob"

"I wish I knew Mac, I got a panic phone call from someone at home to say there was something seriously wrong and Fraser McEwan needed me urgently. That's all I've got, but I know the caller, or did do twenty years ago, we were really close at the time. She wouldn't call like that if it was a wind-up"

Mac already new about that episode in Rob's life, Rob had told him during a long night in the Iraqi desert. Rob recounted the conversation with Mac and the big man's brow knitted into deeper furrows as Rob told him.

"Could be anything Rob, but yer right to be prepared for all eventualities, the lass sounded genuinely scared. What do you need from me other than transport? I've a fair stash of fire-power if you think you might need something there."

Rob sat upright and looked over at Mac "Really! You never fail to surprise me Mac, what the hell do you need with "a fair stash of firepower" in the Scottish highlands. Surely these nationalists are not that scary?"

. . .

"MAN NEVER KNOWS when he might need what" said Mac with a slight peeve in his voice. I do a wee bit of supply from time to time. Only reputable clients mind, guys like yourself, in security, working abroad"

Rob shook his head, "I might have known the centre didn't quite pay for this lot" he said gesturing towards the cottage and the two Land Rovers parked in the drive.

"I think I just need wheels, if you can do that. I have a handgun and a big scary knife in my bag. I won't need any more than that, surely"

"Yer heading for Achravie Rob, no Afghanistan, with any luck you'll no need any o' that. Bang a few heads together and off, back to being a big southern softie again".

Rob rose from the gazebo "Aye, right, as we Scots would say" grinned Rob, "I'm off to bed, busy day tomorrow"

""We Scots" he says, with a southern softies accent like that. You sound no more Scottish than Lulu on the Graham Norton Show." Big Mac laughed and slapped Rob's shoulder with one of his giant hands as they walked back to the cottage.

6

ACHRAVIE January 1996

Robbie's side ward door burst open and there stood Fraser McEwan with an angry look on his weathered face and a rucksack hanging from his shoulder. He tossed a carrier bag on to Robbie's bed. "Right lad, get dressed and make it quick, I'll be outside".

That was the start of the rest of Robbie's life. The start of a journey which would take an eighteen years old Robbie MacLaine from privileged, naïve, gangly lad who wanted for nothing, and mould him into a tall, muscular, confident, worldly wise Rob MacLaine. Ex-army, ex Special Forces covert operative, trained in close quarter battle and sniper techniques. Now Managing Director of Harper MacLaine Security, financial independent and secure, Rob MacLaine was now barely recognisable as the young inexperienced Robbie that Fraser had spirited away from Achravie that cold morning in January 1999.

The journey started in a Glasgow Army Recruiting office with Fraser McEwan and saw a few strings being pulled and favours called in by Fraser and shortly after, entry for Robbie into Fraser's old regiment and that of his father, the Black Watch.

Fraser had stayed with Robbie during these few weeks and had guided a very confused and frightened Robbie through a brief period where he believed he held no control.

Robbie had tried to talk to Fraser about the accident, Bruce, his father and poor Sheila Stewart. What about the police, what about Sheila's family? What about the truth, he wasn't driving the car. Fraser just would not be drawn on these questions. All he would say was that Robbie should forget about that night, it had never happened. His father had spoken to a few people, arrangements had been made, pains had been eased, difficult decisions had been made and Fraser had been instructed to get Robbie off the island as soon as possible. Out of sight, out of mind, Fraser had said

Fraser prepared to leave Robbie in Glasgow and drive back to Achravie, and Robbie packed to leave for Fort George in Inverness later that morning to start a new life. Before he left, however, Fraser stood in front of Robbie and put his hands on the young man's shoulders.

"Robbie it breaks my heart, the way things happened. I never expected to be telling you these things, lad. Your father said never to get in touch with the family or your friends on Achravie. He's put some funds into a bank account to see you started, and I pulled strings to ease you into my old regiment."

Robbie felt a lump in his throat. Basically, his father was disowning him, throwing him out of the family home and off the island, and pushing him away from his friends.

Fraser's eyes filled with tears as he spoke" No matter what you may, or may not have done and if it's any consolation to you, I don't think you've done anything here, but what I think doesn't count. Their minds are made up Robbie and I can't change that". Fraser held out one of his estate business cards. "Regardless of that, here's my mobile phone number on the card. I've scored out the landline 'cause it diverts to the office at the house if I don't pick up. If you ever need me boy, you call me, I'll always be there for you Robbie as long as I have breath in my body."

Fraser embraced Robbie quickly and awkwardly, picked up his bag, walked out of the room and closed the door behind him.

Behind that closed door, Robbie sat on the end of the bed, the reality of it all suddenly hitting him and he burst into tears. His body racked with sobs, tears streaming down his youthful face, he looked up and saw himself in the dressing table mirror. As he looked in that mirror, a coldness descended over him and he felt a change in himself, a determination grew. Robbie wiped the tears, walked into the bathroom, blew his runny nose, then washed and dried his face. Simple acts, but acts that he would remember all his life as the time when he left Robbie MacLaine behind and his new life began.

7

Rob woke early the next morning, not having slept well. Thinking about the events of the past and wondering what would face him today, had kept him tossing and turning before finally falling into restless sleep.

Climbing out of bed slowly, he wandered naked into the en suite and eyed himself in the full-length mirror. Obviously not designed for tall men, it cut off the top of his head. Critically, he eyed the broad shoulders, flat muscled stomach, and brawny, almost hairless chest. The long toned legs belonged to a man who could still run for miles up and down the Welsh mountains, something the SAS was partial to, regardless of the weather, wearing full kit.

While the memories of various trials would be permanently etched in his memory, the body also bore recollections of battles past—via the sundry of scars, times when things hadn't gone to plan. Two bullet scars in his right arm and knife marks in his left shoulder and left thigh bore testament to the fact that Rob had seen much action during his time in the military. All too vividly, he remembered the events that had led to all of them.

He also had that very noticeable white scar that ran diagonally from the centre of his left cheek to his jaw line. Leaning over the wash-hand basin, he touched the scar that was easy to forget as he went about his daily life. He'd hated it at first, was very self-conscious about it, even trying to conceal it with makeup until a colleague had asked, "Are you wearing makeup, you big Nancy?"

He'd never done that again and had slowly gotten used to it being there—and to the fact that most people let their gaze wander to it as they spoke.

THAT WAS one of the things he'd liked about Justine when they'd met that evening in the bar. She had reached over, fingered the scar, and casually enquired, "Cut yourself shaving?"

"My last girlfriend had a really sharp tongue," he'd quipped. "she had to go before she did real damage." He inclined his head and raised an eyebrow. They had laughed and the scar was out of the way, she hadn't even looked at it again as they talked and more.

Now he studied his face in the mirror. It was deeply tanned, a handsome face, no doubting that. There were small creases across the forehead, small lines around the eyes. But the eyes, young Robbie's eyes. Anyone on Achravie who knew Robbie would recognise these eyes.

Time to do something about that. He reached into his toilet bag and brought out two plastic contact lens cases. He had realised during his first deployment in the Middle East that the locals in general had brown eyes. With the vivid blue eyes that Rob had, he stood out a mile, no matter what he wore or how bushy his beard was. Simple answer, brown coloured contact lenses and bingo, instant Arab.

So once again a set of Rob's brown contacts were deployed. He blinked as the lenses settled on his eyes and looked in the mirror again to see the results. He smiled, to anyone who had known Robbie, brown eyes were a better disguise than glasses and a moustache. He then showered and went about darkening his hair, again a well-worn road for Rob to travel. Fair hair and blue eyes in Afghanistan were both dead giveaways, both easily rectified.

He padded through to the kitchen area, following his nose to the source of the coffee aroma and found Big Mac sitting on a bar stool studying his laptop screen.

"Mornin' Mac, heard Pete leave when I was in the shower"

"Yeah, he said to say cheerio. Said he had to fly!" Big Mac smiled at his pun as he raised his head to look at Rob.

"Ah, I see my brown eyed handsome man has reappeared" he chuckled

"I thought it might be a good idea", Rob said with a hint of embarrassment in his voice, "Not many Afghans on Achravie but plenty of people who might just remember blond hair and blue eyes like mine"

"Good thinkin' batman" the big man said, waving Rob over to join him at the laptop. "Have a look at these. One I lifted from my cctv footage from yesterday, the other I Photoshopped from an old photo of you and I, taken about a year into basic training at a night out in Perth"

Rob stared at the photographs on the screen. He didn't have any photos from his early years in the regiment; most of his gear had gone AWOL when they were moving barracks a number of years ago and he had lost most of his personal stuff like photographs.

The difference between the two faces was reassuring for

Rob. Particularly with the colour change in his hair and eyes, he looked totally different to the face of the young Robbie MacLaine that stared back at him from the laptop screen, added to which, Robbie had had fashionably long, curly blond hair when he left Achravie, not the mid-brown crop he wore now. Mid-brown was his colour of choice because dark hair and blond eyebrows look just as out of place and the more natural his facial appearance the better.

"Look at those" Mac pointed to the photographs on the screen, "Your own brother wouldn't recognise you, man"

"I was kinda hopin' that might be the case Mac, being as I might actually run into him at some stage and Lorna Cameron said Bruce shouldn't know I was on the island"

"Did you check the ferry times for me big pal" said Rob

"Sure did wee man, there you go" said Mac, clicking on an adjacent tab at the top of the laptop screen and bringing up the Blackwaterfoot - Achravie ferry timetable.

"How long's the drive to the ferry from here?"

"Well, unless you get stuck behind something agricultural, which is entirely possible or an armoured Warrior looking for IEDs, which is highly unlikely, I'd give it twenty minutes or so, it's a good road all the way down".

"OK, I'll allow 30 minutes. What have you got for me in the way of wheels?"

"You can take one of the Land Rovers outside, like the one we came out here in. They go like stink but don't look that much different to the dozens of other black 110s you'll pass on the road"

Big Mac pulled a pack of twenty business cards out of a drawer and tossed them to Rob.

"Printed these off for you last night, a few people know these vehicles so it makes sense that you are Bob Chapman, my new Senior Instructor here. Bob, Bob, Rob. Not that different, you could equally react to either. You don't start till next month but thought you would come up early and have a look around. I can't do you a full legend with passport drivers licence etc but for a day or two that should do you."

"WELL DONE YOU. Hopefully won't need these but at least I know where to come for a job if I ever need one" laughed Rob. "There's a ferry at 10.35, let's aim for that one. It says here that it only takes 15 minutes nowadays. I just need to make a couple of phone calls. Back in a couple of minutes"

Rob called Joe to give and get updates on a few issues and then called Justine.

"Justine Fellows" she answered in a very business-like tone.

"Hi Tina, its Rob, how are you, you OK to talk?"

"Oh Rob, thank God your safe, I was getting worried"

"Sorry, things got a bit hectic last night, trying to set things up for today, but things are fine. I'm heading down to get the ferry to Achravie in about 10 or 15 minutes, so thought I would give you a quick ring now" Rob explained

"Good, I'm glad you did. Pete said your friend was a really nice guy once he got over his size. Pete says his name is Big Mac is that right?"

"Big Mac to his friends, otherwise Iain MacDonald, I served with him in Iraq and Afghanistan. We joined up to the Black Watch at the same time and went through basic training together. He bought the training centre on Arran when he left the military. It was dying on its feet apparently but Mac worked his magic on it and it seems to be thriving now."

"Excellent, good he was able to help"

"Yeah, speaking of which, I better get going if I'm going to catch that ferry, but I really wanted to talk to you. I'm not very good at this Tina, I normally only do one night stands but I really want to see you again. If you want to, that is, if you don't, please tell me now."

. . .

"Of course I want to see you again, you great lump. I thought I made that pretty clear the other night!"

"That was then Tina and there was alcohol involved. This is now in the clear light of day"

"Stop right there Rob. I don't spend the night with every stranger I meet in a bar" Justine said softly," In fairness I've never slept with someone I'd just met, until the other night. Even now I'm not sure why I did, but I would like to find out. So, clear light of day, I do want to see you again because we might just have something special"

"Wow" said Rob, running the hand over his short, spikey hair. "You know how to get a guy's attention. Can't wait to see you now!"

"Listen, I need to go, the quicker I get this sorted out the quicker we get back together. Look after yourself Tina, see you soon yeah!"

"Will do, you be careful and please don't do anything stupid. I want you back in one piece Rob"

"For sure, bye" Rob said quietly, ending the call.

"Hey, man, you're going to miss that ferry if you don't get a move on" Mac said as Rob walked back into the kitchen carrying his rucksack.

"Phoer, wish me luck Big Mac, wish me luck" said Rob as he caught the keys Mac threw to him across the breakfast bar. He couldn't believe that after twenty two years he was going back to Achravie.

"Ach, you're not goin' to need luck. You're probably over reacting to that phone call. I know what you're like. Now get goin' and I'll see you in a couple days. I've got work to do too, you know" Mac laughed.

Rob and Big Mac shared another bear hug and Rob walked over to the black Land Rover Defender 110 which matched the registration number on the key fob. Rob tossed his bag in the back, climbed into the driver's seat and adjusted it forward a couple of inches. Rob fired up the big throaty V8 engine and with a quick wave to his friend, drove off to catch the Blackwaterfoot - Achravie ferry.

8

THE DRIVE TO BLACKWATERFOOT WAS UNEVENTFUL AND WITH THE power of the big V8 engine, the Land Rover eased past any slower moving traffic. This was the countryside of Rob's boyhood and rather than get nostalgic and even bitter about what he had been forced to leave behind, Rob drove quickly which meant concentrating more on his driving than the past. Given this, he arrived in Blackwaterfoot early, the journey having taken only fifteen minutes.

He parked the Land Rover and walked over to the slipway to watch the ferry as it got closer. The ferry service had now been taken over by a larger ferry operator, which now operated most of the West of Scotland routes to the Isles and now had a bigger ferry than before.

Rob was quite pleased about that as the bigger the ferry, the more passengers it took, the less any one passenger stood out. By this time, the ferry was visible and approaching Blackwaterfoot, albeit still a bit out.

Ten minutes or so later the ferry was disgorging its human cargo with its cars and light vans. The vessels operating on the crossing are of different sizes, the smaller can carry 12 cars and

199 passengers at 9 knots, the larger can carry 24 cars and 150 passengers at 10 knots. The ferries are too small for heavy goods vehicles.

Twenty minutes later and Rob climbed the stairway from the car deck to the passenger deck of the smaller of the two ferries with the Land Rover parked and locked in the small car deck below. He would have been happier to sit in the car, but Health & Safety notices said that passengers and drivers were not allowed on the car deck during the short trip and he had already seen one couple being told to vacate their vehicle as per the notices.

THE CAR DECK was almost full, with nine cars parked nose to tail on the lower deck, but there were only about fifty passengers on this crossing. A few looked like locals but the majority were obviously tourists probably keen to see the standing stones and the ruins of Achravie Castle. Rob did not recognise anyone, which he thought was a good start to his journey, although, at some stage he would meet people from his past

Rod queued at the on-board ticket office as the slipway at Blackwaterfoot was unattended and paid £37 cash for a return ticket to Achravie.

He stood on the passenger deck, looking out over the water to Achravie. Achravie was not a large inland, it covered about 2200 hectares, which was the rough equivalent of just under eight and a half square miles and had a population of around 450 people. About half of these lived in the village of Achravie with the others spread across a few small hamlets or the farms and crofts which provided work for a good number of the residents. The whole island belonged to Achravie Estate, which was the main employer on the island. Andrew MacLaine owned Achravie estate and as such most of the jobs on Achravie depended on him and him alone. It was this fact that had allowed Andrew MacLaine to strike his son's apparent involvement in a road traffic accident and the resultant death of a young girl off the record books.

It seemed no time till the klaxon was sounding on the ferry and the PA system was instructing drivers to return to their vehicles, so Rob made his way back down to the car deck as the ferry approached the slipway adjacent to Achravie harbour. Despite the coolness of the car deck, Rob's hands were sweating as he gripped the steering wheel a little too firmly than necessary. The red Seat Leon in front of him moved off, Rob hesitated momentarily then followed the car off the ferry, up the slipway and on to Achravie for the first time in twenty two years.

By the time Rob drove on to the island it was close on 11.00 and his first impulse was to contact Fraser and find out why he wanted Rob there so urgently. The fact that Lorna Cameron had said that his brother Bruce was not to know that Rob was on the island worried him.

Did that mean that Bruce and Fraser being in hospital were connected? Experience had taught Rob always to plan around a worst case scenario, so he decided that, until he knew more about why he was there, he would try to make contact only with Fraser or Lorna and would otherwise keep a low profile. Rob was well used to operating under the radar so he decided to find out a bit more about Fraser's whereabouts before making any decisions as to what to do next.

Rob turned left from the slipway onto Main Street and drove through the village of Achravie, passing down a street that appeared to have changed little in twenty years. A few of the names over the shops had changed, but little else that he could see. As he approached the Red Lion on his right, he pulled over to the other side of the road to get a closer look. There above the still closed front door was a little polished brass plaque which would display the licensee's name. He slowed to read it. "Hamish Allen". So Hamish was still there, well, well!

Rob pulled back across to the other side of the road again and started towards the Cottage Hospital, just down the road on the edge of the village. He pulled up at the side of the road just as the hospital came into view. It now boasted a couple of Portacabin style temporary buildings which had not been there before, but otherwise looked pretty much the same.

ROB TOOK out his smartphone and Googled the hospital, touching the phone number which was highlighted in blue on the screen. The number rang and then was answered.

"Good morning Achravie Cottage Hospital, Staff Nurse Anderson speaking. How may I help you?" the voice at the other end chirped.

"Yes, good morning Staff Nurse, I wonder if you can help me please" said Rob. Very few people can say no to a request for help.

"Can you tell me when the visiting hours are at the hospital, please?"

"That would depend on which ward you want to visit, sir" came the reply

"Well I'm not actually sure which ward my uncle is in, to be honest. His name is Fraser McEwan, maybe you can help me out there as well."

"Mr McEwan was in one of the side rooms, let me just check to make sure he's still there."

Rob could hear Staff Nurse Anderson shout through her fingers "Is Fraser McEwan still in room F, Mags?

"Uhuh, I've just changed one of his dressings" came the reply

"Thanks, Mags"

"Hello sir, he's in one of the side rooms, Room F. Because it's a side room and he's on his own, we're not too strict with visitors. Are you coming in today?

"Yes, hopefully"

"OK, well I'm the duty Staff Nurse so that's fine by me. Just try to avoid mealtimes. Sister Ingles is on with me, so if you see her, just tell her I said it would be OK. Is there anything else I can help you with?"

"How's the old devil doin' Staff Nurse?" asked Rob, pushing his luck a bit.

"He's on the mend, sir. His cuts and bruises are all fairly clean, but he might need physio on his shoulder and his broken leg once he gets out. Not allowed to give out too much detail on the phone sir, I'm sure you can understand! Can I tell him you're coming in, who can I say called?"

"Oh, just say Robert's going to pop in, I won't stay too long, just wanted to see with my own eyes that the daft old bugger's still breathing!" Rob laughed.

"Oh, here, it'll take more than a quad-bike accident to kill Fraser McEwan, rest assured, Robert. I'll probably see you later, Bye" and she ended the call.

A Quadbike accident! Rob didn't see Fraser calling him back to Achravie because he'd fallen off a quadbike. Time to get a second opinion!

Fraser's phone vibrated in Lorna's inside breast pocket. Excusing herself, she rose from her desk at the front of the classroom where she was in the middle of an English lesson with Primary 4. She hastened into the corridor.

"Hello Fraser McEwan's phone, this is Lorna Cameron" the phone hadn't rung since Fraser told her to retrieve it from his house and use it to get Robbie MacLaine to come.

""If you can't talk, just say "Sorry, wrong number, end this call and phone me back as soon as its safe" the voice at the other end said calmly and with authority.

"Robbie? Is that you?

. . .

"YES, CAN YOU TALK SAFELY?"

"Yes, yes, is it really you Robbie? Where are you? Are you coming to Achravie? How did you get this number?

Rob laughed, "Calm down. Woman, you'll do yerself a mischief! In answer to all these questions. It is me, I'm in Achravie and your call to me is in my call history and it logged the number you called from"

"Where are you Lorna, we need to talk" said Rob.

"I'm at the school Robbie, I teach here now but I can tell them I'm not feeling too good and get someone to cover for me to let me away early. If you're here in Achravie you'll not be safe if Bruce or his cronies find out, Robbie, I mean it, they gave Fraser a real beating, Robbie, left him for dead up by the castle. That's why he asked me to phone you. A couple of tourists found him lying beside his quadbike. It was on its side, so they assumed he'd come off the road and fallen down the banking on to the path. Fraser told me it wasn't an accident, he was attacked by three of Bruce's cronies, but everyone else thinks it was an accident and Fraser said to leave it that way for now."

"Yeah, they said at the hospital it was a quadbike accident but I thought that sounded a bit strange for Fraser to shout for me to come just 'cause he fell off a quadbike."

"You've been to the hospital? Robbie you shouldn't have done that! If they find out you're here they'll come looking for you" Lorna pleaded

"No, I didn't go in, I just phoned to see how he was. I told a Staff Nurse Anderson that I was his nephew, Robert. She's going to tell him that I will be in later.

"YOU SHOULDN'T GO in Robbie. If they find out you're here they'll come after you too, these are vicious, bad people, who

47

beat people up just for the fun of it. Robbie I need to get back to my class, let me arrange cover and I'll meet you in about half an hour"

"No, don't do that. If these guys are as dangerous as you say, we shouldn't be seen together just yet. Can you go to the hospital and tell Fraser that I'm here and that I'll touch base with him when I think it's safe. When you've done that and it's safe to talk, call me back. We'll meet up later. OK!

"OK, right, need to go. I'll catch you later."

Lorna pondered as she walked back to her class. She hadn't seen or spoken to Robbie since he had left the island just over twenty years ago. She had been devastated by the accident and the aftermath which ended in Robbie's departure. She hadn't even known he had gone till Fraser had told her about three weeks after.

He said it wasn't Robbie's decision. His father had insisted that he leave, quickly and quietly, no preparation, no goodbyes, just go! Fraser had taken Robbie to Glasgow and had pulled a few strings, as ex-Regimental Sargent Majors could, and had fast-tracked an application for Robbie to join his and Robbie's father's old regiment the Black Watch. He had stayed with Robbie till he was ready to leave for Inverness, all of this with his father's direction. He had wanted Robbie off the island and knew that the military would guarantee Robbie a home, an income and a career as long as he applied himself.

Fraser had contacts within the Regiment and had been able for a while to get occasional feedback on Robbie, although later on this have pretty well dried up as Robbie had gotten lost in the fog of security which descended on the military as threats of terrorism grew.

FRASER HAD ALWAYS BEEN adamant that Robbie had not been driving that fateful night and somehow Lorna had a sense that he was right. Fraser said he thought that Bruce had been driving and had covered that up by blaming a very drunk Robbie. Lorna knew Bruce through her close friendship with Robbie and neither liked nor trusted him.

She tried to steer clear of him as much as possible after he had backed her into a corner of the back hall in Hillcrest House one evening, tried to lift the hem of her dress and made to kiss her. He had been slightly drunk but knew what he was doing and had raced away when someone opened the kitchen door and came into the hallway.

"All right class, Miss Cameron's back, settle down" she said clapping her hands in the way teachers did, as she walked back into the classroom. "Carry on reading"

She and Robbie had always been close, even at Primary school they had played together and as they grew and matured over the years that friendship grew and matured. They were brother and sister though, there was never anything romantic or sexual between them. When they kissed, they kissed as friends kissed not lovers, but they had loved each other, of that there was no doubt.

Lorna felt as if part of her world had collapsed when Fraser had broken it to her that Robbie was gone. Looking back it seemed as if she had cried for weeks, she just couldn't believe that her best friend who she was so close to, was gone. It was as if he had died, only worse, because she knew that he was alive but that she might never see him again. She felt a tear run down her cheek as she thought about these dark days.

9

Rob put his phone down. It was strange talking to Lorna after all these years. He suddenly realised that he knew nothing about her now, a girl who had been like a sister to him, apart from the fact that she was a teacher at the local school. Was she married, did she have children of her own, and what did she look like now that she was almost twice the age she had been when he had last seen her on that fateful evening, that had changed the course of his entire life so dramatically and so suddenly.

Lorna had tried to tell him to take it easy on the lager that night, but his enthusiasm for the celebrations had gone to his head as much as the drink and he just smiled back to her and said "I'll be fine Lorna".

24 hours later, he was in a hospital bed, his father accusing him of causing an accident which had killed a young girl. 48 hours later, he was in a hotel room in Glasgow disowned by his family, cut off from his friends and told to stay away from Achravie and to contact no one. Not even Lorna

Now he was back!

Sitting in the Four Seasons café on Achravie's Main St,

Rob felt the better for a hearty steak pie, chips and veg washed down with a pot of sweet Moroccan Mint tea, courtesy of Tea Pigs. He pondered on his next move, but decided he needed a bit more background detail before deciding what to do.

He still didn't understand why Bruce's "cronies" would "give Fraser a real beating". Who were these mysterious, vicious people?

"Can I get you anything else?" said the waitress who had just approached his table.

"No, I think I'm good" Rob replied, reflecting the friendly smile on the waitress's pleasant, chubby face. "Can I just have my bill please?"

"Just pay at the till on the way out Sir, thank you" she said as she lifted the empty plate from the table.

As Rob approached the till, a man came out of the kitchen wearing chef's whites and a slightly grubby apron. "Everything OK for you?" he asked as he handed Rob his bill "That'll be £12.60, please"

"Thanks" he said as Rob handed him a £20 note, "Bank of England" the man noted, "I thought I heard an accent that wasn't local. You here on business or just touring around?"

"Bit of both" Rob decided to deploy his new legend "I've just landed a new job at an outward bound training centre about half an hour north of Blackwaterfoot and decided to come up a bit early and have a look around the area. I've never been before and everyone I spoke to said it was lovely up here. And I'll tell you what, they were right."

"Aye, it's beautiful countryside, that's for sure. Are you staying at the centre, it'll be the one at Machrie?"

"It is and I was going to head back there tonight but someone told me about the old castle and the standing stones, so I think I'll maybe stay the night and do a bit of exploring. Anywhere you would recommend for the night?"

"Red Lion's as good as any, if not better. He's converted the old stable block out the back to make four wee cottage rooms, if you get one of these you'll do well for yourself Tell them Billy Templeton sent you over, might just swing one of them for you."

WELL, well, Billy Templeton. Rob hadn't recognised him, He'd been in his last year at school as Rob was in his first year there. More to the point Templeton had not recognised him.

Rob approached the Red Lion with some trepidation, but he had to push the boat out, see how well his somewhat altered appearance would hide his identity from someone who knew Rob better than Billy Templeton. He walked through the front door and into the small front hall which housed the little corner reception desk. There was no one there so he obeyed the little notice and rang the bell for attention.

"Hello, sorry to keep you waiting, what can I do for you" asked a short buxom young woman who appeared from some-where. Her name badge said she was Lizzie and that meant that she had to be Hamish Allen the landlord's daughter. Lizzie Allen had been in Rob's class at school. He'd taken her out a couple of times, but her heart had been elsewhere as he remembered. Thin Lizzie the boys had called her back then but the Lizzie who stood in front of him now was more buxom Lizzie than thin Lizzie, but still an attractive woman. She smiled up at him with not a flicker of recognition.

"I'm looking for somewhere to stay tonight and Billy Templeton from the café up the road sent me here in pursuit of one of your new stable cottages which he highly recommend-ed." Rob explained

"Did he indeed, I suppose this is going to cost us a dram

when he's in next" she laughed as she took out a large book from under the desk counter and placed it open and facing Rob on the desk top. "You better sign in then, can't have you breaking the law, Mr ...?"

"Eh, Chapman, Bob Chapman" Rob replied smiling, I wouldn't dream of breaking the law and he filled in that name and the Machrie Outward Bound Centre as his address.

LIZZIE TURNED the book around and read the entry. "Oh, the Machrie Outward Bound Centre. "

"Yes, well I don't officially start till next month but decided to come up a bit early and have a look around the area. I've never been before and everyone I spoke to said it was lovely up here. I was going to head back there tonight but someone told me about the old castle and the standing stones, so I thought I'd maybe stay a couple of nights, do a bit of exploring so to speak."

"Am sure you'll enjoy the island and I hope you'll enjoy your stay with us. Breakfast is served seven till half nine, dinner is served six till ten and there's a room service menu in your room if you prefer. You're in cottage 4, out the door there into the car park and it's the one furthest away from the main building. Nice and quiet and nearest the rear car cark. There's a barrier on the rear car park, it's for residents only. The code is 1379 to get out. It's the four corners, easy to remember" explained Lizzie as she held up a door entry card. "You need to put this into the wee slot at the door to switch on your electricity."

"OK, thanks, sounds good" said Rob taking the proffered card from not so thin Lizzie. As he turned to leave, he almost bumped into a man who was walking behind him.

"Sorry" smiled Hamish Allen, putting his hand on Rob's upper arm "I really should watch where I'm going, but it's not easy to teach an old dog new tricks" he chuckled. He frowned for a second, looking directly at Rob "You've been here before if I'm not mistaken"

"No, this is Mr Chapman's first visit Dad, he was telling me he has just starting at the Machrie Outward Bound Centre and is doing a bit of exploring" Lizzie interrupted.

"YEAH, I start at the beginning of the month so thought I'd do a bit of sightseeing first" said Rob and as he turned to face Hamish Allen directly he dug a business card out of his top pocket and handed it to him," If any of your guests fancy a bit of adventure, tell them to give us a call"

Hamish's eyes drifted down to the scar on Rob's cheek then caught himself as he realised Rob saw the direction of his gaze. "Sorry son, I didn't mean to stare, that was rude of me" he blushed a deep red and looked intently at the floor

"No problem, I've had it a while, I've gotten quite used to it and the reaction it gets from most people. I usually tell people I cut myself shaving, not sure many believe me"

"Good of you to say so son, if you're in the bar tonight, first one's on the house"

"That's a dangerous promise, you don't know what I drink" Rob laughed

"'s OK son, you decide the drink, I'll decide the quantity" Hamish said turning away" Oh, and do me a favour son, use an electric razor while you're here" he shouted back over his shoulder with a laugh as he walked through to the bar.

The cottage was ideal or Rob's needs, comfortable, with all the expected refinements of recently built hotel accommodation. It was far enough away from the main hotel building to be secluded, close to the secure car park and invisible from the main road. He could park the Land Rover at the side of the cottage and again, it would be hidden to the casual passer-by on Main Street.

Rob took this opportunity to call Joe and update him as he had promised. Joe was not happy and said as much.

"This sounds like trouble waiting to happen Rob, don't get too involved. You told me this was just a recce, you've got no backup if it all goes pear-shaped, I don't like it, I'm coming up"

"No you're not, Joe, I don't need backup. This is a family thing, I just think it's got a bit out of hand. It's nothing I can't handle, don't worry!"

Having calmed Joe down Rob called Justine

"Are you serious, these guys beat your friend to within an inch of his life and you're telling me not to worry! You cannot be serious Rob"

"Tina, I'll be fine, these guys are bunch of pussies, remember my background, I can handle a couple of muscle bound thugs with one hand behind my back" he lied.

"Oh yes, and the other hand holding that gun of yours, that's what worries me, I don't need you up on a murder charge"

Rob held the phone away from his ear a little as Justine went into a rant about his personal safety.

"Oh come on Tina it's not that bad, seriously. If things get out of hand, and there not going to, I'll call "Big Mac" and he can be here within the hour.

"I'm not happy Rob, I'm really not happy, we're just getting to know each other, I don't want you hurt or worse still, dead"

"Tina, this is everyday stuff for me, it's what I do for a living, have done for years. You've seen my CV at SGS, you know what I do, trust me on this one."

Eventually Justine had calmed down and Rob had agreed to call her regularly to let her know he was safe.

· · ·

ROB'S PHONE was a dual SIM phone which allowed him to make calls using one SIM card whilst receiving calls from the other and as he dropped his phone on bed the phone played "Brown Eyed Girl" to tell him that he had an incoming call on the other SIM, the number he had given Fraser and Lorna.

"Who is this?" he said brusquely

"Robbie, it's me Lorna."

"Sorry, Lorna, I wasn't sure. Did you speak to Fraser?"

"Yes, I've just this minute left him. I told him you were here. He says he needs to see you. He has things to tell you about Hillcrest, about you Dad and about Bruce, but he says to keep out of sight. He says that if Bruce and his cronies see you they'll kill you. He says that he asks for his room window to be left open at night and nobody bothers him after lights out."

"OK, I'll go up tonight."

"Can we meet Robbie? I'm dying to see you."

"What are you doing tonight," he asked

I'm just going home to change and I was going to the Red Lion with a friend for a bite to eat and a drink at about seven o'clock, but I can cancel that."

"No, you go ahead, I'll see you at some stage if I know where to find you."

"Will I recognise you Robbie, after all these years?"

"Oh, for sure, I'm still the big, skinny, blue eyed blond lump I always was. You wouldn't miss me Lorna," he lied. "What are you wearing tonight?"

"A RED SILK blouse and a pair of denim jeans."

"OK, don't change your mind, or I might end up chatting up the wrong girl" Rob smiled.

Lorna laughed "I dare say I could give up a woman's prerogative for one night, but don't make a habit of it Robbie MacLaine."

Rob ended the call. He looked at his watch, it was six o'clock. He would have a shower and get changed then head over to the bar for a drink and something to eat and all going to plan, he would follow Lorna out when she left and meet her where no one would see them.

10

ROB WALKED INTO THE BAR AT ABOUT QUARTER TO SEVEN. HE wanted a choice of table rather than having to take what was still free or even worse, be stuck on a bar stool with his back to everyone.

Hamish Allen was behind the bar serving a young couple with a pint and a half pint of Harviestoun Brewery's Schiehallion Cask conditioned lager, 4.8%, strong stuff. Some of the trendy Thames-side bars near Rob's apartment served it in bottles, it was good! He saw Rob come to the bar, "Be with you in a minute son, just rehydrating this poor couple before they die of thirst." Hamish called over.

"No problem" Rob replied, picking up and perusing the bar menu.

"So, what can I get you son?" asked the approaching Hamish.

"I'll have a glass of that Rioja over there and can I have the Seafood Linguini, please."

"What! red wine wi fish, then ye wonder why we Scots want independence from you uneducated lot from the Home Counties, Hamish smiled as he reached for a glass. "Of course you can, son." He laughed again "Where are you sitting?"

"Just over at that table for two in the corner if that's OK."

"A good choice, if I may say so. Sit with your back to the wall; that way, naebody can stab you in the back, and there's a fair few backstabbers in these parts. Aren't there, Ricky?" He laughed as he took a playful swipe at a young lad, probably borderline legal drinking age.

Ricky ducked. "Watch it. It's no backstabbers that worry me in here, but that beer ye serve. Ma dad always said it was passed by the management and it certainly tastes like it." He ducked again as another playful swipe came his way.

It looked like nothing had changed in the bar of the Red Lion. Hamish always enjoyed a bit of banter with his customers, dishing out friendly, well intentioned abuse and expecting to get it back from his regulars.

As Rob sat in the corner of the bar he imagined that he recognised a few of the customs who drifted in and either sat at the gradually disappearing empty tables or stood at the bar, thus becoming front line targets for Hamish's abuse. People's appearances change in twenty two years but while Rob was able to pick out a few well known faces from his past, no one showed the slightest sign of recognising the much physically changed Rob.

Thin Lizzie's appearance had certainly changed in the past twenty years. No more a skinny eighteen year old but now a mature forty year old with generous curves in all the right places. She could not help but display a fair proportion of her ample breasts as she bent over to place Rob's Seafood Linguini in front of him along with a set of cutlery wrapped in a blue napkin.

"Don't pay him any mind" she whispered conspiratorially, pointing her thumb over at Hamish. "He's like that with everyone, doesn't mean any harm, but he's going to get a thick ear one day if he's not careful. Can I get you any sauces or anything else?" She asked standing upright.

"No I'm fine with this" Rob replied and she walked away.

Rob was just lifting a second mouthful of food to his mouth when he heard Lizzie's cheerful voice above the buzz of the bar, "Hi Stella, hi Lorna, I've got a table over here for you girls!"

Rob looked up and almost choked on his Linguini. Lizzie was showing two women over to a reserved table. Stella was a tall angular, not unattractive woman, wearing a just above-the-knee green shift dress and, as many tall women wear, flat shoes. Lorna Cameron on the other hand looked stunning in a sort of, not really trying way, which only naturally beautiful, confident women can achieve. She looked very much as Rob remembered her as an attractive, trim bodied eighteen year old, but she had matured into a woman of real beauty. Her body still looked trim and athletic and her face was that of a classic beauty. Her dark hair was shorter now, cut into an attractive bob. She was wearing exactly what she had said she would wear, a red silk blouse and a pair of tight black jeans.

The two women were sitting side on to Rob but at the far side of the room. Stella looked relaxed but Lorna was showing signs of agitation as she settled into their table with Lizzie fussing around with napkins and menus. Lorna started a slow sweep of the room with her eyes stopping on male customers as they moved across her line of vision. Her eye stopped for moment to stare at two tall men at the bar, then moved on to a couple sitting at a bar side table, then three men sitting eating at another table as she searched the room in case Rob was there.

Then her eyes found Rob. She stared at him for what seemed an eternity but as Rob raised his eyes to meet hers she smiled embarrassedly as she moved her gaze from his scar and looked Rob in the eye for a second or two. Rob smiles at her as he would to any beautiful woman who his eyes met, but Lorna looked away quickly, embarrassed at having been caught looking so directly at someone and started to scan the rest of the room. Satisfied that Robbie wasn't in the bar she turned back to her friend and they started a conversation over the menus, which Rob could not hear over the background noise.

Rob was enjoying his linguini and had to try very hard not to stare at Lorna sitting across the room from him, although he did manage a few surreptitious glances before her friend Stella caught his eye movement and whispered something to Lorna, who in turn glanced quickly and casually across at Rob. Rob smiled, Lorna turned her head back to her friend, said something and they both giggled. Just then Lizzie brought their food and placed it on the table in front of them.

Two large well-muscled men walked in to the bar. Both men were tall, probably just over six foot, their muscle looked like it had been developed with a mix of pumping iron and steroids. They were casually dressed, one with short buzz cut hair, the other with long hair fashioned into a tight pony-tail. Both had an aggressive, arrogant swagger to their demeanour which Rob had seen in many muscle bound heavies. They were not locals and Rob fancied they may be two of his brother's "cronies" as they had been described to him.

As they passed Lizzie at Stella and Lorna's table the one with the ponytail who was nearest to her, rubbed his right hand over her right buttock and gave it a tight squeeze. Lizzie stood upright with a start and an indignant look on her face, but the big guy had moved on to the bar, totally ignoring the furious Lizzie.

As Rob finished his meal, Lizzie came over to clear his table, "Everything OK for you Mr Chapman?" she chirped.

"Yeah, very good actually, really enjoyed it."

"Good, can I get you anything else?"

"No thanks, can you put that on my room please? Who are your large friends?" Rob asked quietly.

Lizzie bent over conspiratorially, once again displaying a fair proportion of her ample breasts. "There no friends of mine, Mr Chapman, they work up at the Achravie Estate. They're trouble with a capital T, come in here as if they own the place, so they do. One of then just helped himself to a feel at my backside, he's lucky I didn't slap him."

"I think you might have come off worst from that Lizzie, best you ignore them. You reckon they work at the estate, they don't look much like your archetypal estate worker."

"Security, Bruce MacLaine has about six or seven of them as security guards on the estate" Lizzie whispered.

"Security! What does he need security from on an island like Achravie?"

"God knows, there're up to no good up there if you ask me, big gates at the road end and that bunch of thugs. You don't need that unless you're up to no good" said Lizzie wiping the table as she spoke.

"I'd better get on" Lizzie said as she dried the table and picked up Rob's plate.

As she passed Lorna and Stella, Stella made the universal "writing in the palm of my hand" request for their bill and Lizzie nodded as she passed. The taller of Bruce's security muscle was saying something to the two women, who in turn, were totally ignoring the man. He gestured to them and laughed, turning to his friend with the buzz cut hair to say something and they both looked over at the women and laughed.

Having paid their bill, the ladies stood up to leave, but the chatty pony tailed heavy stood directly in front of them and said something that Rob couldn't hear. The two women stared at him for a second or two then pushed past him. As he stood laughing at them he stretched out his hand to pat Lorna's bottom as she passed. Lorna whirled round in an instant and delivered a slap to the thug's face which resounded round the bar and literally wiped the smile off the big man's face momentarily. He looked around the bar with an embarrassed grin on his face then tried to look cool by laughing, but no one bought it. He was angry. He had been humiliated by a woman in a busy bar and he was angry.

As the door closed behind the two women, the muscle with the pony tail said something to his companion in a language which Rob instantly recognised from his time in Bosnia. These guys were Bosnians. The friend nodded, drained his pint glass and the two walked towards the door and out into the front car park where the woman were walking to their car.

Rob sensed what could be a dangerous situation for the women and rose from his table to follow them.

Lizzie had appeared from the bar area, followed by her father, "Can you help me here, Mr Chapman. I think these two might cause trouble for my friends" Lizzie confided.

Rob nodded slightly and followed Lizzie to the door. He turned to Hamish, "Stay here Hamish, too many cooks and all that."

As Rob walked out into the car park Lizzie was already shouting to the two men, "Let's not have any trouble out here fella's, can we just go home quietly please."

The shorter of the two thugs was standing in front of Stella blocking her from helping Lorna, who was being pressed against the rear doors of a white van by the man she had slapped. He has Lorna's arm twisted behind her back at a painful angle and was cupping her breast in his right hand. His left leg was pushed hard into her crotch and he was trying to kiss her.

Lorna swung her head from side to side and shouted "Stop it! Stop it!"

The other man holding Stella back saw Lizzie coming and lashed out at her sending her sprawling into some bushes. He turned to face Rob with a gloating smile and beckoned him to come on. Rob did, and before the muscle bound thug could react, Rob attacked him, landing left foot first on the man's right kneecap, instantly shattering the man's patella and sending the joint into a place that it was never designed to go. The man screamed in agony as he fell to the ground. His friend was too intent on Lorna to notice what had just happened but he turned see why his friend was writhing in agony on the ground.

Rob stood about two feet away from the man who was still holding Lorna's arm painfully up her back. "I get the feeling she doesn't want you, so best you let her go" Rob spoke quietly but with an edge of menace to his voice.

"So, you want the tart, do you. Well you can have her" the big man said and pushed Lorna at Rob. Rob sidestepped and Lorna stumbled past him into Stella who was standing behind Rob with Lizzie. As Lorna flew past him, the big Bosnian rushed Rob in an attempt to envelop Rob in a bear hug, but just before his arms closed around him, Rob moved forward like a cobra and hit the man with a head-butt which bore every ounce of fury that Rob felt for this man. The man's nose disintegrated and his front teeth buried themselves in his lower lip and he staggered backward into the back of the white van, one of the doors flew open and the man half fell into the back of the van. As he began to rise unsteadily on his feet, Rob hit him like a sledgehammer in the lower ribcage, breaking ribs and no doubt doing internal damage. The man was all but out on his feet but Rob grabbed his right wrist and holding it against the edge of the closed door of the van, slammed the open door shut on the wrist, breaking bones and severing tendons.

The man yelled in agony and slumped to the ground as Rob grabbed his throat. "If you or any of your pals as much as look the wrong way at any of these people ever again, I will kill you and I mean that literally, I will kill you, not your pals, you!" he growled quietly and stood up. Hamish Allen was standing beside him.

"Last man who stood up to this bunch was in Intensive Care in the Cottage Hospital till a couple of days ago. Bit older and a lot smaller that you, but I'd still watch my back Robbie" Hamish winked, smiled and turned away.

"Shit! He knows who I am" Rob said to himself. "How?"

Rob walked over to where Stella and Lorna were tending to a slightly winded and bruised Lizzie and Hamish was looking on with a worried look on his face, till his daughter said" I'm OK dad, just winded a wee bit."

"They need seeing to dad" she said nodding over to the two thugs lying semi-conscious on the ground.

"Aye, I'll phone Bruce MacLaine to come and get them. If I phone for an ambulance they'll involve the Police. Probably best all round if they don't get involved, don't you think Mr Chapman," Hamish said looking at Rob.

"Just complicate things," Rob nodded

Rob felt a hand on his sleeve, "Are you all right Mr Chapman?" Lorna Cameron looked up at Rob questioningly, "Thank you for doing what you did. I don't know what would have happened if you hadn't got involved. You don't even know me and you might have got hurt yourself. I shouldn't have reacted like that, it was stupid but I was just so angry. Urgh, makes my skin crawl just to think about him touching me."

LORNA STOPPED, stared into Rob's brown eyes and a flicker of recognition crossing her face. "It is you Robbie, isn't it? A don't care what colour your eyes are, it is you Robbie, I knew it was, but they said it wasn't you.

Rob bowed his head and with his thumb and forefinger took out one of his brown tinted contact lenses.

"The wonders of modern technology, Lorna," he smiled, looking down at Lorna with one brown eye and one vivid blue eye.

Lorna squealed with delight and almost knocked Rob over as she literally jumped on him wrapping her arms round his neck and head and her legs round his waist, "I knew it, I knew it was you but they all said it wasn't. I just knew it was you. She was crying now as Rob wrapped his own arms round her trim body and held her close. "I looked at you and I just knew the minute I saw you, but they said it wasn't and that I wasn't to make a fool of myself" She kissed Rob fiercely and held her head back to look at him, "I've got my best pal back." she sobbed.

Hamish came out of the hotel door and walked briskly across the front car park.

"Oh you finally twigged did you" he said to Lorna, laughing.

"You knew! Hamish Allen" She turned to Lizzie, "Did you know? Lizzie nodded.

Lorna looked hurt and let him go and jumped down to the ground, turning to Rob asked him, "Did you tell them?"

"No, I thought I was being clever, I'd convinced with myself that with my brown eyes I could fool anyone, but obviously not" he laughed and a reassured Lorna hugged him again.

Hamish reappeared from the bar "You three better vamoose, tout suite. Bruce and his buddies will be here in about half an hour. I called and told him what happened. He went ballistic, He'll pick up these two but I don't think he'll cause any trouble tonight but better to be safe than sorry.

"I'm not sure that I should stay here tonight, Hamish. Might be tempting fate a bit. Probably best that I sleep elsewhere tonight and I'll maybe head back to the mainland tomorrow night, it's not that far" Rob suggested.

"You can stay with us" Stella ventured.

"No, that's the first place Bruce will look when he susses out who I am" he answered quickly.

"You haven't really met Stella, Rob," Lorna said taking the taller woman's arm," Stella's my partner, we got married in

Glasgow last year. We've been together for about two years. Stella knows all about us, she knows we were always best friends." Lorna looked up at Rob tentatively, "Please say my being gay doesn't spoil what we have Rob."

"Of course it doesn't" Rob smiled and put his arms round the two women and hugged them both. He leaned down and kissed Stella and then Lorna, "Just give each other happiness."

"I hate to break up this impromptu ménage-a-trois but you need to go, now" prompted Hamish. He held out Rob's key for the Land Rover, "Swap you for the cottage key, I took the liberty of clearing your stuff out and putting it in the Land Rover for you so that you could get away quickly. I've left the barrier open for you.

"Lorna, we should go to uncle Charlie's house, figure out what to do from there" said Stella.

"OK, good idea, they won't think to look for us there. You go home and get the keys and I'll go with Robbie and show him where it is."

"OK, I'll see you there" Stella replied and ran off up the Main Street and out of sight.

11

TAKING ONE LAST LOOK AT THE TWO INJURED THUGS STILL LYING on the car park, Rob led Lorna round to the back car park where the Land Rover was parked, passing as they went, a white Toyota Land Cruiser with the Achravie Estate logo on the front doors parked outside the bar entrance.

"Turn left out the car park and head down the coast about two miles or so" Lorna instructed as Rob swung out of the car park and started along Main Street heading along the coast road at a leisurely pace knowing that they would probably get to uncle Charlies house, wherever it was, before Stella.

"Where did you and Stella meet?" Asked Rob.

"She came here on holiday with her uncle about three years ago, we met in the Red Lion one night and just hit it off. She came back a few months later then I visited her in Edinburgh, she came back here and as I said we got together about two and a half years ago. I hope you like her" said Lorna looking over at Rob and studying him." You told me you looked just like you did twenty odd years ago, big skinny blond guy. You look nothing like you did then. You lied to me you big lump" she pouted and thumped his arm.

"Ouch!"

"Fraser said you were in the army. Is that where you learned to fight like that?"

"I joined the army when I left here. Three weeks after I left here. The Black Watch was my father's regiment and Fraser's as it happens, they pulled some strings. The Black Watch became part of the Royal Regiment of Scotland in 2006 and then I served with a Special Forces group for a few years and left the military in 2013. I set up a security company with an ex-colleague when I left the military and I'm still doing that. Yes, I learned a lot about fighting, that's what soldiers do. I try not to fight though, it hurts my knuckles." He smiled.

"Married? Significant other?"

"Um, no, not married but just recently met a girl that I think is a bit special, but that's still early days."

"Turn down here, Robbie" Lorna pointed to a turnoff to the right, leading down a narrow road which after about half a mile opened out into a wide gravel area in front of a reconstructed stone built shepherd's cottage. The big heavy Land Rover crunched over the gravel and Rob parked it out of sight round the far side of the cottage.

"I need to go and see Fraser tonight, Lorna" Rob said as they parked.

"You need to be careful now that they know who you are."

"They don't and if you don't tell them, I won't tell then either" Rob joked."

"It's not funny Robbie, you saw that they were like tonight and they almost killed Fraser."

"I'm not Fraser, Lorna and they will need to catch me before they kill me, which means they would need to see me first and I can be pretty invisible when I want to be." Rob assured her.

Lorna changed the subject. "Fraser says you weren't driving the night of the accident Robbie, he says you didn't kill Sheila Stewart."

"I wasn't and I didn't, I promise you that Lorna. You saw me that night, I couldn't walk let alone drive a car. Bruce and Sheila dumped me in the back seat and Bruce drove. I was so drunk I was hardly even aware of the accident. I felt a massive thump, a lot of noise and falling glass and then I was in an ambulance being sick and trying to answer questions. Bruce was driving that night and told everyone it was me. Sadly for me, everyone believed him."

"I didn't" Lorna touched his arm, "Fraser didn't either. He said the seat was in the wrong place, you couldn't have been driving."

"He said what?"

"He said the seat was in the wrong place, you couldn't have been driving. Don't ask me what he meant, but that's what he said" Lorna repeated.

It was dusk and with fading light, the few cars using the main road above were now using headlights to ensure visibility. Sitting in the Land Rover they heard rather than saw a vehicle coming down the drive then the arc of a headlight swept round the last bend and a motorcycle came into view.

"That's Stella now" said Lorna, getting out to greet her partner as she crunched across the deep gravel and parked the bike.

The two women kissed lightly and headed for the front door, motioning for Rob to join them.

They unlocked the door and went into a spacious open plan area which like Big Mac's Cottage, comprised a lounge and dining area and a kitchen.

"There's two bedrooms and two bathrooms back there" said Stella "and I've brought you a few bit and pieces of food to get you going in the morning.

Rob wandered through to the back and perused the double bedroom, he peered out the window and saw that the trees had been cleared from the back of the house to form a large patio with a gravel surround. The window had a sturdy lock which was comforting.

He went back through to the lounge area as the two women were kissing and Stella turned to Rob.

"Lorna's going to stay here tonight with you Robbie, she says you have twenty years of catching up to do and she's not sure how long she's got you for. I know how close you two were, Lorna and I have talked about it many times and I don't have a problem with you and her. I know your relationship and I know it isn't a threat to what we have, in fact if I'm jealous at all it's because I've never had a friend like that. Can you bring Lorna home in the morning?"

"Yeah sure. I appreciate you honesty Stella and your right, I am no threat to your marriage. I would like to think that my friend's partner could become my friend as well given time. You obviously make Lorna very happy so that raises you in my estimation right away."

"You don't have a problem with a gay marriage then?" asked Stella

"I wouldn't care whether you were a lesbian or a one legged sailor with a parrot on your shoulder, Stella. If you guys are happy that's all that counts."

"Thank you I'm glad to hear it. OK, I'm going to go, see you both in the morning" Stella said leaning in to kiss both Lorna and Rob as she left.

It was dark now and they watched as Stella started the bike and drove up the narrow road to the main road, then heard her gun the big machine down the road heading for Achravie.

"I NEED to go and see Fraser now" Rob said to Lorna "You be OK on your own till I get back?"

"Sure, I'll have a long soak in the bath, wash that scum off me. See you later Robbie and remember, be careful. I've only just got you back, I don't want to lose you" Lorna said and gave Rob a quick hug and a peck on the cheek.

12

ROB FOLLOWED STELLA'S ROUTE INTO ACHRAVIE. HE PASSED THE
Red Lion and noticed that the Achravie Estate Land Cruiser
had gone, no doubt picked up by Bruce's heavies. He drove
beyond Main Street and passed the Cottage Hospital on his
right leaving the village. He had seen a wide layby just past the
hospital earlier that day.

It looked like the road had been straightened at some point
and that this layby was part of the old road. It was partially
overgrown with trees and shrubs so made an ideal place to park
the Land Rover out of sight. He locked the car and set the
alarm. It was a volumetric system which would activate if
someone got into the vehicle.

The hospital lights shone brightly in the main public areas
to the front of the building, but Rob was not going to the public
areas, he was heading for the darkness of the rear of the
building where Room F was situated and Fraser McEwan
would be expecting his nocturnal visit.

Rob was in no hurry though. He slowly crept round the
back of the hospital, keeping to the tree line just inside the
boundary wall.

He pulled the Luna Nightvision Monocle from the little backpack he had retrieved from the Land Rover and positioned it over his right eye. As his eye got accustomed to the Monocle the world of black and of dark shadows turned green and Rob was able to pick out individual items in the grounds. Bushes, trees, an LPG tank and the area for the waste bin storage all became visible.

For twenty minutes Rob knelt motionless watching the area. He saw movement, a rat approaching the bins area, a couple of rabbits hopping across the grass and then a startled cat suddenly ran up a tree. Rob turned his head slowly to look in the direction from which the cat had run and sure enough there was what Rob had been looking for. Fraser's sentry, a near replica of the two men he had left in agony in the Red Lion car park, standing behind a tree trunk watching Fraser's window.

Rob left and crept round the other side of the hospital building and repeated the exercise. This time he found no one watching from the shadows. Rob had seen a door on this side of the building which was visible from the road and had noticed a staff member standing outside, finishing a cigarette. The door was wedged open and remained so when the squat little man returned back inside. He approached the door and found a small rubber wedge under the door to keep it from shutting fully. "Thank you "said Rob to no one in particular and slide into the darkened corridor of the hospital.

Stealthily, he crept round the corridor till he saw Room F. He approached the door and opened it slowly and quietly, crept inside and closed the door back to where it had been, slightly ajar. Rob crossed to the bed and watched a sleeping Fraser McEwan, his chest rising and falling in a slow rhythm. All the tubes had now been removed, which could only be a good thing.

Suddenly Fraser's eyes opened " Fraser, it's me Rob" he said quickly to allay any initial fear or panic Fraser might have, on waking up to find a strange man in his darkened room in the middle of the night.

"Robbie, you came" Fraser whispered "I knew you would come" Fraser smiled weakly

"I can't stay long, someone might come along. How're you doin' Fraser, what the hell happened to you. You didn't fall off a quadbike that's for sure, so what did happen?"

"I was seen up at a part of the estate that Bruce's and his heavy brigade had warned me to stay away from and this was their way of telling me not to do it again and keep my mouth shut."

"Tell me what's goin' on Fraser.

"Oh Robbie, it's a long story. Lorna knows most of it from what I've told her, I don't have the strength to go over it all again. Suffice to say, Bruce and his pals are smuggling something in and out of Achravie. Whatever it is, they keep it in a new warehouse up at the pond below the top field.

"Where's Angus in all this, surely Angus, not Bruce should be running things, he's the eldest?"

"Angus fell out with your father and Bruce, it all started with your accident. I showed them evidence that things didn't happen the way Bruce told them. For a start Bruce had big bruises on his shoulder from the driver's seatbelt, I've seen these before after an accident, he had them and you didn't. Bruce said you weren't wearing a seatbelt, so there would be no marks but he couldn't explain why he did have the bruising. I showed them the seat in the car.

You're six foot three, the first thing you do when you get in to a driver's seat is to push it right back so that you don't hit your knees on the steering wheel. I saw you push the seat in your car right back when you left that night but it had been pulled forward again when I saw the car after the accident.

There were other things, you were sitting on the ground at the driver's door but not in the car for instance. I showed these things to your family, Angus believed me and accused Bruce of lying and fitting you up to take the blame. Your father wouldn't hear of, I think mainly because he had taken Bruce's story and had had you sent away and to believe my version of the accident, was to admit that he had been wrong to do something so drastic.

So ANGUS SAID he was leaving, your mother saw her family breaking up and was ready to admit that they had been wrong to believe Bruce over you and tried to stop him. She failed and Angus left. He's in New Zealand now managing some big farms over there. Eventually your mother and father grew so far apart that she packed her bags and left as well. She filed for divorce and she's living in Hampshire somewhere I think."

"This is crazy Fraser, the whole family has fallen apart because of Bruce's lies. I couldn't have walked across the car park that night never mind gotten into a car and driven it. I don't even remember the accident. Oh sure I felt an impact and was a bit confused about things for a while. But I do know that I wasn't driving, Fraser."

"I know that Robbie and so do the people who really knew you. You've nothing to prove there but you need to sort out this thing, whatever it is that's going on up at the estate with Bruce and his "security people". You'll need help, he's got seven big strappin' lads up there and there all vicious thugs and they're armed Robbie I've seen then with hand guns and automatic rifles. That's what I wasn't supposed to see."

"Well he's only got five as of tonight. I left two of them with broken limbs in the car park at the Red Lion tonight."

"You did what? You don't waste any time do you? Mind you,

you look to have grown into quite a big lad yourself Robbie. I wouldn't like to fall out with you!"

"Not much chance of that Fraser. It's good to see you again, just sorry you needed to be in a hospital bed to get me here. Why didn't you call me earlier?"

"I wasn't sure what was going on with Bruce and these lads of his and even then, I wasn't sure you'd come."

"Fraser, you were the only friend I had in world at one point, apart from Lorna it seems, there is no way I was not going to come."

"Aye, that lass thinks the world of you Robbie MacLaine. I know she's got a woman as a partner, am still getting' used to that, but you cherish that lass, she's a heart o' gold and thinks the world of you. Near as broke her heart when she found out you were gone Robbie."

"Listen, Fraser, I better go before someone comes. They've got a guy in the grounds watching your window. He didn't see come in so I don't want him to see me go out either. You're in enough trouble with them it seems. You concentrate on getting better my friend and leave Bruce to me. He's goin' to pay for what he's done to this family. I'll keep in touch through Lorna mostly but don't worry I'll sort this mess out, one way or another. Take care Fraser."

"Me take care" laughed Fraser "I think it's you that needs to watch your back."

13

With that, Rob slipped out of Fraser's room and headed back to the exit door. He skirted round the "sentry" watching Fraser's window and made his way back to the parked Land Rover. He staying in the cover of some bushes with his night vision monocle on and made sure that there were no surprises waiting in the layby for him. He started the big V8 engine and drove slowly and quietly away from his hiding place on to the open road before he gunned the engine and drove back to Uncle Charlie's cottage and to Lorna Cameron. Once again, taking no chances, Rob parked shy of the cottage and made sure they had no unwelcome visitors before retrieving the Land Rover and driving to the cottage and parking round the same blind side as before.

"Lorna, it's me" he shouted from the front door.

Lorna appeared at the bedroom door "Aye, I heard a car and looked out to check it was you."

"Someone's been quite clever, you can't get near this house without crossing that gravel and making a heck of a noise in doing so" Rob answered.

"I've opened a bottle of red wine, would you like a glass"
Lorna said holding the bottle aloft.

"Sounds good to me, thanks."

Rob went through to his room and took off his jacket. He
took his Heckler & Koch SFP9-SF from his waistband and slid
it under one of the pillows on his bed, kicked off his shoes and
went back through to the lounge area. Lorna was sitting on one
of the chairs holding two glasses of wine.

"YOU OK WITH RIOJA?" she said holding up one of the glasses.

"Couldn't be better, thanks" he answered. Taking the proffered glass and sitting on the settee with his feet up.

"I see you shut all the curtains, we should keep them shut.
Best no one can see that there's someone staying here. If they
are looking for me and see lights on they might come and have
a nosey. Also, if Stella is coming out tell her to text or call you
from the road end so that you know she's there. I'll do the same
and don't answer the door to anyone else, nobody else knows
we're here. If someone knocks on the door or you hear
someone on the gravel, phone me right away."

"Is that not a bit OTT Robbie?" she smiled

"It's called security Lorna. It's what I do and I'm good at it.
I've never lost a client yet" he said smiling back at Lorna.

"OK if you say so."

"I do, better to be safe than sorry, to quote you "I've only
just got you back, I don't want to lose you." OK?"

"How was Fraser?"

"He's on the mend, I would say. Looks as if he took a fair
beating mind you, I need to put that to rights," said Rob, staring
into the far distance.

"He said you would fill me in on the goings on at Achravie
Estate, Lorna. You want to do that? Fraser told me about the

aftermath of the accident that night and the repercussions in the family."

"I NEVER FOR a minute thought you were driving that night Robbie, I knew you too well, probably better than anyone knew you at that time. Fraser tried hard to get your family to listen to his side of events but Angus was the only one who would listen. From what you say, Fraser told you the rest of that story, really sad all round. Your mother and father lost each other, Angus lost his father and both his brothers, you lost your whole family and your friends and I lost my best friend." Lorna drew a lengthy breath and forced the dejection from her expression and tone.

"About two and a bit years ago, not long after your father had his first stroke, Bruce had these big gates built at the entrance and just after that, started bringing in these so called security guards, there're foreign, Eastern Europeans, I think."

"They're Bosnians, I was in Kosovo for a short while and I recognised the language tonight," Rob interrupted.

"Not long after that they built a big warehouse type building at a fairly remote site on the estate. Bruce said he had it built to house equipment rather than leaving it outside and for agricultural supplies for the estate. We all were a bit sceptical but when they built a big high fence round it. We all said "aye right, that'll be to stop the tractors from partying at night." No one is allowed near the estate without "security clearance" or an invite.

A couple of the local lads have decided to have a look from time to time but they all got caught by these thugs and beaten up really badly. Obviously as a deterrent to others and it worked, no one goes anywhere near the estate unless they make an appointment to see Bruce.

There's been a lot more happened Robbie but that's the gist

of it. Pretty much everyone who worked on the estate has been paid off now except Fraser, then he turned up at the cottage hospital a few days ago. Bruce and two of his pals brought him in. Said he'd had an accident on a quadbike and ended up falling down a gully up at the castle.

I went up to see him and he said that four of Bruce's so called security guards had stopped him near the warehouse they built up near the pond. Asked him what he thought he was doing up there and said he had been told not to go anywhere near that part of the estate and proceeded to give him a systematic beating. He said he thought they were going to kill him till Bruce arrived and stopped them. Fraser said the whole thing was getting out of control.

Rob finished the last of the wine. Seeing her glass was also empty, he got up and refilled them, and leaned into a wall. "Sounds like it. You were right to call. And Fraser should have called long before now."

"He wasn't sure you would come, Robbie. It's been a long time, over twenty years. I know that Fraser kept track of you for a while but then he said you disappeared of the radar as he put it and he lost track of you till now. He said you gave him that number years ago and he wasn't even sure if it would still get you."

"You look so different Robbie, you were just a big boy when you left here and look at you now. You are all grown up. You're even bigger now" she laughed "I almost didn't recognise you in the Red Loin. I kept looking at you at thinking is that you Robbie MacLaine. I said to Lizzie but she said not to be daft, then she went over to talk to you and came back and said, "I think you're right". She said to her dad and he said Fraser had showed him a photograph of you in the army and said he thought it was you when you were checking in till he saw your eyes and they were brown. He knew your eyes were blue. So we decided that it might be you but none of us was sure enough to say anything to you, you know that feeling!"

"YOU'VE CHANGED A BIT YOURSELF MADAM" Laughed Rob "when I left you were just a slip of a girl. Look at you now, you're a beautiful, mature woman."

"Hey, we'll have less of the mature if you don't mind" Lorna scolded jokingly.

"OK, let's stick with the beautiful, then."

"You think so?" Lorna teased and they both laughed.

"Are you happy, Lorna? That's what matters in life."

"Yes, I am. Stella's good for me, we're good together. You must be shocked, your best pal a lesbian!"

"No, I 'm not. There was never anything sexual between us Lorna. Sometimes I wanted there to be but I knew you didn't and I suppose I wondered even then. I'm just delighted that you're happy. I've never been as close to anyone as I was to you. I've missed having you as part of my life, I suppose I always expected that you would be a part of my life, although I never saw us as Mr & Mrs, you were just my best pal" Rob said wistfully.

"I was gutted when Fraser told me you had gone. I was so angry that you didn't tell me you were going, but Fraser told me he wouldn't let you, he'd thrown your things to you and told you to go with him there and then. Then I got angry with him for that. Oh, I was just broken hearted, Robbie. I wanted to know where you had gone so that I could go and see you, but nobody would tell me.

Then all my friends started having real boyfriends and I wasn't interested. At first I put it down to not having you and then I started to feel attracted to other girls and again I thought that was just a reaction to losing you and then, finally, I realised that I was gay. It's not easy to have a gay relationship on

Achravie, but I did have a couple of girlfriends when I was at university and then teacher training in Glasgow. I came back here when the opportunity presented itself at the school and then eventually met Stella. The rest as they say is history."

"What about you? You a happy bunny?" Lorna added quizzically.

Rob thought for a second or two "Yeah, I suppose. I hated everybody for a while. Hated Bruce for what he had done. Hated my father for believing him and sending me away. Hated my mother for taking their side. Hated Fraser for doing what he was told. Hated everyone who wouldn't let me contact anybody here. But you can only hate everybody for so long, then you get hardened to it. You accept it and move on. The only way I could do that, was turn my back on the whole scenario. It was as if none of it had happened. I just threw myself into my army career. I became so focussed, almost driven I suppose, really determined to succeed. And I did. I went through the ranks, first in the Black Watch and then it became the Royal regiment of Scotland. I eventually found myself in charge of a small tactical unit and transferred to Special Forces. I got to go to lovely places like Kosovo, Afghanistan and Iraq to name but a few. I wore local dress, grew various beards, got involved in various skirmishes, not all of which turned out as planned" Rob said fingering the scar on his face. I used a lot of my time in these places studying when I wasn't involved. Sat and passed my officer exams and became a "Rupert. An officer to you."

"I eventually knew when I had had enough and a while later, with the cuts in the armed forces, I got the chance to leave, came out as a Lieutenant with a good package. I had met a guy called Joe Harper in Iraq and we got on really well, so when we realised we were both going to be in Civvy Street around the same time, we decided to put our skills to good use and we set up Harper MacLaine Security, a company that provides security and close protection to companies and individuals who need said services. That's going really well now, we're fully established, got a good solid, loyal, client base, very profitable, so making some real money for a change.

"Love life, significant others?" Lorna asked

"Oh, right" Rob laughed "Joe always said I was the king of the one night stands, which was always a bit unfair. He says I was never without a girl, just never the same one, which again was a bit unfair. I just never met a woman that I wanted spend real quality time with over much more than a couple of nights. Until a few days ago. I literally bumped into a woman in a bar where Joe and I were having a few drinks to celebrate winning a really big contract. Spilled some of her gin and tonic on her if the truth be told. We got talking, I bought her a drink, Joe said he had to get back as his wife is expecting their first in a few weeks, we stayed on for a couple more drinks and got on like a house on fire. Turns out she works for one of our major clients, PA to their CEO who is a good friend of mine, we had actually spoken on the phone but never met till that night. So who knows, maybe, I don't know."

"Sounds promising" Lorna teased, "Seriously though, I hope it works out, for your sake. A good partner can bring a lot to your life"

14

THEY TALKED ABOUT THEIR LIVES FOR THE PAST TWENTY YEARS. Rob told Lorna as many of his "war stories" as he felt he was allowed to. Much of his work with Special Forces was governed by the Official Secrets Act and he never spoke about that to anyone. Lorna talked about Achravie and answered questions about "what happened to this one" and "where did the other one end up" and they laughed together for the first time in twenty two years.

Eventually Lorna rubbed her eyes and looked up at the clock on the wall. "You do realise it's now nearly half two in the morning. I've got school in the morning, although thankfully I don't need to be in first thing tomorrow. I'm going to head for my bed Robbie, have you got everything you need?" asked Lorna as she rose from her chair

"Yep, I'm pretty sure I have" said Rob getting up from the settee "It's really good to see you again Lorna, thanks for everything"

"It's me should be thanking you, for goodness sake. It was me that begged you to come" Lorna reached up to put her arms round Rob's neck and buried her head in his chest. Rob put his arms around her and hugged.

"I love you Rob MacLaine" Lorna looked up at Rob, "You were like a brother to me, I never felt so close to anyone and then you were gone. I thought I'd never see you again. I thought I'd lost you" she said as a tear ran down her cheek.

Rob wiped the tear away and kissed her forehead "I love you too Lorna, you were always the sister I never had. Now I've got my best friend back. I won't lose you again, I promise. Now off to bed, I've got things to do tomorrow as well. Good night Lorna.

"Good night Rob."

After Lorna went to her room, Rob washed the two glasses and left them to drip on the drainer. He checked that all the doors and windows were secure, got undressed and went to bed. He didn't get to sleep right away, but lay awake for a while thinking about the morning and what he had to do. Finally he drifted off to sleep.

Somewhere in his subconscious he heard a noise, a creak of a floorboard maybe, or a hinge. He reached under his pillow and his hand found the gun he had put there. He had drifted off to sleep with a bedside light on and it spread a soft glow across the room. There was a soft knock at the door.

"Robbie are you sleeping?" Lorna whispered softly.

"Lorna, what's up" Rob propped himself up on one elbow, his other hand releasing the gun.

The door slowly opened "I could see the light and wondered if you were still awake" she said closing the door behind her. "I don't want to be on my own tonight Robbie, can I sleep with you and I mean sleep, not sex, just sleep and a cuddle."

Rob could see a tear in her eye "Sure, jump in" he said with a smile "Just sleep and a cuddle."

She lifted the pale pink cotton nightdress over her head and dropped it to the floor, revealing an expensive black lacy thong. She was indeed a beautiful woman he thought as she reclined next to him and he covered her with the duvet.

"You didn't keep you're knickers on when we went skinny dipping after school" Rob teased

"YOU DIDN'T KEEP your boxers on either, I'm just following your lead Mr MacLaine" she said as she spooned in to him. She wiggled her bottom against his groin, "Anyway, don't want you getting any ideas" she laughed softly.

Rob settled down on his pillow and put his arms round her. Lorna took his hand and cupped it around one of her breasts "Cuddle and sleep" she said, closing her eyes with a look of contentment on her face.

"Cuddle and sleep" said Rob giving her breast the lightest of squeezes and closing his eyes for sleep.

Despite the late hour of going to bed, Rob rose early and without waking the still sleeping Lorna want through to the kitchen and put on a pot of coffee. He was sitting in his boxer shorts, deep in thought about how to tackle Bruce and his attendant muscle when Lorna came through from the bedroom wearing her nightdress again.

"Mornin'" she said sleepily ruffling her hair with her fingers and then helping herself to a mug of coffee.

She sat down opposite Rob at the small kitchen table and looked at his bare torso. Stretching across the table and touching one of his wound scars on his upper arm said "when you said last night about "various skirmishes, not all of which turned out as planned", I take it that's where you got these from?"

"No, they're just painted on to get women to touch me" he smiled.

"I'm sorry about last night Robbie, I just felt so alone lying there on my own with you next door and not having seen you for so long. I was being unfair to you though."

"WHAT, I get to sleep with a gorgeous near naked women and you think that's unfair? I take it you and Stella sunbathe topless by the way" Lorna slapped his shoulder playfully.

"That's for me to know and you to find out. We might go nudie but I kept my knickers on so you'll never know."

"I'll check with Stella, am sure she'll be glad you kept your knickers on!"

"Don't you dare Robbie MacLaine!" Lorna said almost choking on her coffee.

"S'OK, I'll tell her a kept my boxers on as well," Rob laughed.

"Oh dear, Stella would not understand you and I. I've tried to explain our relationship and am sure she thinks she understands but I can see a wary look in her eye. Despite her wee speech before she left yesterday she wasn't happy about me staying here with you last night."

"She'll get used to us, I hope. Might help when she sees me with another woman "Rob said thoughtfully.

"So, what's she like this other woman?"

"JUSTINE? Oh, "Leggy blond, good tits, nice arse". Her words not mine. She said I was assuming she must be thick because of the way she looked. She misunderstood something I said the first time we met. Having said that, we have actually only met once, when I think about it. We met in a bar and really hit it off, she came back to mine and stayed over."

. . .

"DARE I ask if she kept her knickers on" Lorna teased and they both laughed.

"She was with me when I got your call, I explained what it was about and that I needed to get here sharpish. Next thing she's arranged her bosses helicopter to fly me up here. I told you her boss and I are friends. We've spoken on the phone a couple of times since I got here and there's a real connection Lorna. I think you'd like her, she's intelligent, witty, spirited..."

"But most importantly "good tits, nice arse"" Lorna interrupted.

"Yeah, bit like you."

"Yeah, yeah, I'm goin' for a shower" Lorna said rising from the table and heading for the bathroom. She stopped at the bathroom door, turned and looked over her shoulder in that way women can do. "Do you really think I've got a nice arse?

"Don't know, you kept your knickers on. Good tits though!"

"Cheek!" she said closing the bathroom door.

The room Rob and Lorna had slept in had an en-suite so Rob showered in there and got dressed while Lorna did the same in the other room. They reappeared in the lounge area at the same time. Lorna carrying her overnight bag and Rob had his bag of tricks slung over his shoulder.

"Right, let's get you home to your other half" Rob said picking up the keys to the cottage and heading for the door.

"Robbie, you be careful out there today, please. These are scary people" Lorna said taking hold of Rob's hand as they walked to the car.

"Nah! The Taliban are scary people. These guys are just pussycats in comparison" Rob reassured her, as much to convince himself as Lorna.

They both sat quietly as they drove the short distance to Lorna and Stella's cottage in Achravie. As they stopped outside the cottage, Lorna leaned over and kissed Rob's scarred cheek. See if I'd been around, I could've kissed it better" she said jokingly "Best if we keep last night's sleeping arrangement to ourselves eh!" she said raising her eyebrows.

"Yeah, for sure. Mind you I will need to ask Stella about the nudie sunbathing" Rob smiled.

"Don't you dare, Robbie MacLaine!"

"No, of course I won't." he countered.

"It would take all the fun out of finding out for myself" he added with a smile.

"I'll meet you in the Red Lion about seven tonight, all going well" Rob added as Lorna climbed out of the Land Rover.

With Radio Clyde playing softly on the car radio, Rob drove along the scenic coast road and passed the big iron gates, which hadn't been there the last time he'd been here. He continued up the hill toward the castle ruins and the pond, where the warehouse was situated.

He didn't want to bump into anyone because that would most certainly mean confrontation and he needed to avoid that until he knew what was going on behind these closed gates and high fences. That being the case Rob drove past the ruins and into the Pay & Display car park. Being the start of the tourist season, the car park was about half full, so the Land Rover did not look conspicuous to anyone in the area.

HE CLIMBED to the upper edges of the castle site which gave him sight over much of the Achravie Estate land, include a distant view of Hillcrest House where he was brought up, in what sometimes felt like a different life.

He banished all thoughts of those early years from his conscious mind and concentrated on the here and now. He pulled a set of compact binoculars from his rucksack and looked out over the countryside. He saw the pond and to his right as he looked, the warehouse which he had been told about. It was a prefabricated concrete structure, very similar to some of the storage facilities that the military used in temporary bases although it looked to have been there or some time and was showing signs of weathering and the beginnings of the growth of green algae on the corrugated roof. The only window in the structure visible from Rob's hilltop perch was on that roof and unless there was a window round the far side of the building, which Rob doubted, that window would be the only way to see what was being stored inside, without having to gain access to the building itself. Being as that window was visible from the main road and the castle site, albeit from a distance, it looked very much as if Rob would need to get up there during the hours of darkness. The building itself was surrounded by a chain-link fence which looked to be about nine foot high and topped with barbed wire. There were also floodlights sited at intervals around the perimeter fence which Rob imagined would be motion sensor activated.

Rob lowered his binoculars and looked around himself. The view from where he stood was quite panoramic with views to the east over the island, including the estate and likewise to the south. To the north was open sea and to the west he could clearly see the Mull of Kintyre. He'd never actually been on the Kintyre peninsula he thought, despite having overlooked it for the first eighteen years of his life. His time off the island at that time had taken him to Arran, the main island and then on to Glasgow or Ayrshire, never to the Kintyre peninsula.

He wandered round the back of the castle site, mostly to act like Bob Chapman the tourist and looked out over the water. The sea was almost deserted to the west of Achravie, most of the marine traffic passed a fair way to the east, passing between Arran and the Ayrshire coast. Ships heading for Port Glasgow, Ardrossan and Hunterston. The unseen nuclear submarines heading in and out of the submarine base at Faslane, home of the UKs Trident nuclear missile fleet.

He walked along a coastal path and rounded the next headland and there was a little cove with a small jetty. The jetty was bigger than he remembered and on inspection thought his binoculars he could see where it had been extended fairly recently, which is why it looked bigger. Sitting at the jetty was what looked like a fair sized fishing boat and beside that, on the end of the jetty was a white Achravie Estate Land Cruiser. Rob decided to have a closer look and made his way back round the headland till he was out of sight of the jetty and scrambled down a steep path, which he vaguely remembered, to another small inlet and made his way carefully back round to the little bay which housed the jetty.

He climbed round as far as he thought prudent and slowly raised his head above the rocks. There were four men sitting on deck, at the bow of the boat, two were drinking from mugs and one was smoking a cigarette. They looked as if they were engaged in light conversation, the man with the cigarette talking and gesturing with his arms and the others laughed. The conversation and laughter went on as Rob watched and although he was just too far away to grasp the conversation, he could hear enough to know that they were Eastern European.

They seemed very relaxed, which was understandable as the only people who would see them were liable to be the odd tourist wandering round from the castle and they would think nothing of seeing a small boat moored at a jetty. It was just another boat and another jetty to all intents and purposes, all very innocent. Rob could tell from their general demeanour and dress that two of the men were from Achravie Estate, hence the Land Cruiser. The other two he assumed were crew from the boat. As he looked on, two other men appeared from below deck on the boat and joined the others. One was obviously another member of crew, the other, Rob took a few seconds to recognise as his brother.

Bruce was always shorter and of stockier build than Rob, but over the years his brother had developed a definite paunch and was carrying a fair amount of weight around his middle. His hair was thinning, very much as he remembered his father's had. Bruce shook hands with the other man who had come on deck with him and gestured to the two men sitting at the bow of the boat. They rose and with a bit of backslapping and gesturing, followed Bruce off the boat and over to the Land Cruiser. One of the flunkies opened the back door and Bruce climbed in with a certain amount of effort. With the two others in the front seats, the white 4x4 drove off the jetty and up the steep track back up to the main road.

Rob felt an old anger rise in his chest, an anger he had not felt in years but which once again fired him with an irresistible urge to destroy the man who had destroyed his life and his family with his lies and deceit twenty years ago. Rob sat for a while and let that anger recede. Anger bred impulsive reactions and impulsive reactions bred carelessness and vulnerability, which in turn led to failure. Rob had learned from bitter experience in foreign warzones that vengeance was indeed a dish better served cold.

Rob made his way back round the bay and up to the castle ruins and sat for a few minutes in the Land Rover back in the castle car park.

He picked out his phone and found Justine's number in his call history and hit the call button.

The phone rang five or six times before a woman's voice at the other end said "Rob, are you OK?"

"I'm fine Tina, how are you?" he replied

"Worried sick about you if you must know. Where have you been, you were supposed to keep in touch with me regularly, why didn't you call?"

"Sorry Tina, things have been a bit hectic since I got here and on the odd occasion when I did have time I had no signal", he lied and immediately felt guilty.

"What's happening up there? Justine demanded.

Rob quickly brought her up to date with some of the events on the past 24 hours missing much of the detail of his night spent with Lorna. He would tell her a bit more about that after she had met Lorna. He had been honest when he told Lorna that he thought the two of them would get on.

"Where are you, I'm getting a lot of background noise?"

"I'm in the car with a friend at the moment, but I'm so glad you called. Please don't not call me again Rob, I thought something had happened to you"

"SORRY. There I go again, if you had a pound for every time I have said that word to you since we met, you would be in danger of becoming a very rich lady" he said trying to lighten the mood of the conversation.

"If you don't call me again soon, it's going to take more than "sorry" to get you off the hook Rob MacLaine. I need to go, I've pulled over on a double yellow line to take your call, but, please, please keep in touch and let me know your all right" Justine pleaded.

"I will, I promise, sorry, again. I'll call you later, take care" he said and ended the call.

Rob then hit the speed dial which would connect him to Joe Harper's mobile.

"Rob, where are you, are you OK?" Joe Harper answered.

"I'm fine, just doing a bit of recce, trying to gauge the lie of the land. One of two of the locals who knew me well have recognised me Joe but they're not going to say anything to anyone else. I had a run in with a couple of my brother's heavy's last night at the local pub and broke a few bones as a result, but they don't know who I am. They were just being arses to a couple of the locals, assaulted them in the car park, so I put a stop to it, nothing else I could do, they were people I know."

"I've just seen my brother he..."

"What did he say, did he recognise you?" asked Joe sounding worried.

"He didn't see *me*, Joe, I made sure of that. Fat little bastard he's turned into"

"What the hell's that noise Joe? Rob asked.

"I'm in the car Rob, I'm driving so you're on speaker phone."

"Oh, thanks Joe, hope you're on your own, me slagging off my beloved brother."

"No, you're fine Rob."

"Bloody hell Joe, what is it with everybody today, is the whole world in it's car today? Just phoned Justine, she's in her car. She's not a happy bunny because I didn't phone. It's my fault, I said I would call her, she sounded pretty hacked off with me. I hope I haven't blown it with her Joe, I really like her. I could have babies with her if she'd let me." Rob said wistfully.

"I'm sure you'll be fine Rob" Joe laughed, "The fact that she was hacked off probably just means that she cares and was worried about you, yeah?"

"Maybe, I don't know. She's bloody gorgeous Joe, she could have any man she wanted, what would she see in someone like me?"

"See, now you're doing your insecure bit again, so pack in, you'll have me crying in a minute. Now bugger off and get things sorted on that back of beyond island of yours and you'll see the lovely Justine again before you know it. Need to go, see you soon partner" Joe cut the call.

15

ROB SPENT THE AFTERNOON WALKING ROUND THE ACHRAVIE Estate to try to find the best way to get access to the warehouse, making sure no one saw him. He finally worked out how to do it and made his way sometimes on his hands and knees and sometimes on his stomach to some bushes close to the edge of the warehouse compound.

He looked at the fence and compound through his binoculars even though he was close to the fence, looking for detail that he would not otherwise see. Just as well, because he picked up a series of small cameras around the perimeter and noted down their positions. It was going to be tricky to get to the warehouse, never mind climb up onto the roof to see inside. Rob made his way round to the other side of the building, the side which was not visible from the castle site.

His spirits leapt; there was a small door at the rear corner of the building. Now that was an unexpected bonus, he would not now need to get up on to the roof and might actually be able to gain access to the building rather than trying to peer through a roof sited window. The down side was that the door would probably be alarmed. Rob double checked his notes and sketches and having decided that he had seen enough for the time being started to retrace his steps covertly back to the main road.

He walked toward the car park and crossed the road to retrieve the Land Rover just as a dark blue BMW 5 series estate swung into the car park and stopped in front of him. Three men, excluding the driver, got out of the car and casually but deliberately fanned out in front of him. The man who had been in the front passenger seat stood in front of Rob. He was a dark haired man, taller than the others. but all looked to be in their late thirties or early forties and all looked pretty fit.

"A WORD, SIR" he said "in the car if you don't mind" he added holding the back door of the car open.

"My mother always told me not to get in to cars with strange men and never to speak to strangers" Rob replied.

"My name is Chris Hall, my colleagues and I work for the National Crime Agency" the man said.

"National Crime Agency? That's easy for *you* to say. Show me!" Rob demanded.

The man's left hand moved toward the inside pocket of his short leather jacket. Rob took a step back "Slowly, if you don't mind" he said.

"TRUSTING SOUL", the man quipped, holding his jacket open to show Rob was not reaching for a weapon.

"I'm still breathing and that trumps trusting in my book" Rob replied watching the man's eyes as he pulled a small wallet out of his jacket pocket. He flicked it open and showed the National Crime Agency identification to Rob.

"And you, do you have any ID, Mr..."

"Bob Chapman" Rob said holding out one of his recently acquired business cards.

"Let's walk, if you want to talk, nice day for it don't you think" said Rob.

As Rob moved to walk around the BMW one of the colleagues stood directly in front of him, barring his way.

Rob stared at the man. "Are we going for a walk or not Mr Hall? "he asked.

"LET's WALK" Hall replied

"Rob raised his eyebrows at the man standing in his path and after a pause the man moved out of his direct line. Rob walked forward looking back at Hall who was a couple of steps behind him. "You can bring the three bears with you if you want, 's up to you" he said mischievously.

The three did not wait to be invited but walked behind Hall and Rob into the main car park and over toward the castle ruins.

"I want to know what you were doing trespassing on Achravie Estate land this afternoon" Hall said eventually.

"The Land Reform (Scotland) Act 2003 establishes a statutory right of access to land in Scotland, so I wasn't trespassing. Anyway, what's it got to do with you lot, where I take myself for a walk?"

"My business is none of your business, Chapman and I wouldn't describe your activities this afternoon as a leisurely walk. You were scoping out that warehouse from what we could see."

"You followed me out there?" Rob asked incredulously.

"No we were there before you arrived."

"You're watching that warehouse?"

"Sir?" one of the other officers interrupted and shook his head and handed Hall the business card Rob had given him.

"So, your ID doesn't check out Mr Chapman. Do you want to enlighten me or do we pull you in right now"

"YOU BASED OUT OF CITADEL PLACE?"

"Yes, what's that.."

"You know Tony Urquhart?"

"He's my boss's boss, wha..."

"OK, hang on" Rob said retrieving his mobile and scrolling through his contacts. He pressed the call button and waited.

"Good afternoon, National Crime Agency, Mr Urquhart's office?" the young lady at the other end asked politely.

"Would you put me through to Tony please, it's Harper MacLaine Security" He had turned away slightly from Hall and his colleagues to place this call so they would not have heard the name.

"Tony Urquhart here, who's calling?" the voice asked.

Rob turned back to Hall, "Tony it's Rob, can you speak at the moment."

"Yeah, go on" came the reply.

"Do you know Chris Hall? Says he's one of your guys."

"Sure, good guy, I might add. Why do you ask?"

"He's standing in front of me at the moment, in the car park at Achravie Castle. We are discussing a certain warehouse on Achravie Estate. You know the one?"

"I know why Chris and his team are on Achravie if that's what you're asking"

"OK, I also have an interest in that warehouse and I think we need to get our heads together on this because neither of will back off I would imagine. I don't want to get in your guys' way but I have a vested interest in what's going on. Let me explain."

Rob quickly explained to Tony Urquhart and by default Chris Hall and his team why he was on Achravie.

There was nobody else in the immediate area, so Rob put his mobile on to speaker phone so that as the team huddled round his phone, they could hear both sides of the conversation. At the end of Rob's explanation, Urquhart was quiet for a minute.

"OK, first of all, I can't put you on the books for this one Rob."

"Not a problem" Rob interrupted.

"Secondly, what you suggest makes perfect sense to me am I'm happy to go with a collaborative approach. Can you hear me on that one Chris?"

"Yes Sir, but.."

"No, it's fine Chris. NCA has used Rob's company as consultants in the past with excellent outcomes. I know the man, you two will get on well and that's not an order Chris, it's a prediction."

Chris Hall looked at Rob, who shook his head at Hall and both men smiled.

"OK, can I leave this one with you chaps? Let's get a speedy resolution on it, if we can. Best of luck Rob, Chris."

16

Tony Urquhart cut the call and Rob put his mobile back in his pocket.

Chris Hall's team all looked at their team leader "Seems like we've got a new team member, guys. If Rob here has Tony Urquhart's blessing then I'm happy with that. He's not an easy man to please, he must know you well" Chris Hall said.

"Tony was my commanding officer in Iraq and Afghanistan and I worked with him in other places which we don't need to put names to. I've worked for him at NCA when he needs to work within, shall we say, a less rigid structure. We know each other very well." Rob explained.

"OK, we need to talk about the way forward on this. We've got a cottage on the other side of the Island, rather than draw attention to ourselves in Achravie village. Why don't we go back there and have a pow-wow" Chris Hall suggested and Rob agreed.

"Sounds good, I'll follow you guys" he said Hall turned to one of his team," Ally you want to stay as lookout and report any movement?"

The man in question a wiry man with a boyish face nodded his agreement to the suggestion.

"Rob, this is Alastair Gemmell, by the way, Ally to his mates. I'll introduce the other guys when we get to the cottage."

"Hi Ally" Rob shook his hand briefly, "good to meet you."

"Rob, you too."

Turning back to Hall "I'll head back to the hide." Gemmell said and set off down the path.

THE OTHERS WALKED BACK to the car park and one of Hall's men, a short stocky man with razor cut hair approached Rob.

"Mind if I ride with you?" he asked, approaching the passenger door of the Land Rover.

"No, not at all, hop in."

"I'm Tom Parker, by the way. Nothing to do with Elvis, I might add."

Rob laughed "Good to meet you Tom."

Rob followed the NCA team's BMW out of the car park in silence and it wasn't till they were travelling at speed down the island in the direction of their cottage that Tom Parker said, "So you were a SASS man, then?"

"Yep, did some detective work at the end of Kosovo, then Iraq, Afghanistan and couple of other little pockets. Left nigh on three years ago." Rob replied.

"Mm, I spent a bit of time in the Balkans, nasty war that was, lot of real hatred on the ground. I was under Major Urquhart in Afghanistan. Spent two days in Iraq and got shipped home with a broken leg. You said you worked for him in other little pockets as well."

"Yeah, secret squirrel stuff."

"Oh. OK, so you know him pretty well, then, mate, must do to get through to him easy as you did."

"He was part of a small group that got trapped in a safe

house in Musa Qalah that got compromised. I led a patrol who went in and got them out one night in the middle of a fire fight. Won myself a few brownie points there."

"BET YOU DID, if you'd saved my arse, I think I might take your calls too."

The rest of the journey was uneventful and Tom Parker's interrogation seemed to have satisfied him of Rob's credentials. About ten minutes later, they stopped outside a small detached cottage, which sat slightly back from the road allowing the easy parking of the vehicles.

Chris Hall introduced the other member of the team as Charlie Best, an ex-Metropolitan Police firearms officer from Enfield and they sat down with a brew of strong tea each filled the other in with their activities to date.

Cyber-crime and the use of internet based technology by criminal organisations has become a major issue with the law enforcement agencies in Europe, including the NCA and it was while the Cyber-crime team housed within the Metropolitan Police were monitoring some suspicious internet activity, they came across a site which appeared to be offering to traffic girls from Eastern Europe to the UK. The NCA had been advised of this and not long afterwards had been alerted to some suspicious small boat traffic off the West Coast of Scotland. Further investigation had linked these two activities and with help of Europol they had managed initially to trace this traffic back to a port called Stade, just down river from Hamburg on the river Elbe. Eventually the traffic had been followed to its ultimate destinations. There was no regular schedule being adhered to but the NCA team had been dispatched to monitor the activity on Achravie four days prior to Rob's arrival. The previous night, another NCA team had picked up another boat and it had been followed again to Achravie. This was the boat Rob had seen moored at the jetty below the cliffs by Achravie Estate.

"It took us a while to piece all this together. The gang responsible are not exactly advertising themselves but we have resources all over Europe at our disposal and we're not shy about using them nowadays. People smuggling is big business and as you see on the news almost every day now, there are thousands of people trying to get in to the UK.

You see the tragedies that happen in the Med nowadays with people traffickers trying to get refugees into the EU, putting dozens, sometimes hundreds of desperate people onto boats that were never meant to hold those numbers of people. You can understand how these same traffickers can persuade vulnerable young girls that they are able to get them into the UK and get them jobs. We pretty well know that this is what's happening here, Rob" Chris Hall explained.

"There were two off-loading points that we found, might be more, so we are still watching through Europol. The two that we know of are, Lowestoft and Achravie. We believe the girls arriving here are being kept in that warehouse building and will eventually end up in Glasgow, Edinburgh and Aberdeen, maybe even Newcastle."

"These girls don't exist as far as the authorities in the UK are concerned, so if they get harmed or even killed, nobody is held responsible, Rob" Tom Parker added. "They'll get drugged and raped and beaten. They'll be told if they try to leave or tell anyone, their families back home'll be beaten or killed. When they're finished with them they'll just OD them on heroin and get rid of" he said with disgust.

Rob shook his head. He know his brother could sink pretty low to serve his own ends, but to be involved in the trafficking of young girls and be party to potentially ending their lives in the manner Tom Parker had just describe was way beyond the depths to which Rob ever considered his brother capable of sinking.

"This has to be stopped", Rob growled, holding his head in his hands, his elbows resting on his knees, as he sat in a chair listening to the scenario unfolding from the NCA team.

"No time like the present" Parker chimed in.

"There is a boat at the jetty just round the headland at the castle. We think it has brought another "consignment" of girls. It arrived this morning from Stade. Europol have been watching the group and when the boat left we tracked its position and when it was obvious it wasn't heading for Lowestoft, we were ordered here. As you now know, we've been watching the warehouse today and there has been no movement in or out except for three men who arrived with four large cardboard boxes, which they dumped in the warehouse and left."

"Two big guys, security uniforms and a little fat bastard in a white Land Cruiser?" Rob guessed.

"Yes, you know them?"

"Oh yes, I had a run in with a couple of the bears last night and the little fat bastard is my beloved brother"

"Your what!!" Chris Hall, almost choked on a mouthful of coffee and the rest of his team sat bolt upright and stared at Rob in disbelief. "Please tell me your joking, Rob. This puts a whole new perspective on this. Does Tony Urquhart know this?

"He knows my story, he'll know it's no coincidence that I'm involved in this"

"Involved, in what way, Rob?" Tom Parker asked worriedly.

"Let me tell you" Rob said and started to relate his past history with his family and the more recent history with the situation in hand.

. . .

"I NEED to brief my boss on this Rob. I need to know he's still comfortable with the situation. I need to cover myself here."

"OK, call me on this mobile number once you've cleared it with Tony. He'll be fine with it but I understand where you're coming from." Rob handed Chris a Bob Chapman business card and rose from his chair.

He turned at the door, "I need to get changed and I've arranged to meet someone at the Red Lion at seven thirty tonight. Then I'm going to have a look at the warehouse again, so make sure all your guys know that I'll be snooping around, OK"

"Let me call Urquhart, then I'll call you. We need to do this in a co-ordinated way Rob. We've been working on this for months. I can't let anything or anybody screw this up for us at this stage." Chris Hall said patting Rob on the shoulder as he left.

17

AT SEVEN THIRTY FIVE, SHOWERED AND DRESSED IN BLACK JEANS, dark T-shirt and black hooded sweatshirt, Rob walked into the bar of the Red Lion. The story of his intervention in the car park the previous night had done the rounds of the bar-room gossips and a silence descended over the bar area as he was recognised as Bob Chapman who had beaten off two attackers and done them serious injury in the process.

Lorna was standing by the bar having just taken their drinks from a characteristically ebullient Hamish.

Hamish looked up from a pint he was pouring. "Ah, the conquering hero returns to the scene of his triumph" he beamed.

"Oh, shut up Hamish and pour me a glass of that cheap Rioja you serve" Rob laughed and the general hubbub of the bar was restored to normal levels.

Rob hugged Lorna briefly and kissed her lightly on the cheek as he waited for Hamish to serve him, what was actually a surprisingly good Rioja Reserva.

"Do you want to grab that table over in the corner Lorna, while I wait for my drink?" Rob said.

Rob was suddenly aware of someone standing close behind him and as he made to turn round to see who was there, he felt something sharp press into his lower back.

"Move very slowly out of the door my friend" a deep, heavily accented voice said quietly.

"We have some unfinished business."

Rob could easily have taken the man out there and then, but was aware of the close proximity of the others in the bar and didn't want to attack a knife wielding thug in a crowded bar. He did as the man ordered and moved quietly to the door as he opened the door the man pushed him out into the carpark and Rob found himself surrounded by five of the Bosnian security guards.

"As I said, my friend, we have unfinished business. You hurt two of our colleagues last night and we need to balance things up a bit, so we are going to hurt *you* now. We are going to break your arms and legs, maybe cut you up a bit. Maybe you should even prepare to die."

One of the others opened the tailgate of one of the two Land Cruisers "Get in, we are going to see some pretty sights on the island, get to know each other better" he said and laughed at his own attempt at humour.

Rob was madly trying to look for a way out of the situation, one of him, five of them but no way was he getting into that Land Cruiser. He had just worked out how to get the knife away from his lower back and reach his Heckler & Koch before his closest assailant found it, when he heard a shout from behind him.

"Rob. Darling" the tall blond woman shouted, running towards him and throwing her arms around his neck knocking him away from the man holding the knife, while another shadowy figure hit the man hard on the back of the head. The man dropped like a sack of potatoes, his accomplices too stunned to react.

Rob grabbed the man who had opened the tailgate and as he spun him round, pulled the Heckler & Koch from his waistband and stuck the barrel into the man's right ear. All this had happened so quickly that only now were people in the Red Lion following Lorna out of the bar and into the car park.

"EVERYBODY KEEP WELL BACK" Rob shouted. "You too Lorna, keep back" he said to the approaching figure.

Lorna stopped in her tracks when she saw Rob's gun and caught the expression on his face and the hard cold stare in his eyes. This was a Robbie she had never seen before.

"Right you lot" he turned to the Bosnian's "get lost, go, all of you."

They did not need to be told a second time and they lifted their unconscious colleague as Rob pushed the man he was aiming his gun at into the nearest Land Cruiser. The two big four-by-fours skidded out of the carpark and sped off, leaving Rob staring at Justine and Joe Harper.

"What..? Where the hell did..? Jesus, Tina you could have been killed. Don't you ever pull a stunt like that again, do you hear me!" Rob shouted.

"Joe what were you thinking, she might have been killed for Chrissakes!!"

"Excuse me Robbie MacLaine, from what I just saw, this woman may have just saved your life. She does not deserve to be spoken to like that and would you stop waving that gun around before you kill someone" said Lorna angrily from the edge of the carpark.

"What...? Sorry? Rob said returning the Heckler & Koch to the waistband of his jeans and looking first at Justine and then at a perplexed Joe.

"What the hell are you guys doing here? How did you...?"

"Excuse me. I drive the length of the country, to make sure

you are all right, because Justine is worried about you, not without cause it would appear. Get here just in time to save your sorry arse and the best you can offer is "What the hell are you guys doing here?"" Joe chided Rob. "From what I've heard of the conversation you two had today, the least you can do is give the lady a bit of a hug."

"What do you mean from what you've heard from both of us today?" Rob stopped. "You were in the same car! You were on speaker phone Harper!"

Rob turned to Justine, "Did you hear what I said…?"

"About making babies? Uhuh, sounded interesting, but not in a public carpark"

"Oh God, sorry, I didn't mean you to hear.." Rob blushed.

"I gathered that. Are you going to buy me a drink, now?"

"Yeah, yeah, but first I want you to meet a woman who means the world to me Tina," Rob said steering Justine over to Lorna.

"You say the sweetest things to a girl MacLaine" Justine replied taking his hand in hers.

"Tina, this is Lorna Cameron. Lorna, meet Justine Fellows"

"Hi Justine" Lorna said with an almost embarrassed smile, "I've heard a lot about you over the past couple of days."

"Hi Lorna, I've heard a bit about you too. Nice to meet you. Helluva way to meet though!"

"You're pretty much the way Rob described you" added Lorna "He thinks the world of you too, you should know."

"Oh, and how does he describe me?"

LORNA LOOKED MISCHIEVOUSLY AT ROB, "What was it you said "Leggy blond, good tits, nice arse, her words, not yours."

Rob looked embarrassed "Sorry, but she did ask and I couldn't think of a better description than yours."

"I was pretty mad at him when I said that" Justine explained to Lorna with a laugh. "And would you stop saying sorry, that all you ever seem to say to me Rob MacLaine."

"Sorry" Rob shrugged and they all laughed.

"So are we getting a drink or not?" Joe enquired.

"OK, come on" Rob said holding the door open for the two women.

Rob walked over to the bar and motioned to Hamish.

"Are you OK son, I heard what happened out there. These boys are going to scare you away from my pub. Who am I supposed to sell my cheap Rioja to then?" Hamish joked.

"Can we use the wee back room for a while, Hamish" Lorna asked.

"Aye, sure, Lizzie'll bring some drinks through if you tell me what you want."

Rob ordered a round of drinks and led the way through to the small empty Snug bar.

As they were sitting down, Justine asked Lorna where the Ladies was and Lorna said she would show her where they were.

"So, What happened that you came up here, Joe? "Rob asked.

"Justine happened. She was really worried about you, so was I. We both could see trouble brewing from what you had said on the phone. You didn't call Justine yesterday and when I didn't hear from you, she managed to persuade me to come looking for you. Just as well as it turns out, these guys weren't fooling around. They would have done you serious damage.

Who are they anyway, what's the story here?" Joe asked.

Rob gave Joe a quick rundown on the events of the past couple of days as the two ladies returned from the toilet. Lorna added a bit of local knowledge and Rob told them of his meeting the NCA team and described what they had told him of their investigations.

Almost on cue, Rob's mobile rang

18

"Rob, Chris Hall, I've spoken with Tony Urquhart and he is still of the mind that we should work together on this. He says that under the circumstances, you can operate out with the rulebook if need be, in ways that we can't do. He says you are a hard sod who gets the job done, no matter what the job is and not to get on the wrong side of you."

"Ha! Tony Urquhart taught me most of what I know about the job. He was one of the best I ever came across and if I'm a hard sod, it's because life and Tony Urquhart made me that way."

"So, what's your view on things, Chris?"

Without hesitation, Chris answered "We need to find out what's in that warehouse tonight, Rob. It may not be there tomorrow. Down side of that is that the crew from the boat are still here, there are four of them plus we reckon there's six guys here already. That's a total of ten, there's four of us plus you, that's not the best of odds."

"Well there were seven of them, that's corroborated, I put two out of action last night leaves five plus the four from the boat, makes nine. My partner appeared tonight so that makes six of us. If we watch our backs we should be OK at that, it's less than two each."

"Where are you now, Rob?"

"Red Lion in Achravie."

"Where do you want to meet?"

"Back at yours if that's OK. Let's say one hour from now."

"OK, see you then Rob" said Chris and cut the call.

ROB TURNED BACK TO JOE, Lorna and Justine, "OK, we're going to have a look at the warehouse tonight with the NCA team" he said to Joe. "Did you bring any kit with you by any chance?"

"Does a bear crap in the woods? Rob, this is me you're talking to, of course I brought kit with me. I brought a couple of M27s and a couple of Heckler & Koch SFP9-SF pistols and I know you already have your "Boy Scout stuff" with you. I brought radios, night vision kit and a few other bits and pieces."

"Lorna, would Stella mind if you took Justine back to Uncle Charlie's and stayed with her?"

"No she'll be OK with that, I'll call at let her know" Lorna replied.

"Stella's my partner Justine" she added to Justine.

"Can the girls take your car Joe?" Rob asked

"Sure."

"Good that's settled" said Rob.

The two men transferred Joe's bags hidden in the back of Joe's Audi RS4 Estate into Big Mac's Land Rover and the two women drove off, heading for Uncle Charlie's cottage. Rob and Joe headed over to the NCA team's cottage, which was about a fifteen minute drive from the Red Lion car park.

"So, this is home is it?" Joe asked looking out at the hills and beaches on either side of them as they drove, "Looks very tranquil on the surface, but from what you said earlier, looks are deceptive once again."

"YEAH, if Chris Hall and his guys have got it right, and I've no reason to doubt them, then it's a lot bigger than just what's going on here, Joe. God knows what my brother's got himself mixed up in."

"Do you think your father knows what's going down?

Rob thought for a moment "I don't see it, nobody has mentioned him at all in all this. I don't know if it's because they think I might not want to hear. Not even Lorna spoke about him. Dad was always a bit gullible when it came to Bruce. He would always take his side when it came to disagreements and arguments, not sure why, but he was never stupid, nor was he a particularly bad person. I just don't see him as someone who would tolerate, never mind get involved in something like this. I really need to talk to him."

"How would you feel about meeting him again after what went down?"

"Jeez, I don't know Joe. I've thought about that quite a lot in the last few days and I'm not sure how I would feel. I'll never forgive him for what he did to me, I know that, but meeting him, talking to him. I just don't know, but I know I do need to, at some point."

"What about these NCA guys, Rob, do you know any of them?" Joe asked.

"I don't, but I know a man who does. Do you remember Tony Urquhart, Captain in the Regiment?"

"Yeah, you pulled him out of a spot of bother in Afghanistan, if I remember rightly."

"Yeah, well they work for Tony and I spoke to him earlier. He rates them, particularly Chris Hall from what I gather."

"OK, that can't be bad."

"What about your friend Lorna, she seems a bit of all right. You go back a long way from what you say, bit of history there maybe, something for the future, perhaps. Nudge, nudge, wink, wink. Not that I'm prying my old son, just curious, having spent a good few hours with Justine in the last day or two."

"Lorna and I go back to when we were kids, Joe. We were almost joined at the hip till the accident. She and I were never anything other than best friends, nothing sexual, ever, just best mates and that's way it will always be. I won't let anything come between us, ever again. Besides Lorna is in a relationship with Stella, they're very much together, so even if I did want something other than, it ain't goin' to happen."

"So where does that leave Justine?"

"I'm not sure how she feels about it, I hope she's going to be all right about Lorna. Lorna told her she and Stella were partners and she seemed cool about it. Lorna is not a threat to what I want Justine and me to have."

"And what do you want you and Justine to have?"

"A relationship. A man, woman relationship and who knows after that. I really like her Joe, for the first time ever I've met a woman that I really care about in that way and I get the impression she feels the same way," Rob said

"If she didn't care about you she wouldn't be here, Rob. God knows what she spun Andy Savage, but here she is and just as well for you. She saved your bacon tonight and didn't think twice about it."

"You really like her, don't you, Joe?" Rob asked curiously.

"Yes, I do. I think she would be good for you. I think you would be good for each other, although there is one thing you should know."

"OK, GO ON."

"You mentioned having babies with her, albeit a bit flippantly when we were in the car. She heard you obviously, 'cause you were on speaker and she started to cry. She didn't think I'd noticed at first but, me being me, two feet and all that, asked what was wrong. She told me she can't have kids. She was heartbroken Rob, said you wouldn't want to know her when you found out."

Rob looked across at Joe and shook his head, "Oh God, why do have a big mouth Joe?"

"So that both your feet fit in it!"

"That really is not that important to me Joe. I just want Justine, *she's* what's important."

"You better tell *her* that, not me and whatever you think, she will be feeling a bit insecure about you with a beautiful woman like Lorna on the scene. You need to reassure her Rob."

"I will, trust me. By the time we leave here she will be in no doubt about how I feel about her" said Rob and just at that he slowed down and pulled up at the NCA team's cottage.

Rob did a quick introduction to the team members for Joe as they all sat round the large kitchen table to plan their next steps.

"OK" Chris Hall started, "experience tells us that if there are girls in the warehouse from that boat, they won't be there long. They'll move them on as soon as practical. So we need to move quickly. I spoke to Ally a little while ago and he said that there has been a bit of coming and going at the warehouse, just as it was getting dark. No movement of people as yet, so they may be getting ready to ship the girls out. Ally will brief us on any further activity."

"Sounds good" Said Rob and Joe nodded his agreement.

"Tom's made one of his legendary chicken casseroles last night so I suggest we grab a bite to eat now. That way it will be dark by the time we leave here and who knows when we will get the chance to eat again" Chris suggested and Tom Parker went about serving up a plate of steaming hot food and some bread to them all.

Over their meal, the group discussed their plans for the evening, what they expected, what they knew or didn't know and worked on a plan B just in case things went badly wrong.

Rob and Joe related the events of earlier and said that they still did not think that anyone at Achravie Estate had recognised Rob but that they should be ready for any eventualities.

As they were preparing to leave, Rob stood up and announced that he had a couple of calls to make and that he would see them at the vehicles when they were ready to go.

Rob stepped outside and dialled Justine's number. Six rings later her phone went to voicemail.

"Hi Justine, it's Rob. As someone once sang "I just called to say I love you"" He ended the call and dialled another number.

19

DRESSED FOR NIGHT-TIME SURVEILLANCE, CHRIS HALL AND HIS team came out of the cottage as Rob put the phone away. Joe followed and handed Rob a radio with an earbud and microphone. "We've synced these with the lads' equipment so we're all on the same frequency. The man on watch at the warehouse is with us as well."

"Excellent, so we're all on the same wavelength as opposed to hymn sheet" Rob joked and got a group shake of the heads and groan for his trouble. They all climbed into the two vehicles and drove off, heading back towards the Achravie castle car park and from there to the warehouse on the Estate.

It was fully dark when they pulled quietly into the car park at the castle and parked at the back of the area, furthest away from the road. There were no other cars in the car park and the area was in total darkness. The six men walked stealthily across the road and onto Achravie Estate. Using as much natural cover as they could they headed for the warehouse under Rob's direction as they had agreed, covert operations being his speciality. They approached slowly, stopping regularly to ensure there were no lookouts from the estate watching the approach to the building and the compound.

Suddenly their earbuds came to life "Lookout to leader, movement at the warehouse. Two Land Cruisers have just approached the compound gates and they are opening to let them in. The big roller door at the front of the warehouse is opening and the first vehicle has driven into the warehouse. The other one is staying outside and the door is closing again."

"How many men are with them? "asked Rob.

"Four guys got out of the second Land Cruiser. The first one went straight inside so I don't know who was in that."

"What are the four guys doing?"

"Just standing outside the truck, two of them are having a smoke."

"Rob, looks like they may be on the move, we need to get in there" Chris Hall said.

"Are the gates still open or have they closed them again Lookout?" asked Rob.

"Still open. Hang on, the other guys are going into the warehouse through the door at the side of the building."

Rob brought the team forward slowly, issuing instructions through his radio mic, till they were in sight of the warehouse. To every instruction, each operative in turn gave two clicks of their send button to acknowledge. The white Achravie Estate Land Cruiser sat to the side of the big roller shutter door and there was a single light shining above the small door at the side of building where the four men had entered the warehouse.

Under Rob's direction the team approached the big gates to the compound which were still wide open and from there they made their way round to the back of the warehouse, an area which was in complete darkness. As the five men gathered, Rob laid out his plan.

"I want you to cover the door at the side where the four security guys went in. If they went in there their first reaction will be to come back out that way. When they come out, take them down, *fast*. Ally, can you still see the front door?"

"Yes" came the short answer.

"OK, keep watch on it and report and action."

Two clicks came back.

"I'VE GOT a big surprise for that lot in there, so let's go cover that door." Rob told the others.

"Ally, take your night-vision off, now" Two clicks came back in acknowledgement.

The team moved quietly round to the side of the building at took up position on either side of the smaller side door.

"What now?" asked Chris Hall.

"Achravie Estate is about to lose a Land Cruiser, is what's now."

"It's burger time" said Rob tunefully and there was a sudden flash of light from the trees above the front of the building and the woosh of a rocket propelled grenade a split second before the Land Cruiser parked at the front of the warehouse erupted in a ball of flame and was lifted into the air slamming into the wall of the building. There was silence for a few seconds then shouting could be heard from inside the warehouse and the side door burst open.

As Rob had predicted the four security guards who had entered through the door, plus two others, burst out into the compound, each armed with automatic rifles, which were still swinging by their sides. Hall's team, Joe and Rob were waiting for them and took them totally by surprise. Rob and Joe tripped the first two guards and the others literally fell over them in their rush to get outside to see what had happened. Rob hit the last man out with a savage blow to the ribs with the butt of his M27 and finished him clinically with an equally savage blow to the side of his head with the same weapon. The team were ruthlessly professional as they attacked the Achravie employees, quickly and efficiently disposing of the six guards with savage head and body blows.

As EXPECTED all hell broke loose around the same time.

"Tom, Charlie, tie these up, make sure there secure, we don't want them reappearing.

"Chris, Joe, inside with me" Rob shouted above the clamour.

"Rob, front door opening" Ally Gemmell's voice came over Rob's radio.

"Copy" Rob replied as he, Joe and Chris Hall approached the side door.

A burst of automatic fire sent pieces of the doorway flying and the three men hugged the outer wall.

"Hit the lights, but careful, we don't know who's in there, I'm for the front door" Rob shouted as took off up the side of the building, feet crunching in the gravel as he ran.

He heard Chris and Joe return the automatic fire with short bursts of their own to take out the lights as Ally Gemmell's voice came into his earbud, "Vehicle leaving the warehouse, white Land Cruiser, coming out fast.

Rob careened round the corner of the building with his M27 at the ready and knelt in readiness to fire at the vehicle tyres. As he tried to aim at the fast moving vehicle, his eye was suddenly caught by a head of long blond hair through the open rear window of the Land Cruiser.

Justine!

"Hold your fire everybody, don't take the Land Cruiser" Rob shouted into his radio mic.

He watched, stunned, as the vehicle rocked and bounced down the gravel road towards the main road.

"Status!" Rob yelled as reality kicked in almost immediately.

"WAREHOUSE IS EMPTY", Joe replied in his ear "What just happened there Rob?"

"Justine, she was in the Toyota, Joe."

"What?.."

"She was in the back seat, the window was open, as if I was being deliberately shown," replied Rob.

"You need to see this Rob" said Chris Hall.

Rob entered the warehouse through the open roller door and saw Joe and Chris at the back of the warehouse, standing outside what looked like a row of cells or cages. As he approached the darker end of the building where the fluorescent lights had been shot out he could see that the floors of the cells were strewn with sleeping bags and blankets. There were two rows of three cells and as Rob walked into the first one he could smell the aroma of sweat and human waste. There were metal buckets in the corner which were empty but had obviously been used as rudimentary toilets.

"Looks like three, maybe four to a cage" said Chris Hall.

"No girls though" Rob responded.

"I don't understand" Chris replied "we've been watching this place 24/7 since that boat arrived."

"They knew", said Joe "they knew they were being watched. Could they have known you were here Rob? How did they know about Justine. They must have known that they were at Lorna's friend's cottage. Shit, Rob, have they got Lorna and Stella as well?"

"MY THOUGHTS EXACTLY JOE, something doesn't add up and I think I know what! I hope to God I'm wrong but a few things are falling into place and I don't like what's coming up as the answer."

"We need to find Lorna and Justine" Rob said as he hit a speed dial on his phone.

Justine's phone rang three times before it was answered.

"Well, well, the Prodigal returns with a bang and quite a bang it was too. I wondered when you would show your face. What kept you, you've been here for days Robbie, very remiss of you not to call round and see us after all this time."

"Where are Justine and Lorna, Bruce, if you dare to harm them in any way whatsoever.."

"You'll what, little brother" Bruce interrupted. "I don't think you're in much of a position to make threats Robbie, seeing as you don't know where they are and I do. In fact, I can see them both from where I'm sitting."

"I warn you, if you.."

"Now, now little brother, it's maybe better you don't upset me. Don't spoil my night. You've put me in such a good mood Robbie. Here I am with not one but two of your girlfriends. Lucky me eh! You know I always fancied shagging young Lorna. Not so little now though, turned into a right little beauty don't you think and what about this new one. Now there *is* a rare beauty, maybe I'll have her first then little Lorna. No, I've always fancied shagging Lorna, so she'll be first then your blond goddess will get my attention. Those titties of hers feel real you know. What am I saying, of course you know. How do you do it with that big scar on your face, Robbie? You must tell me when we get together, have a nice wee chat just you and I."

"Just you and I Robbie, just you and I, well maybe just you, me and a couple of my friends who are here with me. Just to keep things fair, you understand and they're going to want their turn with these women of yours" Bruce laughed.

"We're all out at Uncle Charlie's cottage Robbie, so get yourself out here tout suite little brother and as I say, on your own. This cottage has CCTV all round, if anyone comes within a couple of hundred yards of here, we'll see them. That happens and you're dead little brother and your precious girlies will end up as gang raped junkies in some city whorehouse. Do I make myself clear?" Bruce MacLaine ended his threat in a vicious whisper which left Rob in no doubt that he was deadly serious.

Rob put his phone back in his pocket.

"He's trying to wind you up Rob." Said Joe "He wants you mad at him and not thinking straight when you go in there."

Rob turned to face Joe "I know exactly what he's trying to do Joe. Twenty two years ago, he would have succeeded but he doesn't know me now. He has no idea what he is dealing with now" Rod said with a smile on his lips.

Joe knew that his smile went no further than those lips and the look in Rob's ice cold, blue eyes told Joe that if Bruce MacLaine as much as touched a hair on the heads of either women, his life would end violently that night. He had seen that look only twice before and a shiver went down his spine as he remembered the outcomes on those hot dusty nights in Afghanistan.

"Chris, we need to handle this, "outwith the rulebook" as Tony says. Can you lads stand by in case this goes pearshaped?" Rob asked the NCA team leader.

CHRIS NODDED, "Sure, you do what you need to do. We need to report back that there are no girls here and we need to look at finding them. Keep us up to speed and good luck guys"

"Right, Joe, board meeting, lets go" said Rob signalling for Joe to follow him to Big Mac's black V8 Land Rover Defender.

20

THEY APPROACHED THE CAR PARK CAREFULLY, IN CASE BRUCE HAD misled them, but deep down, Rob knew Bruce wanted him at the cottage alive. The two men crossed the open car park and into the Land Rover. Rob fired up the big engine and drove off in the direction of the cottage. Rob removed the radio and earbud, he knew Bruce would not let him keep them anyway. As he drove he outlined his plan to Joe.

Someone was passing information to Bruce MacLaine. He had known that Rob was on the island. He knew about the scar on Rob's face. He had known about Uncle Charlie's cottage. He had been expecting them at the warehouse. He was not expecting Chris Hall's team to be there though, nor had he expected the Achravie Land Cruiser to be blown up, but he knew too much for it to be coincidence or guesswork. He had a good idea who that someone was but he hoped he was wrong.

About half a mile from the cottage and well out of sight of it, Rob pulled over and Joe got out. He opened the back of the Land Rover and pulled out two bags, a rucksack which he put on his back and a large holdall. He waved to Rob as the vehicle pulled away and having checked his bearings, set off into the night across the fields. He felt the adrenalin start to course through his veins, just like old times.

Rob pulled into the drive which ran down to the cottage and stopped. He took out his smartphone and made a connection with two numbers and put the phone into a concealed pocket in his jacket. Having done that he started down the track to the cottage and a reunion with his brother he had not spoken to for twenty years. He thought back to the last time he and Bruce were together, it was ironic he thought, someone died that night too.

THE LAND ROVER hit the gravel parking area in front of the cottage and Rob knew that the noise of the big vehicle crunching over the gravel surface had just alerted everyone in the cottage as to his arrival, even without the cctv. Rob pulled up at the far end of the parking area, to the side of the cottage, took a deep breath, exhaled and stepped out on to the gravel. Showtime!

Rob approached the front door and as he stepped off the gravel on to the slabbed area in front of the door, it slowly opened. Someone stood behind it, out of view. As Rob entered, the door slammed shut behind him. He didn't turn round, the man he wanted to see was standing behind two wooden dining chairs at the far end of the lounge/dining area. Justine and Lorna were tied to these chairs and although looking very frightened, they looked to be unharmed.

A heavily accented voice from behind him told him to stop where he was. Rob ignored the man and walked across the room, watching his brother as he waked, he stopped beside the patio doors at the far side of the lounge and stared across at his brother and the man who had opened the door who was no longer behind him and now walking toward him.

"Take your jacket off and give it to me" the man said pointing a handgun at Rob's head

Rob slowly took off his jacket, looking the man in the eyes as he did so, but instead of handing the jacket to the gunman he tossed it into a corner of the room behind him.

"I said *give me* the jacket" the man said.

"Frankly mate, I don't give a shit what you want, I'm here to see this piece of crap" he said pointing at his brother, "the organ grinder not the monkey if you follow me"

"Ignore him" Bruce said, "He's just winding you up. Check him for weapons, wires, phones, whatever", as he said this, he lifted his right arm to point a large handgun at Rob.

Rob held his hands above his head and the man patted him down as directed, finding Rob's Heckler & Koch SFP9-SF pistol and a mobile phone, both of which he tossed behind him.

"You shouldn't have come Rob, he'll kill you" Whispered Justine.

"He's mad, Justine's right, he's going to kill you" Lorna sobbed.

"Shut up you two, he already knows he's a dead man walking" Bruce shouted.

"Give me the phone, Bruno" Bruce demanded holding out his hand. The man tossed the phone to Bruce as he returned his gun to aim at Rob's head.

Bruce pressed the call button on the phone, it was not connecting to another device. He checked the call log and satisfied himself that the phone was switched off. He then took the back off the phone and took the SIM card out, bent it over and snapped it in two.

"There now" Bruce chirped "No one's going to disturb us and our big family reunion. Isn't this nice, Rob. I believe everyone calls you Rob now" Bruce went on as he walked round the two women and stood in front of Rob.

"I know, long lost brother comes home, I'm supposed to give

you a big hug and a kiss and kill a fatted calf or something biblical, but that's just not going to happen here, is it. We both know that. You've messed up my nice little earner little brother. That's what you've done. But you know that. That's why you came, wasn't it. Little Lorna phoned you "Come home Robbie we need you" And you came, like the Lone Ranger and Tonto all rolled into one. Riding into town to save the villagers from the nasty villain"

"Do you remember the night I killed Sheila Stewart? No, I don't suppose you do. You were pissed out of your tiny little mind. You weren't very bright then Robbie and judging from what you you've got yourself into right now, you're obviously still not very bright, are you?"

Bruce stared at Rob and shook his head.

"My but my little brother has grown. Isn't he big Bruno?"

Suddenly with a speed that belied his paunchy physique Bruce lashed out and struck the side of Rob's head with his pistol then punched him hard in the midriff. Rob sensed both blows coming and swung his head away from the initial blow to the head and tensed his stomach muscles ahead of the second. Both blows hurt though and Rob's head spun as he fought to catch his breath but he stayed on his feet and despite the blood which was running down the side of his head, managed to look his assailant in the eye after an initial few seconds.

"That the best you can do Brucie boy, hit an unarmed man while your hired muscle holds a gun to his head" Rob snarled "You were a coward back then and now you're a fat, pathetic coward, so much for human evolution. I think your safe enough from this one ladies, he doesn't seem man enough to shag sheep never mind a real woman"

Rob laughed, a harsh mirthless laugh.

Bruce swung at him again, a hard punch to the side of Rob's face, Rob felt blood in his mouth, but he laughed again.

"Oh, we'll see about that, will we eh! Let's see what Brucie boy can do with a couple of beauties like these. Bruno, bring the blond over here, now, let's see what she looks like" Bruce shouted

Bruno strode over to the two women, who had not said another word, but were watching in horror as the man they both loved in their own ways taunted the two men who were intent on ending his life.

"He touches her he's a fucking dead man" Rob hissed and stepped forward.

Bruno swung his handgun at Rob's head again but in his haste it just glanced off his forehead.

"I wouldn't touch either of them if I were you, Igor," said Rob.

"Bruno," the man said" Bruno, is my name and Bruno is next in line for these two after Mr MacLaine has his way with them, so I wouldn't be so cocky if I were you."

"Cocky, now there's an unfortunate turn of phrase, Igor. But seriously my friend, have a good look at your own, go on, all joking aside" Rob laughed and looked down toward Bruno's groin.

Bruno, almost despite himself, glanced quickly down at his groin and then quickly looked again, this time he stared at the bright red dot hovering on his groin. As he watched with growing horror, the red dot travelled slowly upwards. Up over his stomach and up, up till it rested over his heart.

Rob saw Bruno's muscles tighten as he prepared to move and so did the man holding the laser sighted snipers rifle. The glass behind Rob shattered and Bruno was almost lifted off his feet as two sub-sonic rounds hit him like sledgehammers, inches apart in the chest and slammed him against the wall, a growing patch of crimson blood staining the front of his shirt.

The two women screamed, Lorna's chair fell over as she tried to move away, Justine tried to turn away but her bonds prevented her from getting away from the scenario which was unfolding in front of her.

Rob had reacted the minute the bullets shattered the glass, he lashed out with his right leg at a totally disorientated Bruce, his toe connecting with his brother's groin. As Bruce doubled up in agony, Rob hit him on the jaw with a roundhouse right hook, knocking him back over the dining table and causing him to lose his grip on his pistol which he dropped on the floor.

As Bruce tried to recover his balance Rob swung a vicious blow into the soft area around Bruce's lower ribcage and heard the snap of ribs as his fist connected. Rob grabbed Bruce by the throat and pulled him upright, pushing him towards the kitchen wall. As he hit the wall, Rob's fist connected with his nose and blood sprayed from the broken bones. Rob hit him again and again, the fury which he had felt for all these years driving him on.

"Rob, Rob, no, please Rob" he heard a voice screaming at him somewhere in his subconscious. He stopped.

"Please Rob, you'll kill him. He's not worth it" Justine pleaded.

Rob picked Bruce up by the scruff of his neck and sat him at the kitchen table.

"Watch him Big Mac." he shouted to apparently no one.

"MAN with the red dots is watching you now Brucie boy, so don't tempt him" Rob said quietly to Bruce as he walked over to the two women and lifted Lorna's chair upright

As he started to untie Justine's hands, he looked at Lorna, tears running down her face.

"Are you OK, both of you? Did he hurt you? Did he touch you?"

"I think we're both OK. A bit sore from being tied up and manhandled in and out of cars but other than that, I think we're OK. Lorna?" Justine answered.

"I'm fine, I just want out of this nightmare."

"It's not over yet" said Rob putting an arm round each of them. Lorna hugged him back but Justine pulled away, sobbing, her head in her hands. Rob tried to pull her back to him

"No Rob, please, don't" she replied pulling away, her arm out to keep Rob away.

Rob sat Lorna down again and looked across at Bruce who was now semi-conscious.

He walked back over to his brother, picked up Bruce's SIG Sauer P220, and tucked into the waistband of his jeans.

Bruce looked up at him in recognition but said nothing.

"The way I see it" Rob said, "You and your cronies are smuggling women, girls from Eastern Europe into the UK. Drugging them up to the eyeballs and selling them on for prostitution in Glasgow, Edinburgh, Aberdeen and other places no doubt. Whoever can meet the asking price. What's a woman's life worth in your marketplace, Bruce?"

Bruce looked up at Rob through slowly closing, swollen eyes "Lot of money, little brother." Bruce smiled, "Family business, why don't you join us, it's not too late, make some real money. Those two over there for starters. They would fetch a pretty penny" Bruce laughed and then coughed.

"Don't think so Bruce" Rob said standing up and walking over to the kitchen. He splashed some cold water on his face and picking up a small kitchen towel dried his face and hands. He walked back over to the kitchen table to look down on his brother sitting where he had left him.

"So, they come from Stade, where do they go from here, how do you move them on?"

Bruce smirked at Rob, "You've been doing your homework,

little brother" he laughed, then coughed as his movement caused his broken ribs to poke at places they shouldn't

"In a van, little brother we get them over to the mainland on the ferries and then we…"

As Bruce was speaking he suddenly noticed movement behind Rob, through the

window and he stopped in mid-sentence as a gunshot drowned out his last word, the window shattered and a neat hole appeared in Bruce's forehead. Rob rolled towards the window on the floor into a position where he could not be seen from outside. As he reached the wall, he heard the sound of feet running on the gravel, then a second gunshot, a grunt and silence. Whoever had been running across the gravel had stopped.

Rob went for the door, flung it wide open and rolled out onto the parking area. He lay, arms stretched out in front of him, Bruce's gun in both hands, pointing it at the prone figure lying on the gravel. A gun lay some distance from the dark shape. Rob slowly got to his feet, keeping his gun trained on the prone figure, he approached it carefully.

"Keep perfectly still" Rob ordered. He stooped and picked up the gun, a SIG Sauer P220. He tucked it into the waistband of his Jeans at the back and approached the figure.

THE SHOOTER WAS tall and dressed from head to foot in loose fitting black track suit and wore a black balaclava. The figure was conscious but obviously in severe pain from a gunshot wound to the hip. Rob bent down to see who the killer was, hoping that he would not find the person he was dreading finding. He reached out, grabbed the balaclava and pulled it off the shooters head. She moaned in pain.

"Stella" he whispered, "Oh God, I hoped it wasn't going to be you."

"Are you OK?" Joe's voice came from behind.

Rob looked round at his partner "Depends on what you mean by OK, Joe."

Stella wasn't going anywhere as she writhed in agony on the gravel from the pain of her shattered hip, so Rob and Joe went into the cottage to tell the two women what had just happened. Justine stood wither arms round Lorna who stared at the body of the man she had known all her life. Bruce had fallen off the chair and now lay staring at the ceiling through lifeless eyes. A small amount of blood had formed around his head. Rob approached his brother's body and slowly bent down and closed his staring eyes.

"Oh Bruce, Bruce, what have you done?" he whispered to his brother.

As he stood, he saw Joe leading Justine and Lorna over to the settee where he and Lorna had sat so recently and reminisced about old times and brought each other up to date with their lives. Lorna was obviously so happy and contented with her life and her relationship which the events of the night had killed as sure as Stella had killed Bruce.

"Joe can you get a hold of Chris Hall, bring him up to speed, tell him we have a live but injured conspirator who shot and killed Bruce. Tell him we need him to be here and take over" Rob signalled for Joe to do so outside.

Rob knew what he had to do next.

"Lorna, a need to tell you something" he said softly, kneeling beside his still sobbing friend.

"I'll leave you to it" Justine said moving away.

"No stay here, I need you to be here."

"I've had enough Rob, I don't want to be anywhere near you at the moment."

"Stay, for Lorna's sake, not mine" Rob said firmly, looking Justine in the eye.

Justine folded her arms in front of herself and stood where she was.

"Lorna, Joe shot and wounded the person who shot Bruce. She is lying out in the car park, Joe is calling for medical assistance. She.."

"She" Lorna said incredulously. She looked at Rob with wide eyes, then at Justine. She held her hand out to the other woman. Justine took her hand.

"You Said "she"" Rob, Lorna said shaking her head "Please tell me you don't mean.."

"Stella, yes, I'm sorry Lorna. It was Stella who shot my brother."

"Oh God no, please no" Lorna sobbed and before Rob or Justine could stop her she rushed out to the car park. Rob and Justine followed her out.

"Stella!" she screamed as she saw her partner lying on the gravel, Joe bending over her, holding a cloth on her left hip.

"Stella, what have you done, did you shoot Bruce?" Lorna asked as she walked slowly across to the prone figure "Did you shoot Bruce MacLaine" she repeated, her voice rising.

"I'M SORRY LORNA", Stella gasped through gritted teeth as she fought against the agony of her gunshot wound "I never meant you get involved. I would never have hurt you, you know that. I'm so sorry."

Lorna, shook her head in disbelief and as she looked from Rob to Justine.

"Lorna" Justine said as she put her arm round her, "Come inside, you need to calm down, Lorna. Please, you need to get your head round all of this," Justine led Lorna back in to the cottage as Chris Hall and his team arrived.

Rob went back into the cottage and picked up the jacket he had thrown into the corner and carefully took his second smartphone out of his inside jacket pocket. He checked that the call he had made earlier was still connected. He took it off speakerphone and lifted it to his ear, "Big Mac, are you there?" he asked quietly.

"Big Mac's got yer back, just like old times" the soft voice at the other end said.

"Thanks Mac, you haven't lost your touch with a sniper rifle and a laser sight, have you?"

"Ach, it's like riding a bike wee man. What now?" his friend asked.

"Joe shot and wounded a shooter, she's going to need medical assistance. Can you get her that fairly quickly? She's the only one who knows any detail of their operation, so NCA are going to need to talk to her. Chris Hall and the guys from NCA will cover you for tonight."

"Sure, let me make a call and I'll be with you in five" the response came.

"Thanks mate, I owe you."

"Chris, can you guys get Lorna and Justine out of here. Take them back to the Red Lion, if you don't mind."

"Sure, Tom can you..." Chris nodded to Tom Parker

21

Rob sat on the low wall outside the cottage, he felt drained. He always did after an operation, when there was loss of life involving someone he knew. Rob had killed many times before and felt little other than, job done. As a covert operative it was what he did. He still hated losing the life of someone he knew, a colleague, a friendly collaborator or a brother.

He had hated Bruce most of his adult life and could have killed him with his bare hands at one point earlier that night, but in the post adrenalin rush reality, which dawned after every battle and which Rob was feeling now, he would not have wished his brother dead. He also knew that Lorna's life would never be the same again.

Stella was not dead but she would no longer be part of Lorna's life. Lorna had also lost someone she had loved, just in a different way, in a way perhaps even harder to accept. He felt sorry for her as he watched them driven off in the back of the NCA BMW.

Joe appeared at his side and sat down.

"I'm so sorry Rob. I know you hated Bruce for what he did to you, but nobody deserves to see their own brother killed like that. I can't even begin to understand what you are feeling just now."

"I don't know what I'm thinking Joe, I've got so much running through my head right now. I can't believe what happened in there. Justine and Lorna have been kidnapped, held hostage, threatened with sexual assault and watched two people being shot dead tonight. They should never have had to witness something like that. Lorna was in pieces, even before she found out about Stella and Justine can't even stand to be in the same room as me."

"YOU DID what you had to do tonight Rob, the girls will see that when things calm down and get a chance to think things through in their heads. You put your life on the line tonight to save then both. Bruce and his cronies would have assaulted them sexually and otherwise and when they were finished with them, they would have killed them. You put a stop to that tonight in what you did. It might not have been pleasant for them, but it needed doing," Joe squeezed Rob's shoulder as he spoke.

"I shouldn't have brought Justine up with me, but she was so adamant that she was coming and I had no idea that she would get caught up in a bloodbath like this" he added shaking his head.

"You weren't to know Joe, even I didn't see this coming" Rob said standing up as Chris Hall approached.

"Rob, I know this isn't a good time but we need to follow up what went down tonight, so we need a quick debrief. I'm going with the big guy and the prisoner. We need to question her before things go cold. We found the girls who were brought on the boat, they were still on board. Your brother must have known we were on to him so he never brought them to the warehouse" Chris Hall said as he stood beside Rob.

"Oh, he knew all right. Stella must have kept him well informed. He knew our every plan, our every move. I didn't see that coming till earlier tonight and it was too late then" Rob replied.

"You knew, when you took off that balaclava you said *"I hoped it wasn't going to be you"*, you *knew* Stella was involved" said Joe incredulously.

"I wasn't sure until earlier but when we came down here for the first time, I noticed things about the place. The way the bushes and trees and been cleared to give a clear area right round the cottage and the floodlights with motion sensors. Look at this gravel Joe, its right round the cottage, everywhere, really deep, really loose and really noisy. Nobody would get near that cottage without being seen or heard. I did a sweep of the place when we arrived that night and found microphones in all the rooms and cameras in the living areas. Someone wanted to know what was happening and being talked about in this place. Deadlocks on all the windows and doors, it's not a holiday cottage, Joe, it's a fortress.

"So Stella, or someone else would know what you and Lorna were planning and talking about from the time you walked into the place?" said Joe.

"I dare say that was the plan, it was Stella's idea to use this place and I remember being surprised at how understanding Stella was about Lorna and I being alone that night. She almost threw us together. In retrospect, she wanted to know how much we knew and what we were planning. But when I set the alarm on my bedside clock I also activate a little jamming device which would have killed the mics and I stuck some tape over the camera lenses, which I took off later. Bruce pretty much said tonight that he knew I was here on Achravie and tonight, they knew we were coming, they were expecting us Joe. We threw them with the explosion but they were expecting us, we were set up by someone who knew our plans and apart from Chris and his guys, only Lorna, Stella, you and I knew."

Rob spent the next minutes giving Chris Hall a rundown of the events of the evening as they had panned out in the cottage. Chris had heard some of it as Rob had included Chris in a conference call, along with Big Mac and Joe, on the second mobile he had secreted in a the lining of the jacket he had thrown in the corner earlier. Rob had instigated the call and left it open when he hid the phone in his jacket lining, banking on the other phone being found easily and no one looking too hard for a second phone. He knew that when Rob had entered the cottage, Big Mac was positioned in the woods behind the cottage with a laser sighted sniper rifle at a distance of almost five hundred yards. This kept him well out of the pool of light generated by the floodlights which surrounded the cottage. He also knew that Joe was similarly positioned in front of the building behind a stone wall. Both men, Rob had explained, were highly proficient and hugely experienced ex Special Forces snipers who had plied their trade as such in the battle fields and war zones that were Afghanistan, Iraq and Serbia.

Rob sat with Joe, watching the NCA team arrange the clear up of the scene and as an ambulance arrived to take the two bodies back to the hospital mortuary, Rob rose slowly to his feet.

"I need to get to the hospital and see Fraser, he's going to hear things when these bodies arrive and I want to tell him first before he hears second hand. Once I've done that, I need to face my father. If he hated me before, he's going to hate me even more when he finds out I've been involved in Bruce's death tonight. What a mess!"

"I'll come with you, stay in the car and make sure there's no other hired muscle about the place. You never know" Joe suggested.

"Yeah, probably best" Rob answered distractedly.

22

THE TWO FRIENDS DROVE INTO THE CARPARK AT THE HOSPITAL and having parked Big Mac's Defender so that Joe could see the front door, Rob took a deep breath and climbed the front stairs into the hospital reception area to find Fraser. He was met by a worried looking nurse, who made to take Rob into a cubical.

"Are you all right sir, what happened to you?" she asked worriedly. "Sit over here and I'll get a doctor" she said looking at Rob's chest.

It was only then that Rob realised that his shirt was stained with blood.

"No, sorry nurse" Rob explained "Most of that's not my blood, it belongs to someone who's already here, I've got a bump on the head but, I'm OK, really."

"I do need to speak to Fraser McEwan though. Is he still in the same room?"

"Yes, but he might be asleep" the nurse countered.

"That's fine" Rob said "Fraser needs to hear what I have to tell him and he needs to hear it now, nurse. It's part of the reason I'm covered in someone else's blood."

"OK, let's go and check him" the nurse said and led Rob in the direction of Fraser's room.

She peered round the door into the darkened room "Fraser" she whispered "are you awake?"

"Whit a daft question!" came the reply "Racket you lot are making out there, you expect anyone to be sleeping, dear God, you'll waken the dead lass. What's going on, what's all the noise. Is that you Robbie?" Fraser asked as Rob stood silhouetted in the doorway of the dark room.

"IT IS FRASER" Rob replied entering the room and standing by the bedside chair.

"What's wrong Robbie, what are you doing here at this time of night?" Fraser asked with a worried tone in his voice.

"You might want to sit him up, before you go" Rob suggested to the nurse.

"Sit me up" Fraser laughed "I can sit myself up for God's sake. See, easy" Fraser said pulling himself farther up the bed, but obviously feeling the effort.

The nurse moved to the other side of the bed and pulled up his pillows to make him more comfortable. "Get away lassie, stop fussing" Fraser protested as he moved to switch on a light.

"Bloody hell, Robbie" he exclaimed as light flooded the room and he saw the blood staining on Rob clothes.

"Aye, Fraser" Rob said touching the front of his shirt "that just about describes it."

"Thanks, Louise" Fraser nodded to the nurse "A wee cuppa might go down well. I think this is going to take a wee while."

"What's happened Robbie" Fraser asked, seriousness returning to his demeanour "Are you all right."

"I am Fraser" Rob answered "but Bruce isn't doing so well. He was shot and killed tonight. Not by me I might add, although I was there when it happened."

"Oh dear God Robbie. What the hell happened? Wait." Fraser held up his hand, now free of tubes and needles, as nurse Louise brought in a tray of tea and some biscuits.

"Sorry, I've nothing stronger" she said "You look like you could use it."

She put the tray down and turned to leave, pulling the door behind her. "If you need anything, give me a buzz Fraser."

"Aye lass, thanks" Fraser replied, pouring two cups of tea.

"You better tell me Robbie. Is this to do with the goings on at the estate?"

"Yeah, everything to do with it."

Rob sat forward in the chair and related the events of the last two nights, while Fraser sat silently listening, every so often shaking his head, as he took in the enormity of what he was being told.

As he finished relating the events, Fraser started to ask questions, wanting some details that Rob might have missed and relating these to information or knowledge he already had, trying to build up a picture of the whole scenario in his own mind.

At last Fraser sat forward and put his hand on Rob's shoulder. "I'm sorry Robbie, if I hadn't got Lorna to phone you none of this would have happened. I don't know what to say, son."

"Fraser, what you did was absolutely the right thing to do. Two people died tonight but we will now be able to save the lives of numerous young girls. These guys were involved in a hideous trafficking ring which had no compunction about killing innocent girls and young women after they had got then hooked on drugs and used them for prostitution. They deserved all they got, Fraser" Rob replied with a note of rising anger in his voice.

"But your brother, Robbie?" Fraser said.

. . .

"BRUCE? Bruce stopped being my brother twenty odd years ago Fraser. I've had no family for the last twenty two years because of him and the web of lies he spun around that road accident and now he has ruined a relationship for Lorna and probably alienated me from a woman that I thought I might have a future with. So you'll forgive me if I don't grieve over his demise Fraser."

"Oh Robbie, I'm so sorry.."

"No Fraser," Rob interrupted "you have absolutely nothing to apologise to me for. When my family basically threw me out, you supported me. You made sure that I got sorted out and got me a future in the military. That got me to where I am today. I did my time in the Black Watch then I served with a Special Forces group for a few years in Iraq and Afghanistan and left the military in 2011. I set up a security company with an ex-colleague Joe Harper when I left the military and I'm still doing that. The company's doing well, we both make a very good living from it. That plus a good military pension and financially I'm more than secure for the rest of my life. I've got a new luxury apartment overlooking the river Thames in London, nice Italian sports car for when I'm not working, cash in the bank, money invested elsewhere and all of that built on what you did for me at a time when you could have walked away like everyone else. You've done more for me than my own father ever did, Fraser and I'll never forget that."

"I just did what I knew was right. You weren't driving your car that night, Bruce was. A blind man running for a bus would have seen that if he had taken the time to look. But, your right, Bruce had such a good story made up and he convinced your father, who convinced everyone else, that it was you're doing, killing that wee lass. Nobody would listen to me, I told them to look at the evidence not listen to the stories, but, no, they had made their minds up. Your father paid everyone to hush the whole thing up and make it go away. Not for you, but for the family honour. But there's no honour in deceit Robbie."

"Speaking of my father Fraser, I need to tell him about Bruce. I'm not looking forward to meeting him again, but I need to tell him Bruce is dead" said Rob starting to rise from the chair. Fraser's hand on his shoulder stopped him.

"Robbie, did you not know! Your father's dead."

23

ROBBIE WALKED OUT TO THE CARPARK IN A DAZE AND JOE HAD TO give a quick blast of the car horn to get his attention. He walked slowly over to the big black Defender and climbed into the driver's seat, staring out of the windscreen.

"Rob, Rob, you OK mate?" Joe asked with his hand on Rob's shoulder.

"My father's dead, Joe. Fraser said he died of a heart attack, over a year ago. He said Bruce told everybody he had tried to get me to come to the funeral, but I said no, that my father had died long ago as far as I was concerned. He said he begged me to come but I refused, put the phone down and wouldn't answer to him again."

"Oh Rob, I'm so sorry."

"What must people here think of me, that I wouldn't even come to my father's funeral? My mother came and my brother even came over from New Zealand. He said Bruce was raging afterwards because my father's solicitor said at the reading of the will that I should be there, as a beneficiary. He apparently had a fight to have the will read, but when he did, it was announced that the whole estate was to be divided equally between his three sons. Apparently Bruce went ballistic, tried to get me excluded but old man Hogg, his solicitor, refused to change it, said he couldn't change my father's wishes."

"So, you own a third of Achravie estate?" Joe mused.

"Yep, funny isn't it, although I'm not sure what will happen to it now, with Bruce gone."

"To be fair, I'm not sure "funny" is a word I would use tonight" Joe muttered.

"So what now, you should really try to get a few hours' sleep, you look shattered" said Joe.

"I want to talk to Justine and Lorna before I do anything else, Joe, so let's head down to the Red Lion" Rob said and turned the key in the ignition, the big V8 engine giving a deep rumble as it started.

"They're not there Rob." Joe cautioned.

"Oh, right, where are they?"

"Justine took my car and left and Lorna went home."

"Justine left, to go where Joe?"

"London, she is going to Machrie and Andy Savage is having her picked up from there."

"London? She didn't tell me she was leaving" Rob said in disbelief.

"No, I think she just wanted away."

"From me?"

"Partly, but there's a bit more to it, I think. Lorna might be able to tell you more, they talked for ages apparently. Give her a call in the morning, it's late or should I say early."

"Oh, OK. I hadn't realised" Rob sounded lost.

"I've got keys for two of the cabins at the Red Lion, let's go and get our heads down for a bit while we can."

"OK" was all Rob said and he put the Defender into gear

and drove through and out of the carpark to the Red Lion a few hundred yards down the road.

ROB DIDN'T THINK he would sleep but he undressed and pulled the duvet up as he lay staring at the ceiling, his mind filling with a multitude of thoughts about what had happened, things he had been told and plans for the next day and what he needed to do before he left Achravie. Sleep did interrupt his thoughts though and Rob woke to a soft knocking at his cabin door.

"Yes, who is it?" he called, sleep clouding his thoughts.

"It's me" Joe's voice said from the other side of the door "You OK in there?"

"Yeah, yeah, just waking up, didn't think I'd sleep but I did. What time is it?"

"Time you were up and about, we got a lot to do today. I've had breakfast but Lorna hasn't and she's waiting for you in the dining room."

"Oh! Right, OK. Give me time to grab a quick shower and I'll be right there" Rob shouted as he made for the shower-room."

He showered and dressed quickly in a blue denim shirt and beige jeans, inspecting the damage to his face from the night before in the process and made for the dining room and Lorna. What would he say to her?

The dining room was empty as he entered and he was about to go and find Hamish or Lizzie when Lorna and Lizzie walked in, obviously deep in conversation as they walked. They stopped when they saw Rob.

"Let me go and get some coffee for you Robbie" Said Lizzie, looking a bit embarrassed as she left Rob and Lorna on their own.

"God, you look worse than me" Rob said with a half-smile and a look of concern.

"THANKS ROBBIE, you always did know how to make a girl feel good about herself" Lorna replied with a half-smile of her own and a coy look which betrayed the fact that she was not sure what to say next.

"How are you" Rob ventured.

"Probably about as good as I look. You?"

"Not sure yet, still having difficulty in taking it all in. My father's dead, did you know that?"

"Yeah, everyone knows that."

"I didn't" Rob shrugged

"But Bruce said he told you, said you argued and refused to come to the funeral. That's why I didn't say anything. I thought you knew! The bastard, he didn't tell you!"

"No, I found out last night from Fraser, he thought I knew too" Rob felt a tear form in his eye as he spoke.

"Scrambled egg for you Lorna and a full Scottish for you Robbie, I thought you'd be hungry" Lizzie interrupted Rob's downer as she breezed into the dining room with two break-fasts and a pot of coffee on a tray.

"You OK?" she asked looking at Rob "Can't believe a just asked that Robbie, a'm sorry" she said and a tear ran down her face.

Rob, walked over and put his arms round her "S'OK, its fine Lizzie honestly" Rob laughed "As long as there's people like you in this world Lizzie Allen, it's a place worth being. Any chance of some HP sauce?"

· · ·

"AYE, NO BOTHER" she said and disappeared, returning a few seconds later with a bottle of HP sauce. "There you go, I'll leave you two to talk, if you need anything else just holler."

"Will do, thanks Lizzie."

Rob and Lorna sat in front of their respective breakfasts and although Rob had not come in to the dining room with much of a notion of food, the smell of the cooked breakfast made him realise he not eaten since early the previous day and he ate the meal along with toast and coffee with gusto. Lorna ate her scrambled eggs with a little less enthusiasm.

Rob sipped his coffee, "What are you thinking Lorna?" he asked.

"Up until a wee while ago I just couldn't think. Yesterday seems like a dream, a nightmare, more like and Stella. I still can't get my head round Stella, what she did. She used me Robbie. She used me and I loved her, I just can't believe it. We all knew Bruce was a bad one, but even at that, nobody could have imagined he was capable of what he did yesterday. He would have killed you Rob, his own brother. Killed you without a second thought. I shudder to think what he would have done to Justine and I. You didn't hear what he was saying to us, what he was going to do to us, then pass us on to those thugs he employed. It was filthy and twisted. Who shot that guy, Bruno was it?"

"Big Mac. He was up in the forest with a laser sighted sniper rifle."

"Is that what the red dot was?"

"Yeah."

"BIG MAC, is he the guy from the training centre in Machrie?"

"Yeah, I served with him in the Regiment, one of the finest shots I ever came across" Rob explained.

Rob hesitated for a second "What did Justine say when she left?" he asked.

Lorna likewise hesitated, then replied. "Justine had a very violent partner a few years ago, violent towards her. She suffered a lot because of him. He is in prison for what he did to her one night and she hasn't had a serious relationship since. She finds it difficult to trust men because of that, but for some reason she felt she could trust you. I think she genuinely cares for you and saw the chance to build a life with you. She never ever saw you as being violent till last night and it freaked her out."

"Have I lost her Lorna?"

"I don't honestly know Robbie."

"You know me Lorna, I would never harm anyone I care about. Life has taught me to be fiercely loyal to people that I care about and if anything or anyone hurts or threatens someone I care about, then I will react to protect them. The only thing I cared about last night was stopping Bruce and his cronies from hurting you and Justine. They were a serious threat to both of you last night. They would have killed us Lorna, all three of us and I reacted in the only way I know how, but I would never hurt Justine or you for that matter."

"I know that Robbie, you need to convince Justine, not me" said Lorna.

"What will happen to Stella, Robbie?" Lorna asked, tears starting to form in her eyes.

"I don't know Lorna. I can ask Chris Hall. She will be in hospital for a while I would think, that hip looked to be in pretty bad shape from what I could see. She will be charged in connection with the trafficking and with Bruce's murder. When she is fit, she will go to court and then it will be a lengthy prison sentence, I'm afraid. Do you want to see her?" Rob asked.

"No, I never want to see her again, ever." Lorna replied sharply "She used me Robbie, all this time. I feel so stupid."

"You know what Lorna, I think she genuinely loved you, I don't think she *was* just using you. Even the hardest criminals have wives or husbands and children sometimes and they love them like other people love their families. Don't be too hard on yourself."

"Oh Robbie, what's to become of us, eh" Lorna sighed.

"That's called fortune telling and if I could see into the future I could *make* a fortune" Rob smiled. "You've still got kids to teach and I've still got a company to run. I guess we start with that and see where life takes us. I found out last night that I own one third of Achravie Estate, courtesy of my father's will. He left a third of his estate each to Angus, Bruce and me Not sure what happens to Bruce's third now, come to think of it, but I guess that means I will be coming back to Achravie pretty regularly from now on, so we'll see each other fairly soon I would imagine. I need to get in touch with Angus and tell him what's been going on here and I suppose I better try and find my mother and tell her that her son is dead. I need to talk to Justine as well, I guess we both need to start to rebuild our lives."

Rob looked up as Joe stood at the dining room door "Time to go?" he asked Joe.

"Yes, sorry, we should make tracks, there's a ferry in about half an hour and Big Mac's going to meet us at the other end to swap cars."

ROB SAID his thanks and goodbyes to Lizzie and Hamish, with a promise to come back soon. As he and Joe stood in the carpark beside Big Mac's black Land Rover. Lorna hugged Rob with tears in her eyes.

"At least this time I get to say goodbye, I should be grateful for that at least" she said with a slight quiver in her voice.

Rob hugged her back and kissed the top of her head. "I'll

need to come back up shortly to sort out the Estate, Angus and I need to decide how we are going to run the place. Angus being in New Zealand's not ideal so I probably need to take a lead on that. If you ever fancy a city break, I know a pretty good boutique B&B on the Thames embankment. Take care, if you need anything, you've got the numbers, give me a ring. If I'm not around talk to this man" Rob said.

"See you soon Lorna" He waved as he and Joe climbed into the big Defender and drove off to catch the ferry.

They met Big Mac with Joe's Audi RS4 Estate at Blackwaterfoot and having swapped vehicles, thanked Big Mac for all the help he have given Rob and said their goodbyes they set off to catch another ferry to take them to the mainland and from there by motorway to London.

The big powerful Audi ate up the miles with Joe driving and Rob staring out of the dark tinted windows and saying very little. Joe left him to his own thoughts, knowing that Rob had much to think about and a good few answers to find. Rob tried to call Justine's mobile but it eventually went to voicemail. He tried a few times after that but it went straight to voice mail every time. He tried the SGS office but was told that Justine was not in the office and Sir Andrew was also out for the day.

HE EVENTUALLY GOT THE MESSAGE, Justine did not want to talk to him. When they reached London that evening, Joe offered to take Rob to his house and have his wife cook supper for them, but Rob said that he just wanted to get home and have an early night. Joe dropped Rob off at the front door of his apartment block and Rob took the lift to his penthouse apartment. He dropped his bag in the hallway and went through to the open plan living area, opened a bottle of Malbec Reserva, poured a large glass and stepped out on to the terrace overlooking the Thames. He stared out over the river and recalled the last time he had come out to the terrace. He remembered standing holding Justine as she enthused over the views and how they had gone back inside and made love, passionately at first, then more slowly, savouring each other and then fallen asleep in each other's arms. Then his phone had rung.

24

ROB HEARD HIS PHONE RING SOMEWHERE IN THE DISTANCE, NOT Van Morrison this time, Springsteen's, "Darlington County". That was good, it was his normal ringtone, although it didn't tell him who was calling him, he needed to answer it find that out.

"Hello?" he muttered, his voice thick with sleep.

"Hello yourself sleeping beauty" Joe's voice seemed far too bright and cheerful for this time of morning, Rob thought as he stretched for his clock to see the time. Shit! Twenty past ten. Rob could not believe that he had overslept, then he vaguely remembered an alarm clock in the dim and distant early morning and stretching out to silence it. Oh God, he'd gone back to sleep, if he was ever awake that was.

"Joe, I must have..."

"It's OK, I don't need to know, we're all consenting adults after all" Joe chortled

Rob squinted over at the wine glass and bottle, both sitting empty at his bedside.

"Ha, ha, very funny. The only thing I came to bed with last night was a bottle of Malbec, which is half my problem this morning. The other half being that I was just knackered last night".

"Look, mate, there's no rush at this end, everything is pretty much on track and you don't have any appointments today, or for the rest of the week for that matter." Joe hesitated, "Am I carrying you here MacLaine?"

"Naff off, as certain other royals would say."

Joe laughed, "Listen why don't you get your shit together in your own time and we'll see you when we see you. I really just wanted to make sure you were OK. Yeah?"

"Cheers mate, I do have a few things to clear up from the last few days, including finding my mother and letting her know what happened up there before she hears courtesy of the BBC or ITN".

"Ah well, maybe I can ease that burden for you. I'll email you an address a found for her via a few phone calls to a few friends" Joe teased.

"You found her?"

"She wasn't lost, Rob. You just didn't know where she was, others did."

"Where? Is she in Hampshire right enough?"

"Yep, Crawley. Not the naff one near Gatwick. Crawley in Hampshire. Apparently it's all thatched cottages and duck ponds, very picturesque by all accounts. I'm just pinging you her address now. She remarried as you know, so she is now Mrs Elizabeth Reynolds" Joe typed out a quick email as he spoke."

"You told me you didn't have any friends, said I was the only friend you had" chided Rob.

"No, I said you were me *best* friend, not my *only* friend. I'm not a total saddo, I don't need to take a bottle of wine to bed for company. Anyway, go and see your mother. Have a shower and smarten yourself up first though. Remember, she hasn't seen you for twenty two years."

"God, you nag like a woman, Joe."

Rob's phone pinged at that moment and Rob saw an email from Joe on his screen.

"OK, I'm off Joe. I'll let you know how I get on."

"Do you want me to tag along Rob, all joking aside, it has been twenty two years, for both of you."

"No it's OK Joe, but thanks anyway, I appreciate the offer. I can't believe you've got other friends, I really…"

"Sod off to Hampshire" Joe laughed and ended the call.

25

ROB LIKED HAMPSHIRE AND HAD AT ONE TIME THOUGHT OF buying a house there when he left the military. He had spent a number of training stints at RAF Odiham in Hampshire where the RAF Heavy Lift Chinook helicopters were based. One of the variants of these had been adapted for Special Forces needs and Rob had been involved with these.

It was a beautiful warm, sunny day as Rob drove out of the underground car park of his apartment in his pride and joy, a blue Maserati Grancabrio MC. Powered by a 460bhp, 4.7ltr V8, the Maserati would hit 60mph in less than 5secs, boasted a top speed of around 180 mph and very importantly, growled like an alpha male lion in heat.

He paused long enough at the car park entrance to power down the top and listen for a second or two as that growl resonated around the car park. Rob turned left towards the Chelsea Embankment and the Hampshire countryside.

Being a week day rather than weekend and late morning rather than rush hour, the roads leading out on to the M25 and M3 heading south were relatively quiet and Rob made good progress till he hit a 50mph speed restriction on the M3. The extensive roadworks were covered by average speed cameras and a few times Rob became aware that his speed was creeping up beyond the legal limit. Simple answer, engage the cruise control.

All Rob was doing now was keeping the Maserati between the lane lines and he soon found his mind wandering to the events of the past few days. During that time he had seen his brother shot and killed, had been told of his father's death over a year before and he had lost Justine. Justine who he had just found and in such a very short time had fallen in love with.

That was out of character for Rob. He was normally slow to trust or like people and as a result had few friends, not something that bothered him. People let you down, they hurt you when you least expect it. So he had built walls to stop people getting too close. One or two, like Joe Harper had managed to get through these walls and had become really close friends. Justine had sailed straight past them as if they didn't exist. But once again, someone he had loved had hurt him, Justine was gone, didn't want to speak to him, never mind live with him and what hurt most was that he didn't know why.

"In 500 yards take the exit, Junction 8" the woman in Rob's Satnav said bringing him back to the moment and he manoeuvred off the motorway on to the A303 heading for Salisbury and Andover. He followed the Satnav instructions until he reached the outskirts of Crawley, his mind occasionally wandering back to Justine.

The village was as picturesque as Joe had eluded to. There were thatched cottages in abundance and straight ahead, a large duck pond. Rob pulled out his smartphone, took a photograph of the pond, managing to get a thatched cottage in too and WhatsApped it to Joe with a message which said "Hey, you really must have friends".

Rob looked at the phone and on the spur of the moment, called Justine again. The phone rang out at the other end but once again, no reply and it went on to voicemail. Rob didn't leave a message, Justine would know from the display on her phone, who the caller was.

According to the address Joe had given him, Rob's mother who he had not seen on spoken to in twenty years, lived just round the corner. What was he going to say to her? Would she even acknowledge him? Did she still blame him for the accident that killed Sheila Stewart? Had she told her new husband about him? Suddenly he was unprepared for meeting his mother. Should he just go back to London and have his solicitor break the news to his mother? He almost did, but something deep inside him said "No, you need to face this yourself Rob MacLaine"

ROB STARTED the car and drove round the corner and up a hill till he came to the address Joe had given him. The house was thatched, he would need to tell Joe that his mother lived in a thatched house. "Funny what runs through your mind when you are nervous" thought Rob. He took a deep breath and turned into the gravel drive. "They'll hear me coming" Rob thought.

The drive curved round some high hedging to a parking area to the front of the large, traditional, red brick built house which was surrounded by well-kept gardens with large areas of lawn and well-tended beds with shrubs and flowers in full bloom. As the Maserati crunched to a halt a woman who had been tying up an errant delphinium stood up and turned to face the source of the noise in her garden.

Elizabeth MacLaine, or Reynolds as she was now had not changed much in twenty years. She was tall for a woman and still slim and elegant and almost exactly as Rob had remembered her. Her hair was shorter and maybe a little greyer, her face had a few extra lines but she was still instantly recognisable. As she walked forward to meet the car and its driver she held her hand to her brow to shade her eyes from the sun.

"Good afternoon, can I help you?" she said in a positive, almost challenging tone of voice. She was obviously not accustomed to strangers disturbing her in the garden.

As she approached the car, Rob opened the driver's door and got out.

"Yes, I think maybe you can Mrs Reynolds, maybe we can help each other" he said walking slowly towards her.

For a moment, neither spoke as they stood facing each other and slowly Elizabeth Reynold's defiant look faded and an expression of disbelief spread across her face.

"OH DEAR GOD, no! It can't be, Robbie, is it you?" she started to sob. Rob thought she was going to faint and moved forward to support her but she pulled away. The look on her face was almost one of horror, her hands flew to her mouth and she stood staring wide eyed at him, shaking her head in disbelief.

"It can't be, it can't be, he said you were dead."

"Who said I was dead, Mother?" Rob snarled, "who said I was dead?"

"It is you Robbie. He said you were dead. Bruce said you were dead."

His mother walked unsteadily over to a wooden bench seat at the edge of the lawn and sat down heavily, still staring at Rob.

"Oh Robbie, is it really you?"

Rob stood in front of her and stretched out his hand to her shoulder "Yes, it really is me. I must admit I felt as if I was near death's door when I woke up this morning with a bit of a hangover, but I can assure you, I'm very much alive, despite what my brother might have said. Just one more lie in a whole series of lies Mother"

"Lizzie, Lizzie are you all right? What's going on here? Take your hand off my wife" a voice from behind Rob shouted.

Rob half turned slowly and found himself looking at an elderly man with a certain ex-military bearing and a very intense expression on his tanned face.

"Move away from my wife, slowly and keep your hands where I can see them, do you hear."

"MR REYNOLDS, I'm Rob MacLaine, I'm sorry if I..."

"Richard, its Robbie, it's my Robbie. He's not dead, why did they tell me he was dead?" Elizabeth Reynolds sobbed.

"Robbie? Are you sure Elizabeth?"

"Yes, Richard I may not have seen him for over twenty years but I know my own son" Rob's mother sobbed. Richard Reynolds' expression softened as he realised that Rob was not a threat to either of them, much to Rob's relief.

Elizabeth Reynolds stood up and took an unsteady step towards Rob. She reached out her hand and stroked the scar on Rob's face.

"Oh Robbie, you must hate me so much. I'm your mother and I let them talk me into believing that you killed that little girl, I let them send you away."

"No Mother, I don't hate you. It took me a long time to understand why you did what you did, but, hate you, no, never that Mother." Rob said reaching out and folding his arms round her sobbing body.

"Maybe we should go inside, get you sitting down Lizzie" Richard Reynolds said worriedly "This must be a bit of a shock to the old system, come on" he said taking a hold of her.

"You too young MacLaine, let's get you both inside, come on."

The three walked up to the house and in through a set of Bi Fold doors into a large sitting room. Elizabeth Reynolds walking rather unsteadily, supported by both men until she was sitting in comfortable looking armchair.

"Sit down lad, you two have a lot to talk about. I'll go and put the kettle on, shan't be long" he said and disappeared through a panelled door.

"Are you OK Mother" Rob asked "This must be quite a shock. I didn't know that you thought I was dead or I would have approached this differently. I'm sorry to have upset you like this."

"Upset me, Robbie, how can I be upset, I thought you were dead and here you are, large as life."

"And twice as ugly" Rob laughed, touching the scar on his cheek self-consciously.

"Oh no. No scar would spoil that face of yours Robbie. You were a beautiful wee boy when you were growing up and look at you now you're a man, Robbie, not a wee boy any more. I don't know what to say to you Robbie. I let you down, I did something a mother should never do. I deserted you when you needed a mother most. I don't know how I let them talk me into it."

"I realized afterwards that the version of events Bruce gave was a load of lies. Fraser had taken photos of your car and showed me things that belied Bruce's story. I tried to tell your Father but he didn't want to know and warned me not to do or say anything about that night. He threatened Fraser with the sack if he ever spoke about it again".

"You don't need to say anything Mother, I.."

"But Robbie you don't understand..."

Rob held up a hand, "Mother, I'm just back from Achravie" Rob said as Richard Reynolds reappeared with a tray of tea and biscuits, "I've spoked to Fraser McEwan, Hamish and Lizzie at the Red Lion and Lorna Cameron. I've spoken to Bruce as well, so I understand a lot more than you think."

· · ·

"You've spoken to your brother, what did he have to say for himself, more lies I've no doubt. I hope he burns in hell for what he did to the family," Rob's mother started to cry again.

"I hope you mean that Mother, because I have some things to tell you and I hope you won't be too upset."

Elizabeth Reynolds looked up at Rob, "I don't think I like the sound of this, you better tell me."

"OK, there's no easy way to tell you this Mother, so, I need to tell you that Bruce is dead, he was shot dead two days ago."

Rob's Mother wailed "God forgive me, Robbie, I almost said thank God. I know I gave birth to your brother but he was an evil, spiteful, twisted individual who would go to any lengths to get what he wanted. What did I say Richard, an evil person who would meet an untimely end."

She looked at Rob for a moment, then a look of horror crossed her face, "You didn't shoot him. Robbie, did you, please tell me you…"

"No Mother, I didn't kill him, I came very close at one point but no, I didn't kill Bruce, but I was there when he died."

"What happened, Robbie, tell me."

"It's a long story, Mother, but first, did you know that my father was dead?"

"Yes, his solicitor, Alan Hogg, wrote to me a few days after he died and told me, otherwise I would have been none the wiser. He said he suffered a heart attack, apparently he was found dead on the floor beside his wheelchair. I went up for the funeral but I didn't stay, neither did Angus. He came too, Bruce had told him. He said he told you too, but you refused to come and put the phone down on him" Rob's Mother dabbed her eyes with a small handkerchief. "The next thing he said you were dead, killed in Iraq, he said. That's the last I heard from him"

"I found out my Father was dead from Fraser a few days ago, Mother" Rob replied sadly.

"As you can see though, rumours of my death have been grossly exaggerated" he smiled.

"What about Angus, I take it your still in touch with him?" Rob asked

"Yes, we keep in touch, he phones nearly every week from New Zealand, he's doing well out there Robbie.

"Judging by the car this young man arrived in, he's doing pretty well too, Lizzie" Richard Reynolds ventured. "I'm Richard, by the way Richard Reynolds"

"Good to meet you Mr Reynolds, albeit the circumstances could have been more congenial"

"Please, call me Richard and sorry about the welcome, I had no idea who you were" said Richard apologetically.

"No, not at all, why would you know, after all, I'm dead, or so it seems. At least I know my Mother is well protected," Rob laughed.

Richard smiled, "You're the healthiest looking corpse I've ever seen and I've seen a few of those in my time."

"ME TOO, RICHARD."

"Tell me about Bruce, Robbie" Rob's Mother asked.

Rob told her the story from the phone call from Lorna to the night of Bruce's death. He only told her what she needed to know as he did not want to upset his Mother any more that was necessary. At the end of his recollection of the events leading up to Bruce's demise and his revelation that he had not known of his father's death, Lizzie Reynolds cried.

Once she had composed herself, she asked about Rob and his life away from Achravie after he had been banished so summarily by his father and again Rob gave an edited version of his life for the last twenty years. He spoke of his time in the military, of meeting Joe and his new life as CEO of Harper MacLaine Security. He told her where he now lived and said they must come and visit him when they were next in London. By the time Rob had finished, his Mother wore an expression which was a mixture pride in his achievements and regret of not having been part of Rob's success.

"What about Achravie, Robbie? That's your home, son and you now know you are part owner. Angus sold his part of the estate to Bruce after your father died, he didn't want any part of it. He invested the money in the estates he worked for in New Zealand and he's a director of the company now, so Angus won't come back to Scotland again, not now, if ever."

"Looks like it's up to you then Robbie, you either take on the family estate or you sell up" said Richard.

"YOU CAN'T SELL Achravie Robbie, sorry Dickie, it's been in the family for generations" Lizzie said, horrified at the very idea of the estate being sold.

"Mother, I hadn't even started to think about that aspect of things yet" Rob protested.

"If you sell an estate that's been in the family as long as Achravie has, it will be like Bruce has won and he has finally destroyed the MacLaine family" Lizzie sobbed.

"Lizzie, Lizzie, you can't put that kind of pressure on Robbie, that's unfair, particularly after what he's been through. Achravie must be the last place on Earth he might want to be. Plus he has a life and a business down here" Richard pleaded.

"I need to think long and hard before I make any decision on that Mother and I would need to talk to Angus, so let's not get ahead of ourselves."

"Look" said Rob, "I should be getting back to London"

He pulled a business card out of his wallet and scribbled some numbers down on the front of it.

"Take this card Mother. I've written my private numbers

down on it as well. Can you give me your numbers too and an email if you have that."

Let me", said Richard, "I'll give you our card and write both mobiles on it. It's got the house number on it and we share an email account lizrich@xmail.com."

"Excellent" said Rob as they all stood.

Rob's Mother flung her arms around Rob's neck and hugged him tightly, "I can't believe you're here Robbie, after all these years and they told me you were dead, the bastards" She cried, but this time tears of real happiness at being reunited with a son she thought was gone.

Rob and his Mother embraced each other again on the drive as Rob opened the door of the Maserati and Rob shook hands with Richard, who, Rob felt, was a good man who would look after his Mother more so than his Father had ever done.

His Mother had also given him contacts for Angus so that he could re-establish contact there and discuss what was to happen with Achravie. As Rob drove back up the M3 toward London, he mulled over his options. He may have lost his Father and Bruce, but there again, he lost them twenty two years ago he told himself. On the bright side he had established contact with his mother again and it seemed that she and her second husband would be a part of his life going forward and hopefully Angus would too, once he had spoken to him. His Mother had said that Angus was married to a lovely New Zealand woman and had two sons. It suddenly dawned on him, he was an uncle!

As the late evening sun dipped in the sky away to his left, Rob pulled onto the hard shoulder quickly, powered the Maserati's roof back into place and as he re-joined the main carriageway, he hit the Bluetooth button and dialled Joe's personal mobile number. Joe, like Rob, carried a dual-SIM smartphone which allowed the use of separate numbers for business and private use on the two SIM cards housed in one phone. Joe's phone rang three times before he picked up the call.

"How did it go buddy" Joe asked.

"Great, brilliant, I think. I've got my Mother back in my life, Joe and that feels great. Her new husband seems right, they fit well together if you know what I mean. She'd sussed Bruce out for what he was and hated him with a vengeance so wasn't too upset by my news. Oh, and I'm an uncle, Angus has two kids, I've got his contacts in New Zealand so I can talk to him."

"I sense a "but" right about now" Joe interjected.

"YES, well, my Mother wants me to take on the running of Achravie Estate, *"It's been in the family for generations, it's part of the family tradition, you can't just turn your back on the MacLaine family history, you can't just sell it"* all that kind of stuff.

I can't run Achravie Estate Joe, even if I wanted to and I'm not sure that I do want to. What do I know about running an estate for God sake?"

"Sounds like you've got a deal of thinking to do mate" Joe said thoughtfully.

"Sorry Joe, it's not fair to burden you with all this, you've got enough on your plate with Suzy and the pregnancy and all. It just that, I've got no one else to talk to about it and you make things make sense in your own perversely logical way" Rob replied.

"Oh, thanks, Rob. I think I detected a compliment in there somewhere" Rob chuckled.

"Listen, Suzy and I were talking at lunchtime today. We booked a villa in Corfu for a holiday. We booked it when we left it last year before we knew Suzy was pregnant, but the way things are, we can't go. We had arranged for Suzy's sister and their kids to go out but they've got chickenpox and they can't go either now. We took it for a month and it's about a week or so into that as we speak. Things are pretty quiet in the office just now and as we were to be going away anyway, why don't you take yourself out there, get away from things, bit of peace and quiet, all that stuff and just have a good think about everything" Joe suggested.

"You know what, that sounds like heaven right now, but I can't just up and leave you at the drop of a hat" Rob said.

"Yes you can, Rob. The workload in the office has been planned with me not being here this month so where's the problem?"

"Are you sure, Joe? What if Suzy goes into labour early or something?"

"Corfu is about three hours from Gatwick and EasyJet do daily flights, so if we really needed you tout suite you could be back next day. The Villa in Pelekas has good robust Wi-Fi and a reliable mobile signal, so again we could still talk day to day if it came to that." Joe said.

"Villa in Pelekas?" Rob asked with an edge of curiosity in his voice.

"Yeah, it's beautiful, sits just outside the village of Pelekas, four bedrooms, big terrace area, stunning views. Twenty minute walk to the beach, lovely big pool and it's absolutely spotless. You know Suzy, Rob, she wouldn't go to a villa that wasn't spot on, never mind go to back to it again and its sitting there empty."

"I could phone the owner, tell her you're coming out and EasyJet have got seats on a flight at 05.55 tomorrow morning, Suzi checked. This time tomorrow you could be on Corfu, sitting with a G&T with a slice of lemon from the trees in the garden, munching on a local takeaway meal. What do you say, do you the world of good?" Joe added enthusiastically.

"Right, you're on, go for it" Rob laughed.

"I already have, mate. I know you too well. Suzy booked you a flight and a rental car this afternoon and she emailed Vicky to tell her you'd be coming. She'll email you all the details now, it will all be in your inbox when you get home" Joe replied smugly.

"Eh, excuse me, what if I'd said no?"

"YOU WERE NEVER GOING to be allowed to say no. Even if I'd had to set Suzy on you. Seriously, you need this space, Rob, for your own sanity. Just get out there, relax and try to make sense of all this, work out a way forward. Once you get your head together, get your fuzzy butt back over here and we'll get on with things" Joe laughed.

26

At 05.56 the next morning, EasyJet flight EZY8751pushed back from Gatwick Airport's North Terminal to start its flight to Corfu. Speedy Boarding which Suzy had booked worked well and Rob sat in seat 2A watching as London disappeared behind him and as he read and dozed his way to Corfu he began to think about the people in his life.

His father and Bruce, now both dead. His mother, who had now realised how wrong she had been to believe the web of lies spun by Bruce and accepted as gospel by his father and who had believed him dead, another of Bruce's lies. His eldest brother Angus, who he had not spoken to in twenty two years and was now a successful businessman in New Zealand where he lived with his wife and family. Lorna Cameron, his soul mate when they were both at school and whose life had now also been left in tatters by recent events on Achravie. His business partner and best friend Joe, who with his wife Suzy, had been the closest he had had to family in recent years and who were instrumental in organising this trip to Corfu. He could not forget Justine Fellows. She had come into his life so unexpectedly and it felt as if someone had switched on a light in his life and in turning her back on Rob, Justine had taken that light away and left his life a darker place than it had been before. He would not have believed it possible to miss someone so much, having known them for such a short time.

The flight landed on time and Rob picked up his luggage from the carrousel and made his way to the car rental desk where he was given the keys to a little Fiat Panda. "You're just on your own, so you won't need a big car" Suzy had said, ever practical. However, a photograph on the desk of a Volkswagen Eos convertible caught his eye, as it was no doubt intended to, so he treated himself to an upgrade, having negotiated himself a good deal with the cheerful young lady behind the desk.

Rob set up the satnav on his smartphone and started to follow its directions to the village of Pelekas and to the villa. Having reached Pelekas, Rob stopped briefly at one of the little minimarkets in the village and stocked up with a few essentials and headed to the villa where he was to meet the owner who would give him keys.

The owner, turned out to be an attractive, gregarious, friendly lady, who showed Rob all the things in the villa she thought he would need during his stay. She gave him a few pointers as to where to go and what to see in the area, how to get to the beach and the other places of interest locally. She then handed him a set of keys and gave him a business card with her contacts, telling him to get in touch if he needed anything and left him to settle in.

It was lunchtime, so Rob made himself a light lunch with the bread, cheese and cooked meat he had bought in the village, poured himself a glass of wine he took these out to the terrace overlooking the pool. He sat by a low table and eat his lunch, taking in the spectacular views of the surrounding countryside and admiring the well-kept pool area and gardens which were accessed by a small gate at the bottom of the drive or by means of a large sliding, electrically operated gate if vehicle access was required.

Once Rob had finished his lunch he went in to unpack his clothes into the extensive wardrobes in the master room and laid out his toiletries in the bathroom next door to the bedroom. He decided at that point to have a swim in the pool and spend the rest of his first day there, relaxing.

That evening, he found a menu in the kitchen from a local restaurant which did deliveries, so he phoned in his order and waited for the restaurant owner to deliver his food on a noisy little scooter. He ate the meal out on the terrace and washed it down with the remainder of a bottle of red wine. The villa had a large flat screen television and was equipped with a generous satellite package, so after dinner, Rob sat on a large comfortable settee and watched the BBC World News and then a movie. By that time he was struggling to stay awake and headed for bed. He was asleep almost as his head met the pillow.

Early the next morning, because the heat of the day had not quite developed, Rob decided to go for a run. He donned a white cotton vest-top, running shorts and trainers and set off. He ran up the hill towards the village and cut off the road on to a little track which was signposted for Pelekas Beach. The track became a road which wound its way steeply down to the beach. It took Rob a good fifteen minutes, running at a fair pace to reach a long curved sandy beach, which was still reasonably quiet as it was not yet nine o'clock and most of the tourists who would populate the beach later would still be at breakfast or still in bed for that matter. Rob was hot by the time he reached the beach, so he took off his top and trainers and ran into the water. He swam for a few minutes, savouring the gentle warmth of the shallow water, then collected his clothes and continued his run. He noticed another road snaking up the hillside so decided to investigate the possibility of a round trip rather than running back the way he had come. The road was steep and Rob was soon sweating profusely in the gradually increasing heat of the day. By the time he reached the main road at the top of the hill, Rob was soaked in sweat and breathing heavily from the exertion.

The road up had brought Rob out on the main road on the far side of the village from the villa. So he ran through the village and down the hill to the villa. After catching his breath, he stripped off, had a cool shower and dressed in a light linen shirt, shorts and leather flip-flops. He walked back into the village and bought some fresh bread from the local bakery and stopped for a coffee in one of the village cafes. He sat sipping his coffee and checked his emails on his smartphone. Nothing that needed his urgent attention and a load of advertising junk mail, he decided and finishing his coffee, he walked back to the Villa. As he was walking up the drive, his phone rang in his pocket.

"Hey Mr Holidaymaker," Joe chirped, "How is the villa?"

"Brilliant, very comfortable, you certainly look after yourself."

"Ah well, that's Suzy you see. I would camp as you know, nice little tent, a sleeping bag and a primus stove would do me fine but I'm prepared to make sacrifices where Suzy is concerned, so a luxury villa it is, sadly" Joe replied

"Joe Harper, you are so full of bullshit, you are actually a health hazard" Rob laughed.

"Getting back to reality, Rob. I've just e-mailed you a couple of documents, one will be part of a proposal and the other one is part of a contract we are about to sign. Can you find time in your busy schedule of swims and G&Ts to have a read of them, make sure they're all in order and get back to me? If you think they need amended, just type them up in red and we can do the needful at this end."

"Yeah, fine, I'll do that after lunch," Rob replied. "By the way, tell Suzy thanks for this, the flight was excellent and the villa is just beautiful. Just what I needed Joe, thanks mate."

"I'll pass that on, must go, talk later, Rob" and Joe ended the call.

During the next week or so, Rob got into a morning routine of run, swim, run back, shower, and then walk into the village for bread and a coffee, sometimes lunch. The local shop-keepers were getting to know him and his needs. His coffee arrived without having to ask, as did his fresh daily bread. Courteous greetings became conversations with the proprietors and staff, all of whom spoke English surprisingly well. By the end of the first week, Rob was being greeted like a long lost friend.

Rob's afternoons were a mixture of reading, relaxing around the pool, odd phone calls from Joe and attending to his e-mail. He was feeling a lot more relaxed and had thought out some of the problems that the events on Achravie presented him with. His skin was taking on a deeper tan and his blond hair was lightening even more with the sun and the sea and he found that he was not quite so out of breath when he got to the top of the hill running up from the beach, as he had been that first morning.

On the Sunday evening of the second week, his smartphone started playing Springsteen's "Darlington County". That will be Joe, Rob mused as he picked up the devise.

"Joseph, to what do I owe the honour of your attention this fine evening?" Rob said to the phone.

"Someone sounds relaxed" the woman's voice at the other end replied.

"Joe, you're not wearing Suzy's underwear again are you, what have I told you about that, she's going to find out. It makes you voice go all funny and high pitched" Rob responded.

"Very funny, do you and my husband ever take anything seriously?" Suzy Harper asked.

"I think Joe wearing your underwear is serious Suzy, his voice will stay like that if he's not careful" Rob said seriously.

"God, you're like Morecombe and Wise the pair of you. You should take to the stage not the Welsh mountains."

Rob laughed.

"You sound as if Corfu's doing you a bit of good Rob. Enjoying it?" Suzy asked.

"Yeah, really good Suzy. I'm feeling a lot more relaxed and getting my head round a few things, starting to make a list of things I need to do when I get back."

"How's the baby" Rob added, "He, she or it behaving itself in there."

"Lot better thanks Rob, still got a way to go, so fingers crossed" Suzy replied.

"Listen Rob, Joe had to nip out but he asked me to ask you if you can do a conference call with a client, he didn't say which one, something about a change of requirement. He asked if he can Skype you at twelve thirty your time tomorrow morning."

Rob thought it strange that Joe should not have called himself. Even if he were out he still had Bluetooth in his car.

"Yeah, that's fine by me, Suzy. Is Joe alright, he usually phones himself, not that I'm complaining about your dulcet tones you understand."

"Yeah, yeah, he's fine. I asked him to nip out for me Rob, and he was a bit concerned about phoning you too late with the time difference so he said he would go if I gave you a ring while he was out. Seems this is quite important tomorrow and he was getting a bit uptight about it" Suzy explained.

"You don't know who the client is Suzy?"

"No, I'm not even sure he told me who it is and if he did, it didn't register, sorry" Suzy replied.

"OK, no problem, I'll talk to him at half twelve."

"Thanks Rob, good night" Suzy said and Rob heard the line go dead.

27

MONDAY MORNING, ROB WAS RUNNING BACK UP FROM THE BEACH "Should be getting ready to go into the office" Rob thought to himself as he realised that it was if fact Monday morning and the start of a new working week. He had left a bit earlier as the days were getting hotter earlier now. He was amazed at the difference a week could make to the average temperatures in an area like Corfu. Back on to the main road, back through the village, wiping the sweat from his eyes again as he approached the villa.

His phone had pinged coming through the village. A text from Joe "Still OK for half twelve?" without breaking stride he had replied "Sure, no problem." Joe obviously felt this was an important call and he knew that Rob was better at talking to clients than he was. Rob was the silvery tongued salesman of the two, Joe happier behind the scenes, the organiser.

Rob showered and dressed in a plain white shirt as the mystery client was on the Skype call and a pair of loud shorts, which he would ensure no one would see during the call.

As 12.30 approached Rob opened up Skype on his laptop,

prepared a coffee from the espresso machine in the kitchen and carried both out on to the table on the terrace overlooking the garden and the drive. At 12.30 on the nose, Rob's laptop sprung into life telling him that Joe Harper was calling. He clicked on the icon and a few seconds later Joe smiling back at him from the screen.

"Good morning campers" Joe shouted in his best Hi-Di-Hi impression.

"It may be morning for you mate but its afternoon here. Some of us have already done half a day's work" Rob chided.

"Half a day's work?" Joe responded "You haven't done half a day's work this month never mind this morning. You're probably just up you lazy sod."

"I wish" said Rob laughing. "I've been for a run and a swim this morning. It's a beautiful morning Joe. In fact it's been a beautiful morning every morning, truth be told. This is a cracking place, mate. Lovely and quite, beautiful scenery, lovely beach and the villa itself is amazing. Bit big for just me but there you go."

"Like I said, it was all Suzy's doing, so it was always going to be first rate. How are you spending your time now?" Joe asked.

As Rob explained the routine he had gotten into in the mornings, he noticed a black Mercedes taxi had stopped at the big entrance gate and someone wearing a wide brimmed hat got out. A few seconds later the intercom buzzed.

"Joe, there's someone at the gate and the intercom has just buzzed. Hang on, let me answer it and find out who it is. Back in a mo." Rob said and rose to answer the caller as the taxi drove away.

"Hello?"

"Rob?" the woman's voice replied tentatively.

Rob stood in stunned silence.

"Rob, are you there?"

"Tina? Tina is that you?" Rob replied in disbelief.

"Yes Rob. Can we talk please?" Justine replied, her voice quivering slightly.

"Tina, what on earth are you....No wait, of course, come in" Rob spluttered and pressed the entry button, opening the gate.

He replaced the handset and walked down from the terrace, past the pool and on to the drive as the gate swung open and there stood Justine. She was wearing the same pale blue suit she wore the night they first met and a wide brimmed straw hat. She had a suitcase with her. Rob could not believe his eyes as he strode down to meet her standing at the gate. As Rob approached, Justine took off the straw hat and he could see tears running down her cheeks.

"Rob, I'm sorry, I've been so stupid. I don't know what I've done to us, but I just know I love you so much. You risked your life for me and I just ran away from you and..."

"Whoa, whoa! Stop right there." Rob said as he stepped forward and put his arms round her and pulled her to him. "I don't quite know what's happening here but I do know that I love you too Tina and I want you to be a part of my life."

"Please don't cry, darlin', please" said Rob as he wiped her tears away with his thumbs.

"Come on up to the house Justine, let me grab your case."

"Oh God, hang on" Rob said as they passed the pool on the way into the house. "Joe's on Skype, we were talking when you arrived.

Rob turned onto the terrace, swinging his laptop round so that he could see the screen. Joe had ended the call and just at that moment his smartphone pinged to tell him a new message had arrived. He looked at the message, "*I love it when a plan comes together!*"

Rob laughed, "I've been set up here. Haven't I?" Rob pulled Justine to him and they held each other tightly.

"It was Suzy and Joe's idea. I didn't know how you would react, I thought you might hate me for the way I treated you. Suzy invited me out to theirs's for lunch on Saturday and they said you had been trying to talk to me but were not getting any response from me. Joe said you were really upset that I wouldn't talk to you.

Suzy and I had a long talk about my past and my hang-ups and I told her that I really loved you but was totally phased by what happened on Achravie. She said that, if I wanted you, I should come out here and talk to you. She booked me a flight and arranged the call from Joe to make sure you would be here when I arrived."

"Do you *really* love me Rob?" Justine asked, pulling back and looking up at Rob's eyes

"Yes, Tina, I do love you and I thought I had lost you, because of what happened on Achravie. Please believe me, I could *never* hurt someone I care about. That never has to be a worry for you."

"I know that now. I suppose I panicked that night and the next day. I just couldn't stand another violent relationship. Suzy, Joe and I talked about you and they both said the same, that you were so fiercely loyal to people you cared about. They said that both you and Joe had killed men in the past, as soldiers, but that was what you had been trained to do. They assured me that never crosses over into your personal life.

We talked for ages about you and I told them what I felt about you, but that you had really frightened me that night. As Joe said though, you walked into a situation to save Lorna and me, knowing full well that you were risking your own life, but you did it all the same.

You've got two really good friends there Rob. They told me a lot about you and your past. There are things about me that I need to tell you and talk about. I don't want any secrets or any surprises if we can sort things out between us." Justine said as she looked up at Rob.

"Do you remember this suit?" Justine asked, lifting her jacket by the lapels.

"Yes, you were wearing it the first time we met. I'll try not to spill G&T on it this time" Rob replied.

"Glad you remember, 'cause I'd like us to start again Rob" Justine said as she dropped the jacket on the settee and started to unbutton her blouse.

They left their clothes on the lounge floor and Rob led Justine through to the bedroom, where they fell on to the bed and lost themselves in each other for the next few hours. As the afternoon wore on they made love repeatedly holding each other without speaking at any great length about anything apart from in lovemaking until they eventually dozed in each other's arms late in the afternoon.

"Let's go eat" said Rob eventually.

"Sounds good to me" replied Justine, stretching lazily by Rob's side, "I haven't had anything all day apart from an EasyJet sandwich."

"OK, let's go shower and head into the village to eat" Rob suggested as he walked around the bed towards the bathroom.

"Rob?"

"Yeah?" Rod stopped at the door and turned

"I can't have children Rob. You said you wanted to have babies with me" Justine looked sadly at Rob. "I can't"

"I know. Joe told me what you said in the car that day and I told him then, what I'll tell you now. That was a glib figure of speech. I don't care about babies, you're what's important to me. That was just my clumsy way of telling Joe that I was falling in love with you Justine."

"I sometimes feel as if I'm not a whole woman because I will never be able to give birth to a child" Justine said, "And when I heard what you said to Joe, I just cried. I felt so inadequate."

"Oh Tina, am so sorry. I really do not care about children. As long as I've you, I'll have all I need. As for not being a whole woman, that's nonsense. You once accused me of treating you as if you were some sort of leggy, blonde bimbo whose only assets were good tits and a nice arse. Well trust me, you've got all those and more. You *are* beautiful Tina. But more than that you're intelligent, you're witty, you're good fun and you're sensitive. You're everything I have ever wanted in a woman and till I met you, never been able to find." Rob explained, holding his hand out to Justine and pulling her off the bed to hold her close to him.

"I didn't believe Joe when he said you wouldn't care. I was dreading your reaction, but I knew I had to tell you" Justine said with a touch of relief in her voice.

"Well there you go, let's add honest to that list of assets" Rob smiled, "But seriously, it's not an issue." He leant forward and kissed her forehead. "Shower?"

A hot shower on a June day on Corfu is not a good idea so Rob and Justine stood under a cool, refreshing spray of water and slowly lathered each other's bodies exploring the curves, muscles and recesses of their partner. Justine wanted to know what the wound scars on Rob's arms, leg and shoulder were while Rob just marvelled at the smooth texture of the skin which covered Justine's perfectly proportioned body. They rinsed off the lather and dried off using the large fluffy bath towels which the villa supplied in abundance then got dressed in the bedroom. Justine wore a pair of white linen trousers and a floaty blue and white top with a pair of white Sketchers casual shoes, while Rob opted for a pair of pale grey jeans and a navy shirt with a pair of navy GEOX moccasin shoes.

It was still daylight when they left the villa but as it would probably be dark when they returned and there were no street lights on the road to the village, Rob took a little Maglite torch from his bag and put it in his pocket. It was dusk as they walked through the village and the lights were on in all the small local shops, bars and restaurants as passed. They stopped at Jimmy's Restaurant and asked for a table outside. A cheery, chatty waiter showed them to a table, then brought over menus and a wine list.

"Can we have some bread with oil and balsamic vinegar to nibble on till we decide please?" asked Rob.

"Certainly Sir" the waiter replied and returned a few minutes later with the bread.

They ordered their food and a bottle of wine and started with the bread, tearing pieces off and dipping them into the oil and balsamic mixture.

"So what made you decide to come looking for me then?" asked Rob.

"A combination of Joe, Suzy and Lorna. I think they could all see that I didn't want to lose you and they seemed adamant that you felt the same, so they all tried to convince me that the Rob MacLaine I saw on Achravie was not the Rob MacLaine that they knew on a day to day basis.

Joe said that he had worked with you in some very hot war zones and said that professionally, you were an outstanding soldier and operative who he would choose, above all others, to have with him in a tight spot. He also said that if you or yours were threatened you would react with appropriate but never excessive force and under these circumstances you would kill someone without a second thought. He said that was why both you and he were still alive, you having saved both your lives on a number of occasions. Hence the strong bond between you. He also said that the Rob MacLaine I witnessed on Achravie was a Rob MacLaine who knew that my life and Lorna's was under threat as was his own and he reacted with appropriate force.

Suzy said she couldn't argue with that description of you

because she had no experience of you in a war zone, but she knew that you had saved Joe's life a couple of times that she knew of. She said she thought you were a lovely guy who needed the right person to love you. They both said you could never hurt someone you really cared for."

"And where does Lorna fit in to the equation. Have you spoken to her since you got back to London?" Rob asked

"Yes, she came down to see me, came to the office, which I didn't expect. Begged me not to finish our relationship, said you were devastated that I wouldn't talk to you, she told me you loved me. She told me all about the Robbie MacLaine she grew up with, the things you did together, how you were taken away after the accident and she lost touch with you till the other week. She thinks the sun shines out of your backside by the way, loves you to bits, not in a sexual way but like a sister loves a brother. She says that was always the case and always will be. I wish I had a friend like Lorna, your very lucky Rob."

"I know. I love Lorna very much Justine, but as you say, just like I would love my sister if I had one. How did she know where to find you?"

"SHE CALLED Joe and he told her. Listening to what these guys said about you and seeing how they felt about you helped me to understand where the violence came from that night. As Joe said, if you hadn't reacted like that, *we* might have been killed.

I also understand where Lorna fits in, I must admit I was very jealous of Lorna's presence initially, but I've got to know her now and I actually like her a lot. I know she's not a threat to you and me."

Justine went on, "About 4 years ago, I met a guy at the gym I went to at the time. We went out, became a couple and after a while he moved in my flat with me. A few months down the line he lost his job in the City. I found out later he had been reported by one of his female colleagues for sexual harassment and had been sacked when he reacted badly to the accusation and had hit the woman involved. He started drinking quite heavily and was getting very frustrated at not being able to find another job.

He said it was because his boss was being childish and wouldn't give him a decent reference. Again, I found out later, it was because the City is a very tight community and word had got out about the accusations and the assault. The more frustrated he got the more he drank and he started to get very aggressive. Not with me at first but gradually he started to shout at me and throw things around the flat and eventually he started to hit me. Not often at first, but again as time passed it happened more regularly and with more aggression. People started to notice my occasional bruising and started to put two and two together.

I was really stupid and allowed myself to get pregnant which he was none too happy about and in turn made him more aggressive and abusive. I was about 6 months pregnant when I got home a little late one night from work. He was pretty drunk when I got in and started to go on about being hungry and me not being there to make his dinner in time. I said something about one of us having to work to pay the bills and so on and he just went ballistic. He said I was a lazy, ungrateful cow who didn't know when I was well off and started to slap me. I tried to get out of the flat but he pulled me back into the room and started to punch and kick me, told me I was going nowhere until he had been fed. He gave me a real beating Rob, I passed out at one point and when I came round he was taking money from my bag shouting that if I wouldn't feed him, he would go down to the pub for his dinner.

He stormed out leaving the flat door open and almost knocked the woman next door off her feet as he passed her. She realised something was wrong and came in to check if I was alright. I wasn't, I was badly beaten and was haemorrhaging badly internally. She called 999 and got me to a hospital but by that time I had lost a lot of blood and even worse still, I was losing the baby. I had an emergency operation, but they couldn't save the baby and as a result of all the trauma the hospital said that I would not be able to have another child.

The medical staff had called the police and they found my so called boyfriend in the flat, blind drunk, breaking up furniture and ornaments. They tried to calm him down but he hit one of the policemen with a stool and lunged at another with a kitchen knife. He ended up in court facing a string of charges ranging from attempted murder, assaulting a police officer, GBH and drunk and disorderly, having caused mayhem in the local pub that night. He's still in prison and will be for quite a few years yet.

Until I met you, I hadn't been with another man. That's why I can't have children Rob and why I am so frightened of another violent or abusive relationship and that's why I had to be certain before I even considered committing to you." As Justine finished her story, her voice was beginning to falter and a tear rolled down her cheek as she recalled the pain of her past ordeal.

"Wow! I'm not surprised. I don't know what to say Tina. I can't even begin to understand how it must have felt to go through that and I am even more amazed that you are here now. Joe is right Tina, when he says that have killed people in the past. I didn't enjoy it, but I did what was necessary at the time and given similar circumstances, I would do so again.

But life has taught me to be loyal to and protective of the people in this world that I care about. I could never hurt you like that, it's not in my nature. I don't trust people easily and I don't have a lot of friends either, for the same reason, but I promise I will always love you and protect you Tina. I started to fall in love with you the moment I set eyes on you. I knew you were the one for me that first night. I've never felt like this about anyone before, that's why I took it so hard when I thought I'd lost you" Rob said as he stretched across the table and took Justine's hand in his. He squeezed her hand and smiled "As I said earlier, the baby thing isn't important. For me it's all about you and me. I think we can make a life together, be happy, make memories".

"I've got things to sort out with the estate on Achravie, that's my other priority. My mother is adamant that it shouldn't be sold. She is also quite positive that Angus won't be interested, he apparently sold his share of the estate to Bruce after my father died and used the cash to invest in the farms he managed in New Zealand. He's now a director and shareholder, with no desire to come back to the UK my mother says, although I haven't actually spoken to him yet.

Speaking to Alan Hogg the estate's solicitor, he said that there was a fair bit of cash in the estate which would more than cover inheritance tax and other costs, so there's no worry there he says. I pretty much live off my army pension and I've invested most of my income from Harper MacLaine. I could possibly use that to buy Angus out, if that was what he wanted and he was prepared to be reasonable with his price.

The main problem would be the running of the estate, most estates with an absentee landlord struggle, so I would need to either spend a fair bit of time there or have a full time estate manager that I could trust. I would probably need to do the later because there's Harper MacLaine and Joe to consider.

That's a business I know and I enjoy running it and Joe is more like a brother to me than a business partner. I couldn't just walk away from either, they've been my life since I came out of the Regiment. Plus, if you and I do make a life together, how would you feel about the possibility of going back to Achravie?" Rob asked.

By this time their food had arrived along with a bottle of wine and they ate and drank as they talked.

"I liked Achravie" Justine replied "what I saw of it and Lorna's there. I like Lorna, I'd like to keep in contact with her. She's hurting too you know. Stella really caused her a lot of pain Rob."

"I know" Rob agreed.

"Just don't ask me to go back to that cottage" she shuddered."

"So, what exactly does Achravie Estate consist of?" asked Justine,

"Pretty much the island of Achravie, which is about 6000 acres, about 9 square miles in layman's terms Hillcrest House which is about 6000sq ft, 8 bedrooms 5 reception rooms, including a main hall with a massive staircase and high vaulted ceilings. There are about 15 various houses and cottages, plus the Red Lion the pub in the village. All told probably worth somewhere around 12 to £15million in today's market I worked out. Most of the other properties on the island are leasehold although some of the newer ones are freehold, the estate sold the plots to the builders."

Rob caught the waiter's attention with the universal sign which said *can I have the bill please* and having paid the bill, Rob and Justine started to walk back down through the village towards the villa. The village was relatively busy, with the village's limited selection of bars and restaurants doing a steady trade. The evening was still warm, as they walked back to the villa with their arms round each other and as they left the lights of the village behind them, used Rob's little Maglite torch to light their way.

"I could help you put together a plan for Achravie if you like. I'd need to have a look at the accounts with the P&L and cashflow spreadsheets. Do an inventory of the assets and if you can give me an idea of what you want to do with the place we could knock up a first draft business plan, see what it looked like and we could refine it from there once you've spoken with your brother."

"Umm" Rob replied, "sounds good, if you could do that I'll have a look over it with you"

"You sound sceptical Mr MacLaine, but to someone like myself with a first class honours in Business Management and a Masters in Strategic Marketing, it would be a walk in the park. I worked as a project manager with a firm of management consultants before I lost my baby. I suppose I lost a lot of my confidence along with the baby.

Andy Savage's my uncle, not many people know that and he's happy to leave it at that. He kind of took me under his wing afterwards and took me on as his PA on maternity cover, but the girl decided not to come back to work, so I stayed on. Truth be told, it really doesn't hold my interest anymore and I would love to get my teeth into a project like this. Not just a pretty face you know" Justine joked.

"No, you've got good tits and a nice arse too, you told me so" Rob chuckled and smacked Justine's bottom lightly.

"Oh God, I'm never going to be allowed to forget that am I?" Justine said with a laugh.

"Absolutely not!" Rob exclaimed in response and they kissed as they walked.

They reached the villa and Rob locked up as Justine unpacked her case, hanging clothes in one of the wardrobes, stowing her smaller items in various drawers and lining up her lotions and potions in the bathroom alongside Rob's toiletries. They both undressed and slipped naked into the firm king-sized bed.

Rob and Justine wrapped their arms round each other and holding each other close, kissed slowly. "It's been a long day" said Justine quietly, "I've been on the go since before 4 o'clock, but it was worth it" she added tucking her head under Rob's chin and resting it on Rob's chest while Rob gently ran his hand over her lower back and her right flank.

"I'm glad you came, I was really missing you, you know" Rob said softly as he stroked her soft smooth skin. No response. He looked down and saw that Justine was already sound asleep in his arms. He smiled and closed his eyes "Good night Tina" he whispered and closed his eyes.

28

THE NEXT MORNING, THEY BOTH WOKE EARLY AS THE SUN SHONE through the fabric of the curtains flooding the room with light. They kissed each other and began to make love, slowly, exploring each other and enjoying the fact that they did not need to rush. Afterwards, Justine dozed. The previous day had been long for her and she was obviously still tired, so Rob slid out of bed and stepped into the shower. He had almost finished in the shower when he became aware of another presence in the room, turning, he found Justine smiling up at him.

"Am I too late to soap your back for you?" she enquired mischievously.

"Certainly not" Rob replied and lifted her into the shower with him.

Later as Justine washed her hair, which she said would *"take ages"*, Rob set out a breakfast of cereal, bread, honey and coffee for them both out on the terrace. While he was waiting for Justine to make an appearance, Rob had texted his mother to ask her to send Angus's contacts so that he could make contact and discuss the Achravie estate.

His mother had replied almost immediately, much to Rob's

surprise as it was still early in the UK. She told Rob that she had contacted Angus to tell him that his brother was still alive and to expect a call from him. She said that she had related the story that Rob had told to her about the situation on Achravie which had led to Bruce's untimely death and to her finding out that Rob was in fact not dead, as Bruce had led the family to believe. She added Angus's contact details and said to expect a call from Angus as he had asked for Rob's details.

"She ended her message with *"Please don't sell Achravie!!"*

"Not going to sell, want to buy Angus out if possible. Did I wake you mother?"

"Not you darling, *Dickie's snoring!! Delighted you're not selling. Expect a call from A, he's delighted you're still with us!!"* came the reply.

Justine finally arrived "Oh I love a man who feeds me" she teased Rob rubbing her hands at the sight of the food and the coffee, and while she ate copious amounts of breakfast, Rob told her of the exchange of messages and the gist of the conversation.

"So, you've decided you're definitely not going to sell Achravie?" Justine enquired, through a mouthful of bread and honey.

"I'll only sell if I can't afford to keep it and a lot of that depends on Angus and what he wants for his share. In theory, I already own one third of the estate and if Angus sold his share to Bruce, Bruce then owned two thirds. Now that Bruce is dead, I inherit half of his share apparently, he'd turn in his grave if he knew that, and Bruce the other half." Rob explained, "That means that Angus again owns one third of the estate and I own the other two thirds, so I need to buy that third from him. This all assumes that my mother is right and he doesn't want to hang on to it."

"The other aspect of that is that if, as I think, the estate is worth around 12 to £15million then Angus could reasonably ask up to around £5million for his share, which would use up a great deal of my working capital, so I would need to be a bit inventive when it came to raising that cash" Rob mused. "I own 75% of Harper MacLaine, so if Joe was up for it, I would sell him 20% which would leave me with a controlling interest and still realise a million or few. The problem is that Harper MacLaine makes healthy profits and is about to take a big hike in turnover, and profit, with the new contract we were celebrating the night I bumped into you. Achravie on the other hand, is profitable but not to the same extent as Harper MacLaine, so if I need to sell a chunk of that to buy Achravie, I'm going to lose substantial income."

"Unless we can increase the turnover and profit at Achravie" Justine interjected.

"If we can increase the turnover and margins at Achravie, it would be helpful and make the whole exercise worthwhile, but, we would need to do that without making life for anyone on the island more difficult" Rob insisted.

"Can you get me access to the Achravie accounts and inventory?" Justine asked.

"It's all over there" Rob said, pointing to a pile of plastic folders and papers on the large dining room table, "I got it all from Alan Hogg before I left and printed off the important parts. It was Alan Hogg who told me that I inherit half of Bruce's estate as he didn't have a will made out and Angus and I are the only family left. The rest is on my laptop if you need back-up data. If you need anything else, I can ask Alan to send it or get it from the accountants."

"OK, while I look at that, why don't you try to speak to your brother, his asking price is important in the whole scheme of things? New Zealand is 10 hours behind us here so you would get him about now."

"OK, let me try him" Rob said and watched as Justine went into the villa and sat at the table with the Achravie files and folders.

Rob pulled up his brother's telephone numbers and dialled his landline. He suddenly became aware that he had not spoken to Angus for over twenty years and wondered what he would say to him. Rob and Angus had been good friends as boys and shared many hobbies and interests as they were growing up. Neither really had much in common with Bruce when they were young and most of their friends were not big fans on Bruce's. Rob's thought train was broken by a young boy's voice answering the phone.

"Robert MacLaine, can I help you" the voice said. Rob was stunned, Angus and his wife had given their son *his* name.

"Hello, Can I help you?" the boy repeated.

"Yes sorry, may I speak with your father please, Robert. Tell him it's his brother, your uncle Rob" Rob said eventually.

"My uncle Rob? I'm named after you" the young lad exclaimed, "but you were dead" he added.

"No I wasn't dead, Robert" Rob laughed. "Some people just said I was dead because it suited them, but it wasn't true. I was in the army and I'm very much alive young man" Rob added.

"Robbie, who is it?" a man's voice in the background asked.

"It's Uncle Robbie and he's not dead, you were right Dad" said you Robert innocently.

"Hello, Robbie, is that you?" Angus asked taking the phone from his son.

"Yes, Angus, it's me and I'm not dead, your son is perfectly correct" Rob replied.

"Aw heck, sorry about that Robbie. Young Robbie just says it as he sees it, bit like you when we were kids. How are you, you OK now? Mother told me about you and your adventures on Achravie. She said you were there when Bruce was killed."

Angus asked the questions with an enthusiasm which reminded Rob of his elder brother as they were growing up.

"I'm pretty good Angus, all the better for being alive again. How about you, we have so much to catch up on Angus. We haven't spoken in over twenty years, that's unbelievable."

The brothers spent the next twenty minutes just catching up and reminiscing then got down to the specifics of the Achravie estate. Angus confirmed that he had no interest in the estate he was raised on, it held too many bad memories for him. A bad tempered, sometimes abusive father, a brother, Bruce, who did his best to make Angus's life a misery and the reaction to the car accident which had seen him lose his brother so suddenly and cruelly when Rob had been sent away.

He had left Achravie after a violent argument with his father and vowed never to go back and had instead made a happy family life for himself in New Zealand. He had married a local girl and they had brought two sons into the world, who along with a collection of dogs and cats made up their family. He was happy where he was, thank you very much. Rob told Angus that his mother was adamant that she did not want to see the family estate sold, having been the seat of the MacLaine family for generations and that he had assured his mother that he would do his best to keep the estate and broached the subject of buying Angus's share of the estate.

"I sold my third share of the estate to Bruce when our father died. I sold it then because I didn't want it Robbie and I still have no interest in Achravie Estate. I've already discussed it with Val my wife and she agrees that we sell it. You being here now and wanting to buy it put a new slant on the whole scenario, so when mother told me, I talked to Val again and what we decided was this.

Val's father owns the share of the farms out here that I didn't buy from him and he's looking to retire. If I sell you my part of Achravie, we can buy the rest of the farms from Val's dad and that would be great. So, the upshot of that is. I sold my share of Achravie to Bruce before and I'm more than happy to sell it to you now.

I know you want to make a go of things and I respect you for that Robbie, it *is* our family home after all. We've spoken to Val's dad and agreed a price with him, it's way under valuation because he said if he died tomorrow, Val would get it for free anyway. That means if you agree to give me what we have agreed with Val's dad, we are set up here for life. Achravie estate was valued when father died at £14million and I sold to Bruce at market value. This is almost a second bite at the cherry for me, I get to sell something twice." Angus hesitated for a second "Val's dad needs the equivalent of £2million Sterling from me, so I would like to ask you for that price for my share of Achravie. How does that sound Robbie?"

Rob hesitated, thinking, then said eventually, "That's way under value Angus."

"I know, I don't need the full value Robbie, as I said, buying the rest of the farms sets us up for life here. You are going to be more in need of your money than I am if you're going to invest in Achravie and much as *I* don't want Achravie, I don't *really* want to see it go out of family ownership. I know our mother is quite passionate about that. This way we all get what we want. Yeah!" Angus explained.

"Say something little brother" Angus said after a few moments of silence from Robbie.

"I don't know what to say Angus. £2million is way less than its worth" Rob reiterated.

"Why don't you just say yes, then I can go eat my supper here" Angus chuckled.

"Yes, then. Thank you Angus, thank you" Rob replied.

"It's no more than you deserve after the way this family treated you Robbie. Get in touch with Alan Hogg and have him draw up a document on the basis we have agreed, send it over to me, I'll sign it and when you pay me the funds, Achravie is all yours. I'll give you a call in a couple of days, Give me your ID and I'll Skype you, let you meet your sister-in-law and two nephews."

"OK, will do, good to talk to you again Angus and thanks, again" Rob ended the call in a state of disbelief. "£2million" he said to no one in particular.

Justine was so engrossed in the Achravie paperwork that she hardly noticed Rob's hesitant return to the table till he stood beside her, still with a glazed look of disbelief on his face.

"Well, how did it go, what did Angus say?" Justine looked up at the still bemused Rob.

Rob looked down at her and a smile slowly appeared on his face. He shook his head. "£2million!"

"What, you got him to agree to £2million?" Justine exclaimed, her hands grabbing Robs forearms.

"No, he got *me* to agree to £2million. I told him that was way under valuation, but he said that's all he wants, all he needs. He doesn't want me to sell Achravie and I think he sees this as payback, his contribution if you like" Justine squealed and jumped up, throwing her arms around Rob's neck and hugging him tightly.

She pulled back and looked at him, "You can do this Rob, at that sort of price, you can do this. Even a cursory look at the accounts says that Achravie is actually a fairly healthy cash generator even as it stands. Oh Rob, you can *do* this" she enthused.

"No, I can't Tina. *I* can't do it, not...."

Justine's jaw dropped, the enthusiasm gone, "What are you saying Rob, you can, *you must!*"

ROB LAID his right forefinger on Justin's lips, "If you'd let me finish. As I was saying before I was so rudely interrupted", he smiled, "*I can't do this*, not with everything else I've got on the go. But *we* can, you *and* me. You said yourself last night that you managed projects with a big management consultancy and you said that being Andy's PA wasn't exactly holding your interest. If we work on this project together, we can do it Tina, but it's too much for me on my own. What do you say, come and work with me on this, help me make it work."

Justine stood, dumbfounded, her hands on her face. "Are you serious?" she asked in a soft voice.

Rob smiled "I haven't taken the decision to buy Achravie lightly. It's "our ancestral home" to quote my mother and this is a second chance for me to make it *my* home, something I never dreamed would actually happen. A lot of people on the island rely on the estate for a living. I need to make sure I don't let them down, so I need to make it work, for them as well as for me."

"You once asked me not to play with you Tina and I promised I never would. I knew that first night sitting in the bar by the river talking to you, that I was going to want more of you in my life. Then I thought I'd lost you, but here you are and I love you Tina. I really don't think I could effectively manage the Achravie thing without Harper MacLaine suffering and that wouldn't be fair to the company or the guys we employ and it certainly wouldn't be fair to Joe. You've got the expertise to solve my problem and I get to have more of you in my life. So, yes, it's a serious offer."

JUSTINE ALMOST KNOCKED Rob off his feet as she jumped at him, wrapping her arms around his neck again and her long legs round his waist. She held him tight. "Oh Rob, I thought I'd lost you too, but I'm here now and I'm not going anywhere, if that's what you want."

"Is that a "yes" then" Rob gasped.

Almost as unexpectedly, Justine let go and ran out to the terrace down the steps leading to the pool area and on down to the pool. By the time she got to the edge of the pool she was naked and she dived into the cool water, surfacing when she reached the other end. As she surfaced she saw his dark silhouette through the water cascading down her face, "Of course it's a yes" she shouted clearing her vision and looking up at the pool man who had been quietly cleaning the pool.

"Aaarg" Justine screamed and tried her best to cover her modesty as the pool man turned away, theatrically covering his eyes. While Rob stood at the top of the steps from the terrace down to the pool and laughed as he hadn't laughed in ages.

29

THEY WERE STILL LAUGHING AT THE INCIDENT WHEN THEY recalled it a week later as they sat on the EasyJet Airbus A320-214 lifting them into the cloudless skies above Corfu to begin their journey back to London Gatwick. During the week since the incident, Rob and Justine had worked tirelessly on a business plan for Achravie.

They had spent hours pouring over spreadsheets and projections and deciding what the finished Achravie would look like as a business. "We need a vision of what we are trying to achieve" Justine had said "What do we want Achravie to be and what do we need to achieve that?" she had prompted Rob. They had completed their first draft business plan and had worked out roughly what it would cost to implement and how much revenue they could reasonably expect it to generate. They worked various scenarios, different outcomes, costed them and projected income streams.

Justine had phoned Sir Andrew Savage and told him that she wanted to leave and explained why. To say that Sir Andrew was pleased at the outcome of Justine's flight to Corfu would be a gross understatement. He was delighted for both his niece and for Rob, who he privately looked on as a surrogate son and told Justine that as he was just about to leave on a family holiday, her services as his PA would not be needed and that he would get a temp in when he got back.

This meant that Justine could concentrate on Achravie right away and she could not hide her delight at that possibility. Rob had set up meetings with his solicitors and bank to finalise the transfer of Achravie shares from Angus's name to his and the transfer of £2million to Angus as agreed. Further calls were made to Joe and to his mother to bring them up to date with the situation. Joe was in turn, pleased with the outcome of his and Suzy's little deception, surprised by Rob's intention to buy out Angus, although supportive of the plan once he knew that Rob would still be committed to Harper MacLaine and relieved that Rob would retain his shareholding in the company.

By the end of that working week, Rob owned Achravie Estate and Justine, who had taken to her new role like a duck to water, had employed an architect to work on plans to alter Hillcrest House. Further plans were to be drawn up to form two separate sites, one to the north of the island and one to the east, each for the installation of twelve luxury log cabins and ancillary buildings. Saturday was spent preparing Justine's flat in town for renting out as both had decided that she should move into Rob's river view apartment in the short term until they had time to make longer term plans. Justine wanted to keep her flat as it had been bequeathed to her by her grandmother and it would give her an independent source of income.

SUNDAY MORNING FOUND them headed to his mother's for lunch, an invitation she'd sent early that week and one he happily accepted. Joe Cocker playing in the background, he headed along Chelsea embankment and eventually on to the M3 with the roof down and the wind ruffling Justine's long ponytail.

. . .

"YOU LOOK WORRIED JUSTINE" Rob commented as he drove at an infuriating 50mph as per the temporary, if long-term speed limit on the roadworks.

"I am worried that I don't meet with your mother's approval or that she just won't like me. I feel as though I'll be on trial" Justine replied with a frown.

"That's not why we are going, Justine. We're going because I want to bring her into the loop with the plans for Achravie, I want her on side and the best way to do that is to make her feel a part of what we are doing. Yes she wants to meet you but I think my mother has learned her lesson when it comes to being judgemental. Apart from which, I do actually believe the two of you will get on. Mother and I were close when I was young, we agreed on most things. I suppose I was her baby, being the youngest." Rob explained.

"Some baby, you're over six foot for goodness sake" Justine laughed.

As Rob drove, Justine asked about Rob's childhood on Achravie and his relationship and interaction with his parents and his two brothers. Rob had gone to primary school on Achravie and then to a private school on Arran where he boarded during the school week but came home at weekends at his mother's insistence.

Rob took after his mother in physical appearance and temperament, being tall and skinny as a boy and generally placid in nature, unless riled and then his bite was much worse than his bark. Both his brothers were shorter and stockier in stature, more like their father and darker in complexion than Rob, who again had his mother's blond hair and vivid blue eyes.

Soon they were passing through the beautiful picturesque

village of Crawley and Justine went quiet as they turned into the drive of Elizabeth and Richard Reynold's thatched house.

Two golden Labradors were playing on the lawn as they drove up and the dogs bounded over to investigate the new arrivals as they got out of the car.

"Oh, aren't they gorgeous Rob. You didn't tell me your mother had these beauties" enthused Justine, kneeling on the drive to play with them as they did their best to lick her to death, as only Labradors can.

"I didn't know she had them" said Rob in his own defence

Just then Elizabeth Reynolds opened the front door. "Boys! Come away!" she shouted to the dogs, only to be totally ignored "I'm so sorry" Elizabeth shouted to Justine, "Jock, Rory, behave, don't be a nuisance, now" she chided the dogs again.

"Oh, never a nuisance, Mrs Reynolds" Justine replied laughing, "I grew up with two beauties like these, I just love Labradors, they're such great soft lumps and just so full of love."

By this time one of the dogs had found Rob and had decided that he too needed licking, while the other lay on his back to have his belly rubbed by Justine, who duly obliged. Justine stood as Rob's mother approached.

The older woman held Justine's shoulders and kissed her lightly on both cheeks," You must be Justine" she declared, "I'm very pleased to meet you. Rob speaks very highly of you, my dear. I hope he looks after you well. If not you're to let me know" she added, turning to Rob. "This is becoming a habit Rob, twice in twenty two years!" she said laughing.

"Come in to the house my dears, if these dogs will let you" she added shooing the dogs away from Justine and Rob's feet and leading them indoors. "Dickie's in the kitchen. He's stirring the gravy and says he can't stop stirring till it's ready or it gets lumpy. I wouldn't know, can't cook, won't cook, that's me. Dickie's the family chef, much to my delight, I can tell you."

"I'm not the best of cooks either, Mrs Reynolds" admitted Justine "as Rob is about to find out"

"Call me Lizzie, Justine, Mrs Reynolds sounds very formal and I don't think we are going to want to be too formal"

"OK Lizzie, but my friends call me Tina" Justine smiled.

"That's it settled then" Lizzie Reynolds pronounced, "and what about you, young man, I believe everyone calls you Rob now not Robbie" she said turning to Rob.

"I get both now but yes, most of my friends nowadays call me Rob. Having said that, I've been called a lot worse than Robbie, trust me." Rob chuckled.

Just then Richard appeared in the doorway, wearing an apron with *"I cook with wine, sometimes I even put some in the food"* emblazoned across the front "I thought I heard voices" he declared.

"Dickie come and meet Tina" Rob's mother said shaking her head, "Do you have to wear that awful apron dear, it's embarrassing."

"Tina, I'm delighted to meet you and trust me, if didn't wear my apron I would be told, *"You've got a stain on your shirt, why don't you wear your apron"* Richard chuckled and kissed Justine lightly on her cheek. "Rob, good to see you again, my boy" he added shaking Rob's hand firmly.

"Lizzie why don't you pour the young ones a drink and get them seated, lunch is pretty much ready, so I'll bring it out. Richard said and disappeared into the kitchen again.

Rob's mother poured the gin and tonic Justine had asked for, a mineral water for Rob the driver and sat them at the large dining table while Richard brought in a traditional Sunday roast beef with Yorkshire pudding with all the trimmings. Richard served and they all started to get to know each other a bit better, the Reynolds finding out a little about Justine's background and her family, who Rob was still to meet and Justine learning a bit more about the Reynolds, who seemed, Rob thought, to have rather taken to this woman that he had so recently fallen in love with.

They moved to more comfortable chairs in a large, bright library and over coffee and home-baked ginger cookies, Elizabeth broached the subject of the estate.

"What finally made you decide to buy Angus out? When you left here last, you seemed undecided as to what you wanted to do."

"Oh no mother, I knew what I *wanted* to do, I just hadn't decided *how* if it was feasible at all. I had no idea what costs were involved and I knew that I had a duty of loyalty to Harper MacLaine and to Joe Harper in particular. Actually you must meet Joe, he's a lovely guy and he's been like a brother to me over the years" Rob said.

He took another biscuit as Richard refilled his cup "There was no one factor that made me decide that it would work. I did a lot of thinking out on Corfu and did a lot of sums, but I still had two major concerns.

One, I didn't know how much Angus would want for his share, assuming he was interested in selling. If he had wanted market value, or more, I would have had to look very closely at it from a financing point of view.

Two, could I devote enough time to Achravie to ensure that I was doing it justice, without it having a detrimental effect on Harper MacLaine. Harper MacLaine by the way, is close on a £20million turnover company and needs a lot of work from both Joe and I. When Angus told me that he only wanted £2million for his share, I knew I could probably manage it financially, if I did a bit of juggling.

That just left the workload aspect, which was almost the major stumbling block, not the finance one. Tina and I had a little bit of a wobble in our relationship, for reasons which I'll let her explain to you at a later date and which are not that important, because we are now back on track and very much an item" Rob said smiling over at Justine who was sitting beside him on the settee. He reached over a gave her hand a gentle squeeze.

"While we were both looking for ideas and solutions, this young lady announced that she has a first in Business Management and a Masters in Strategic Marketing, and, that she is not all that fulfilled at her present job. Now, if that's not a job application, I don't know what is." They all laughed and Rob continued.

"The upshot of all that is that Tina here solves the workload problem. As of last week, Tina is taking on the project management of the Achravie Estate rejuvenation project, I'll oversee and get involved when Tina says she needs me to get involved. That means that I can still do justice to Harper MacLaine, although I may need a bit of extra support from Joe or an extra resource if we feel we need it. Once we get the project completed, the workload will lessen and Tina and I will look after the management of the place together. So, does that sound like a plan to you?" Rob finished.

"Wow, you don't hang about, do you?" Rob's mother chipped in, "And how does Tina feel about all this, I hope you're not bullying her into something."

"Trust me, Lizzie, that's not the case. I've been through a lot in my life, but I've come out of it a stronger person and certainly one who would not be bullied. I'm doing this because I want to. Rob knows how I feel about him and he's made it quite clear how he feels about me. We want to share our lives with each other Lizzie and if rejuvenating Achravie Estate is part of Rob's plan for the future, then I would want to be a part of it. In fact I think I have a lot to bring to the project."

"Good for you, you don't strike me as being anybody's fool Tina and believe you *will* add something to the Estate. Will you keep me in the picture as to what you are planning?" Lizzie asked.

"If you will help me, yes" Justine replied.

"Help you my dear? How can I help?"

"You lived on Achravie a lot longer than Rob did and I hardly know the island. You know the island better than Rob and I put together. Your advice would be invaluable Lizzie" Justine said.

"Oh, that would be good Tina, I would love that. Rob's father and I had issues, but I loved Achravie, still do if I am truthful." She answered and Rob thought he could see a tear form in the corner of her eye but she dabbed it away quickly.

"OK, one last thing before we need to get going. We moved Tina into my flat last night, so it's now our flat. As Tina said, we want to be with each other and we want to be seen to be making that commitment" Rob said as he stood.

"Oh Robbie, I'm so pleased for you. Dickie and I have done a bit of checking up on you since we found you again" His mother said through a great big mothers hug, "Dickie was in the Regiment you know, I know were not supposed to talk about that but we're family.

He knows what you you've been up to these last years, won't tell me all of it but I can guess. He tells me you "didn't leave footprints" in some of the places you went to. You need a good, strong feisty woman to keep you out of trouble by the sounds of things" she turned to Tina, "And by the sounds of things, that's exactly what you've got" she added to hug a slightly surprised Tina "You show him who's boss, my dear, keep him out of dark places."

They said their goodbyes to Rob's mother. Richard and the two dogs before heading back up the road to the riverside apartment which was now home to both of them.

"So" said Rob "That went well, mother was very impressed with our plans for Achravie and you seem to be a bit of a hit."

"What did she mean about not leaving footprints and

keeping you out of dark places?" Justine asked as they drove slowly up the M3.

"When I was in the Regiment, the SAS to you, well you've seen my CV at Savage, I got involved in covert, undercover operations, black ops as we refer to them, in places where British forces were not supposed to be and it would be very embarrassing for government if it were common knowledge, hence the "not leaving footprints".

As for dark places, I don't do that kind of work anymore, you know what I do. Someone was a bit naughty giving that kind of information to Richard, he must have some pretty high up contacts" Rob replied.

"Thank you for including my mother in the Achravie planning by the way, I think she was quite touched" Rob added.

"Makes sense Rob, I meant what I said. She knows the island better than you or I and you know what they say about local knowledge. That wasn't me just being nice to your mother, although she's a lovely lady and I really took to her too. So is Richard, they suit each other, don't they?" Justine observed.

"I'd like to take the architect up to Achravie this week if you don't mind and if he's available. What do you think?" She added.

"Yeah, sounds about right, but it's your project, your decision Tina. By the time this project takes off, you're going to know what needs to be done better than I will, so you do what you feel you need to. I know he's on holiday, but why don't you email Andy, ask him how much he would take to rent you the Agusta for a couple of days to take you up and down. Save a lot of time!" There are a couple of Land Cruisers on the estate, you could use one of them for getting about." Rob suggested.

"Good idea, he's not using it, I know that." Justine said then hesitated. "How would your mother feel about coming up with me Rob?"

Rob laughed, "Do you know what, I'm sure she'd jump at the chance. Give her a call once you set things up and ask her, Achravie and a helicopter, I reckon she'll bite your hand off."

"Ok, I'll do that."

Rob frowned thoughtfully "If I'd known I was going to end up owning the estate I might not have been so quick in blowing up that other Land Cruiser that night."

Justine looked horrified, "You blew that Land Cruiser up!"

"Yeah, who did you think did that?"

"I, I really hadn't thought. You blew up a Land Cruiser? How did..." Justine started incredulously.

"Well, when I say I blew it up. Big Mac actually blew it up. He hit it with a rocket propelled grenade when I told him to. Wish I hadn't now" Rob explained ruefully.

"Rob MacLaine, you're unbelievable, you just..... blow up a Land Cruiser!" Justine shook her head.

"I've done it a good few times Tina, I knew exactly what I was doing" Rob said in his defence.

"You've done it a few times!" Justine mimicked "And that makes it all right? You know what Rob, you know what they say about being in a hole? I think you need to stop digging, *now!*"

They drove in silence across the M25 and on to the M4.

Eventually Justine looked at Rob and shook her head "It's like your two different people Rob, you're so gentle and thoughtful one minute and then talk about blowing up a Land Cruiser with a rocket propelled grenade as if it were an everyday event. *"I went out to get a sandwich at lunchtime. Oh, and I blew up another Land Cruiser on the way back".* Life with you is never going to be dull is it?"

"Well, actually, I hope it will be. I was a soldier for years Tina. Covert operations means getting behind enemy lines, living undercover, sometimes killing some nasty people before they torture and kill you. The one driver in those situations is "survival". Survival at all costs, because sometimes a lot of other lives depend on your survival. I might have killed someone in Afghanistan, who if he had lived, could have been instrumental in killing you, or your parents or anyone who happened to be in the vicinity of his bomb blast somewhere in London. That's why we did what we did, but that was me as a professional soldier and it was the professional soldier in me that blew up that Land Cruiser on Achravie that night and I hope you never need to see that guy again. But be aware he still exists Tina" Rod explained.

Justine sat quietly for a few minutes, "I've never thought of it that way Rob, I'm sorry. You must have seen some terrible things. What finally made you decide to come out of the army?"

"I'D HAD ENOUGH, basically. I never baulked at killing someone who was a threat, but I didn't enjoy it either. I believed that the end justified the means. End one of two lives to potentially save a few hundred innocent men women and children. But I'd had enough and I'd survived a few scrapes from knives, bullets and explosions and you can't do that for ever. So I thought I'd quit while I was still in one piece. You've seen all these guys on telly who come back from war zones minus arms or legs, traumatised and generally messed up. I operated beside guys who ended up like that and didn't want to be one of them." Rob explained.

"I'm glad you came out safe" Justine said softly and reached across to lay her had on Rob's thigh, giving it a gentle squeeze.

"Have we just had our first argument?" Rob ventured.

"If and when we have an argument MacLaine you won't need to ask that question, you'll know we've had an argument!" Justine told him and punched his upper arm.

"Ouch!"

As they approached the Chelsea Embankment, Justine asked "So, who is this Big Mac then?"

Rob laughed, "You didn't actually meet Big Mac that night did you?" Rob recalled "Big, because he is just over six foot seven tall and build like the proverbial brick shithouse wall. Mac, because he's actually Iain MacDonald, I think Pete Hall mentioned meeting him, he was a bit wary of him because of his sheer size but he's just a big pussycat. I served with him in Iraq and Afghanistan and now he runs this outdoor centre on Arran. It was his Land Rover I had on Achravie."

"Was it him who shot that big guy at the cottage?"

"Yes."

"Some pussycat!" Justine mocked.

"He's like me Justine, an ex-soldier who is very good at what he does. Which in his case involves shooting things from a long way away. He was about a quarter of a mile from the cottage when he took that shot. He saved all our lives that night."

"In that case I would like to meet this big pussycat" Justine said.

"Let me know your schedule on Achravie once you get organised and I'll get him to pop over and meet up with you." Rob suggested.

"That would be good, Thanks" Justine replied.

ROB AND JUSTINE stood on the balcony of the apartment where they had stood that first night less than three months ago. Justine sipping at a glass of New Zealand Sauvignon Blanc and Rob with his Malbec Reserva. They stood quietly for a few minutes watching the traffic on the Thames, such as it was on a Sunday evening and the traffic crossing Vauxhall Bridge, which was even at its quietest, fairly constant. Justine appeared to be in another world.

"Is all this moving too quickly for you Tina?" Rob asked finally.

"No! Oh God no! Why. What makes you ask that Rob? Are you having second thoughts?" Justine replied quickly. "Please tell me you're not!"

"No, no! I'm not having second thoughts, I just wondered if you were. You've been very quiet since this afternoon and I just wondered if we were moving a bit too fast for you, that's all."

Justine took Rob's glass from him and put along with her own on the glass topped table on the balcony. She turned and placed her hands behind Rob's neck and looked up at him. "I love you so much Rob" she said with real feeling. "You are the loveliest, most sensitive man I have ever met and I feel safe with you. I know you would never do anything to hurt me, the very opposite in fact. You risked your own life that awful night to save me from God knows what and you did it without thinking twice about it. I know what you did in the past, as you said this afternoon, I've seen your CV and I know that Andy hires you and Joe for protection in dangerous parts of the world, but when we talk about killing people and blowing things up. I don't know, it kind of freaks me out a bit I guess.

I also know that if it wasn't for your past, I might have been raped and killed by these guys that night. When you talked about it this afternoon in the car, it made me think. I'd never thought about what you did in that night and I think I understand a bit more about your motivation for doing it. I suppose it's just taking me a bit of time to get my head round that side of you, that's all. Just give me time, I'll get there, but am I having second thoughts? Absolutely not and yes, we are moving our relationship along quite quickly. But you know what, it just feels like the right thing to do."

As she finished, Justine became aware that she had been

running her thumb up and down the scar on Rob's face, "What happened to the man who did that to you?" She asked

"He died about 30 seconds after he stuck the same knife into my left leg. He really didn't like me!" Rob answered.

"That's what I struggle with, the flippant way you talk about death" Justine shook her head.

"I survived the knife wounds physically, although only just, because of blood loss from the leg wound. Surviving mentally is more difficult sometimes. The closer to death you go, the harder it is to recover mentally, so you get flippant, make jokes about it. It's that or go mad."

"Just help me to understand, it's not that I don't love you Rob" Justine said quietly and picked up their drinks from the table. She carried them into the apartment. "I think you need an early night Mr MacLaine" she called over her shoulder as she headed to master bedroom."

30

THE NEXT MORNING ROB WENT IN TO THE OFFICE TO MEET A client with Joe and one of their senior security personnel for a scheduled quarterly review meeting. He left Justine in the apartment to work on the Achravie project and to make arrangements for the proposed visit to the estate with the architect. She got agreement for the architect him to accompany her on Wednesday and Thursday of that same week then phoned Rob's mother to ask her if she might want to go with them. Justine got a very excited and resounding *"Yes!"* to her proposal just as Rob had predicted.

They arranged that Lizzie would come up to London on the Tuesday evening and stay with them at the apartment as opposed to braving the rigours of a rush hour Winchester to Waterloo commuter train on the Wednesday morning. If Rob was agreeable, he could drive them over to Chiswick where they would meet up with Pete Hall. Justine had already spoken with Sir Andrew Savage, rather than emailing him to propose the use of his otherwise temporarily redundant helicopter. Justine then emailed Rob to let him know and to ask if he would be available to take them to Chiswick. She got a reply about an hour and a half later confirming that he would take them and saying how delighted he was that his mother was going with Justine.

Rob and Justine picked Lizzie Reynolds up from Waterloo station on the Tuesday evening. The station was busy with commuters heading out of London to all points south of the capital. The three of them enjoyed dinner in the apartment with the sliding glass doors open and the sounds of the river and the bridge being carried in with the warm air from outside.

Rob called Fraser McEwan, who by this time was back at work on the estate and told him of his purchase of Angus's shares making him sole owner of Achravie. Fraser was delighted and listened intently to some of Rob's plans for the future.

"I'm going to need a good reliable estate manager Fraser because I won't be there all that often, someone I can trust. I hope you're up for the challenge Fraser" Rob finished his precis.

"Me," replied Fraser, "I'm jist the ghillie Robbie, I've no got the business experience to run an estate like Achravie."

"I don't mean you to, I just need you to run the land side of things. I'll have to get someone to manage the business side and the house on a day to day basis, a kind of general manager if you like, as opposed to an estate manager. Fraser, you know that estate like the back of your hand and to be fair you've been pretty much running that side of it since my father died, from what I gather. All I'm proposing is a little more decision making and a change of job title and a bit more money to boot" Rob explained.

"Aye well, I suppose I could manage that all right, if that's whit ye want" Fraser replied reluctantly.

"Good, because the last thing I need is someone poaching you and you disappearing on me Fraser. I need you where you are" Rob laughed.

"Oh, I'll see off any poachers, young Robbie" Fraser chuckled. "When're we goin' tae see you up here again? I need to ask.

"Not sure, Fraser, but do you remember Justine who came up with Joe Harper?"

"Oh aye, no an easy woman to forget Robbie, wi these great big long legs of hers"

"WELL JUSTINE IS GOING to be running the project for me, great big long legs and all Fraser. She is coming up to Achravie tomorrow, that's why I'm phoning tonight. She's bringing my mother with her, so can you get a couple of rooms in the house ready for them, they'll be staying till Thursday. Oh and they'll need one of the Land Cruisers to get about Fraser."

"Here, don't you tell her whit a said aboot her big long legs. Robbie" Fraser said quietly.

"Too late Fraser, she's here with my mother and you're on speaker phone."

"Oh God no, why did ye no tell me, laddie" Fraser spluttered.

Rob laughed, "Only kidding Fraser, your secret's safe with me."

"That's no funny Robbie, you could gie a man a heart attack like that. Ye say yer mither's coming up, yiv been in touch wi her then, that's good Robbie, she's a guid woman, too guid fir that faither o' yours."

"You'll see her tomorrow Fraser and you can have a good chinwag then. Give Justine all the help she needs, will you and I'll try to get up soon. Cheers for now Fraser" Rob said, ending the call.

Rob went back through from the study and found the two women deep in conversation till they saw him and they stopped suddenly.

"What was all that about?" Rob asked.

"Nothing, just woman's talk" Rob's mother chirped.

"OK" Rob replied sceptically, "OK, Fraser's expecting you tomorrow. He knows what you need and he'll organise things for you."

"I hate to be a pest Rob..." said Justine.

"Well don't be" Rob interrupted her.

"Ha, ha, very droll" Justine chimed back," I'd like to pick up a couple of things from my flat on the way out Rob and it's not really off our way by much. I said we would meet the architect at 10.30, if we leave about 09.00 we could swing by and I could nip in, won't take me a second."

"OK, let's do that then."

31

AT 08.55 THE NEXT MORNING, ROB, HIS MOTHER AND JUSTINE climbed into Rob's "business" car, a Black BMW 4.4L X5 M with darkened rear windows for passenger privacy. The car was fitted with light Kevlar armouring and bullet-proofed glass which offered extra passenger protection, voice activated Bluetooth phone connectivity for ease of use in an emergency and GPS tracker for tracking the vehicle's whereabouts if the need arose.

Like Rob's weekend Maserati, it was fast. Very rapid from a standing start to get out of bad situations fast and had a top speed of in excess of 150mph. Both Rob and Joe had undergone defensive driving training in the Regiment and like their own security operatives were subjected to frequent refresher courses, which Rob secretly enjoyed.

The three were in fairly high spirits as the car took them along the Chelsea Embankment and turned off down a side street to Justine's apartment which sat one block from the river and had views of the river from a corner balcony.

"Don't bother parking Rob, just sit on the double yellow and move if a warden appears, I honestly won't be more than a couple of minutes" Justine suggested as Rob neared the building which housed Justine's third floor apartment.

As Justine jumped out and ran across the pavement heading to the lifts, Rob's phone rang. He stabbed the answer button and Joe's voice rang out over the speakers. He asked if Rob remembered a particular Middle East client they had dealt with about two years back. Rob said he did he was an Emirati and remembered him as a really nice guy, good to work with. Rob had provided him close security for a trip to Jordan. Joe said the client was planning another such trip and had asked if Rob was available to provide the same service.

Neither Rob nor Joe had time nowadays to undertake work which took them out of circulation for two to three weeks at a time and they agreed to diplomatically inform the client of this and to offer him the services of one of their most trusted senior operatives, who now did most of the close security work in the Middle or Far East. They discussed day rates and Joe said he would put together a proposal to the guy and let Rob read over it when he got into the office.

Ron ended the call and subconsciously glanced at the dashboard clock, he had been on the phone with Joe for almost fifteen minutes. "Honestly, a couple of minutes, the woman said mother, you heard her. Is this what my life is going to be like" Rob protested jokingly.

"Better get used to it Rob, this is only the beginning" his mother warned him with a smile.

Rob punched the Bluetooth again and carefully called *"Justine's mobile"*. Seconds later the sound of a phone ringing, it rang for a few seconds then stopped.

"Justine, Justine are you there?" Rob asked but there was no reply "Justine, it's me Rob, speak to me" he persevered, but still no reply.

"Oh sod this" he said impatiently and undid his seatbelt. "I'll go and get her mother, she's probably packing another suitcase. Won't be long. If wardens appear just humour him till we get back" he added as he jumped out of the car and followed Justine into the building.

He took the lift to third floor and turned left into the carpeted corridor heading for Justin's apartment. He was just about to knock and go in when he heard a clatter and a cry of pain from inside the apartment. Rob froze. Another noise, a man's voice and another cry of pain. Rob tried the door, it wasn't locked and Rob entered the hallway. He could see into the lounge and he could see Justine lying on the floor with a man standing over her about to hit her again. Justine's left eye looked red and swollen and she was bleeding from her mouth and nose. The man seemed to sense someone else's presence and looked up, his fist in mid-air.

"Who the fuck are you, what do you want? Get out of here" he snarled.

Justine looked up "Rob!" she sobbed.

Rob saw for the first time that the man had a knife in his other hand and he grabbed Justine's hair and pulled on it.

"Oh, you must be soldier boy, she's told me all about you soldier boy, didn't tell me you were with her though" he jeered at Rob "She didn't tell you about me though, did she?"

"No" he added, "I just did seven years inside because of this one" he looked down at Justine, "but you didn't know I got early release, did you, bitch." And he pulled on her hair again, Justine yelled in pain.

"Let her go and move away from her" Rob said quietly.

Justine's ex-boyfriend laughed, "Oh no, I came here to make sure she never gets another boyfriend. I'm going to mark her so bad that no man will look at her again"

He looked down at Justin again, "Do you hear me bitch?" he shouted at her and tugged her hair again, raising another cry from her. Then he punched her again.

"I said, let her go and move away from her" Rob repeated in

a voice that left no doubt that he meant it. Rob's eyes now had a fierce glint in them and the man didn't realise that he was now about to die.

"And if I don't big soldier boy, what are you going to do about?" he shouted in reply "Eh, what you going to do."

"If you don't let her go by the count of three, I'm going to kill you." Rob answered calmly "Simple choice, one, live, two or die, three". Suddenly Rob looked sharply to his left and unconsciously the man spun his head to follow Rob's sharp movement. In that second, the man took his attention off Justine and Rob launched himself at him right foot first. His foot connected with the unsuspecting man's knee and Rob heard the knee cap shatter. The man screamed in agony as Rob moved behind him trying to stay out of the way of the man's knife and grabbed the top of his head and his jaw. He twisted the man's head viciously and heard the snap of vertebrae at the same time as he felt a sharp pain explode in his right leg. As the man fell and Rob's leg gave under him they both fell backwards on to the floor.

Rob lay still for a second, then pushed the man off him. He raised himself onto one elbow and surveyed his leg. The man had plunged the knife into his right leg and as they fell it had opened up a deep gash in his thigh which was bleeding profusely. He looked across the room to where Justine lay motionless and seemingly unconscious. Please God, let her just be unconscious.

The pain in Rob's leg was sickening and he felt light headed, but he needed to know that Justine was alive. He tried to drag himself across the floor but the world started to go round in circles and stars twinkled somewhere behind his eyes.

"Hello... hello... excuse me, is that your BMW on the double yellow down stairs?" a voice from somewhere called. "Hello."

"In here" Rob managed through the pain "In here" louder this time he thought.

. . .

"WHAT, oh dear God, what's this?" a man in a traffic warden's uniform said as he entered the room and surveyed the mess of bodies and blood.

"Don't just stand there, check Justine, make sure she's alive" Rob said through the pain.

"Rob, are you there, what's happening, the warden was going to ticket you but... Oh my God Rob, what on earth..." Rob's mother stuttered.

"Check on Justine mother, just check on Justine" Rob shouted at her, frustration getting the better of him.

"She's breathing OK" the traffic warden said, "She's taken a bit of a beating, but she's still alive, OK."

"She's coming round Rob" his mother said, now calm and together.

"What about you sir?" the warden asked, "That looks like a nasty gash, you need to stem that blood flow or you'll bleed out in no time."

The warden tool off his belt and wrapped it round Rob's thigh, tightening it as much as he could. He grabbed his radio, calling in the incident and requesting an ambulance and police.

"What about this man?" the warden asked Rob making to check on him.

"He's dead" Rob said with a coldness that stopped the warden in his tracks.

"Rob? Rob?" Rob heard Justine's faint voice, "Rob are you there?"

"He's there Justine darling, he's there, just not very mobile at the moment by the looks of things." His mother replied.

Rob could not believe how calmly his mother was taking all this.

. . .

"I don't understand, what's wrong?" Justine asked trying to sit up and only managing to do so with Lizzie's help.

"It looks as if he has a nasty cut on his leg, my dear" Lizzie explained.

"Rob! Where's Harry, where did he go?" Justine sounded in a panic.

"Harry won't bother us again Tina, don't worry."

"You don't know that" Justine replied.

"Yes, I do, trust me he's not a problem any more" Rob reinforced.

The sounds of sirens outside signalled the arrival of the emergency services and a couple of minutes later the room was full of paramedics, ambulance crews and uniformed police.

Justine by this time was coming round to a more cohesive state and seeing Rob's injury crawled over to him and hugged him tightly. "Oh Rob, what have I done to you?" she sobbed.

"You haven't done anything to me Tina, I should have been more careful" Rob replied "Your Harry stuck the knife in me, not you. He obviously didn't like me either" He added then passed out through pain and loss of blood"

32

THE NEXT THING ROB KNEW HE WAS LYING IN A HOSPITAL BED, with tubes and sensors plugged in everywhere. He looked round the room to find his mother, Joe Harper, nurses, doctors and a policeman, all peering down at him. One of the doctors was checking the monitors which he was attached to and smiled when he saw Rob open his eyes.

"Good of you to join us again Mr MacLaine. We thought we we'd lost you for a while back there in the ambulance. Thankfully your mother remembers your blood type so we got some into you PDQ which helped."

"Justine, where's Justine?" Rob asked.

"Miss Fellows?" the doctor replied, "Just back from an MRI, precautionary measure. We think she has a concussion, but the rest looks worse that it is. The bruising will disappear in a week or so and unless the MRI show something we aren't expecting she'll be right as rain in a couple of weeks."

"Can I go and see her now" Rob asked the doctor. "I need to be sure she's OK,"

"Mr MacLaine, I've just explained her condition to, she is

going to be fine, really, or do you think I am lying to you for some reason?"

"No, of course I don't, I just want to see her, that's all."

"Of course you do, I appreciate that, however just for the time being, may I suggest you stay where you are. You arrested on the way here in the ambulance Mr MacLaine and when we first looked at your leg our initial thought was that you would lose it. However once we got in, we found that it was not as bad as we first feared so we let you keep it.

It is rather sewn together at the moment but provided you don't go galloping across the hospital to see Miss Fellows any time soon, it should mend itself with no long term consequences. Now you can either do as I suggest or you can suffer the ignominy of having your mother tell you what to do in front of everyone in the room. Your decision!"

"OK. OK, I get the message" Rob said in surrender.

"Good, once I've seen the MRI results I'll ask one of the staff to bring her to see you" the doctor suggested as he turned to leave the room.

"No you won't" a tall, slim serious looking young policeman interjected "Not till I get a statement from this one" he said nodding in Rob's direction. "I'm Police Constable Farthing, Metropolitan Police and I'll decide when and if they get to talk to each other" he told the doctor.

"You" he said to Rob, "will stay where you are till I say you can do otherwise. There was a dead man in that room with you two and my job is to investigate the circumstances of his death." He added, a superior, arrogant, nasal twang in his voice."

"Well, I hope you're not expecting overtime on this one sunshine" Rob responded, "There were three people in that room, when the traffic warden arrived, Justine, who was unconscious, the dead guy that you're so worried about and me. So either he killed himself or I killed him and as of now you can take your pick."

"So you admit you killed him, then" the young policemen said in response.

"No I said we were fighting over the knife he was threatening Miss Fellows with, I hurt his knee, he stabbed me in the leg, we both fell over and he must have hit his head, bingo, dead knife wielding thug."

"So that's your statement is it, that's the way it happened according to you. Funny though, his neck was broken, he didn't hit his head" the constable said mockingly

"Joe, should I know that, or should he not have told a suspect, how the victim died?" Rob asked Joe.

"OK so he fell over and broke his neck when he landed, oh dear me, isn't that a pity, what a shame" Rob glared at the policeman, "So there you have it, you've got my statement, case closed. I would like to see my fiancé now please doctor."

"Not going to happen, you're seeing no one till I say so" the constable held out his hand, palm forward facing Rob.

"I'd take a step back from that if I were you" Rob retaliated, "you're getting your ambitions mixed up with your capabilities there. Careful you don't fall over and break your neck while you're biting off more that you can chew."

"Are you threatening me sir" came the reply.

"Me, threaten a police officer, never" Rob replied "Just issuing a bit of a health warning, in *your* best interests of course."

"One more remark like that sir and I'll charge you with a breach of the peace as well as the murder of Harry Goodchild" the young policemen bristled.

"I like that "Getting your ambitions mixed up with your capabilities", yeah, I like that, in fact, I might well use it sometime" said a gravelly voice from the back of the room and all eyes turned to investigate the newcomer.

He held out a Metropolitan Police warrant card as he stepped forward. "DCI Mark Green, Serious and Organised Crime Command. I have just been outside listening to the scenario Mr MacLaine has described. I have also spoken with Miss Fellows, who asks kindly after you Mr MacLaine and am satisfied that the sad and untimely death of Harry Goodchild appears to have been the result of an unfortunate fall. As I seriously out rank you PC Supercilious Twat, I think we can dispense with your investigative skills. So why don't you disappear before I decide to have you stuck out on the streets as of tomorrow morning wearing a pointy hat and helping old ladies across the road and if I ever hear you talking to a witness in that manner again I'll have you do it on the M25. Do I make myself clear?"

"Yes Sir, thank you Sir" PC Twat stuttered and retreated from the room.

"Sorry about Constable Farthing" Green said apologetically, "just spoke to his sergeant down the corridor, he was speaking to Miss Fellows. He says Farthing is straight out of university, full of his own importance and sees himself as fast track material, God forbid. Apparently the lads down the local nick call him Penny, 'cause they're for ever telling him to get on his bike" Green added and they all laughed, except Rob who grimaced in pain when he tried to laugh.

The doctor had been summoned into the corridor but just then stepped back into the room, "That was my colleague telling me that Miss Fellows scan was clear, as we had expected. Let me go and get her to you for a little while, but you need rest Mr MacLaine. Rest, yes?"

"You must be Joe Harper" Green addressed Joe," you spoke to Tony Urquhart earlier. He explained the circumstances and was keen to clear things up for you as soon as possible. I heard what Miss Fellows told sergeant Patel and what you told Farthing, Mr MacLaine and I'm satisfied that any actions you took were well justified. There will be a report go to the judiciary obviously, but we will say that we see on further action being required. It won't even go to court, Rob, no worries there. I'll head off and report back to Tony, leave you to rest as the doctor said."

Green shook hands with Joe and very gingerly with Rob then made for the door. He almost tripped over a porter with Justine in a wheelchair followed by an older man and woman, obviously her parents. Obvious because Rob had just seen a vision of what Justine would look like in later life, tall, slim, elegant and still possessing a beauty which only came with maturity. Her father was also tall and slim with a full head of white hair and a white goatee beard both contrasting with his tanned face. He was walking with the aid of a stick.

Justine looked pale and her right eye was very swollen and bruised as was her bottom lip. She had a butterfly stitch over her right eye, adding to the general puffiness and bruising around the eye.

"Rob" Justine cried when she saw him, "Oh God, Rob what has he done to you?" she asked taking a hold of his hand. "They wouldn't let me see you earlier, they said your condition was serious and that you were still unconscious. I imagined all sorts of things, I even thought I might lose you at one point" she sobbed and kissed his hand.

"You should be so lucky" Rob replied "he stuck a knife in my leg and I lost a lot of blood apparently but they refilled me and sewed me up again. They say I'll be as right as rain in no time"

"Oh Rob, I'm so sorry. This is all my fault, if I hadn't wanted to go back to the flat this would never have happened."

. . .

"Maybe not today Tina, but he would have got to you some other time and I might not have been around to help. He might have killed you on another day and I wouldn't have wanted that. At least now I know you'll be safe, he can't harm you again and OK, I'll have a sore leg for a few weeks but it worth it to know you're safe."

"Is it true, he's dead Rob...?"

"End justifies the means Tina, remember" Rob interrupted.

"You mean...?"

"End justifies the means!" Rob smiled at her, "remember we talked about that?"

Justine looked around the room "Yes, I understand that now, thank you."

"Rob, Lizzie, this is Ingrid and Matt my mum and dad, the hospital called them when I was admitted" She turned to her parents, "Lizzie is Rob's mother, we were flying to Scotland this morning, then this happened. This is Joe Harper, he's the Harper in Harper MacLaine." Justine explained and her parents acknowledged Joe with a wave of the hand and a smile.

"Hi, it's my job to keep this man safe and out of trouble. I'm pretty good at my job too, you should see the states he's come back in when I'm not around" Joe smiled, trying to raise the mood of the room.

There were tears in Ingrid Fellow's eyes as she looked at Rob, "You saved Justine's life today, that monster would have killed her. I can't thank you enough for what you did and look what he did to you" she said her voice starting to break. "Is it right that he will be OK soon? She asked Lizzie.

"So the doctor says" Lizzie replied "he lost a lot of blood but he has had transfusions and there should be no permanent damage to his leg either so, hopeful he will be fine, yes"

Justine's father stepped forward to Rob's bedside and shook his hand gently, "I can only add my thanks Rob, although "thank you" hardly seems adequate when we are taking about our daughter's life. You are a very brave young man, to do what you did. Justine speaks very fondly about you and Andy Savage speaks very highly of you, very highly. We must have you all out to dinner when you feel up to it."

The doctor appeared at the door at that juncture "OK, this young man needs some rest now so can I suggest that we all adjourn till tomorrow" he said to the room and to Rob," the more you rest the quicker you recover. You're young lady here will be just down the corridor tonight so no midnight canoodling the two of you, plenty of time for that when you both get home.

Speaking of which, Miss Fellows could be ready to go home tomorrow although to be on the safe side we may hang on to you for a day or two. You can help us keep this man in check" he joked. They others all said their goodbyes and filed out. Justine was last to leave and she kissed Rob and stroked his hair before saying good night and being taken back to her room in the wheelchair.

33

THE NEXT MORNING, ROB LAY AWAKE IN BED, LISTENING TO THE sounds of the hospital. His leg was throbbing despite the pain killing drip which was inserted via a cannula to his left wrist. During the night the duty doctor had made regular checks on his monitors and at one point had decided to give Rob a further top up of blood, which was now dripping down another tube into another cannula. Rob wondered idly those blood it was that he was now getting.

There was a soft tap on the open door and when Rob turned to see who was there, he saw Joe pushing Justine into the room in a wheelchair. Justine's bruising look darker and more pronounced than it had the previous evening, which Rob had come to expect with bruising. Her eye and lip were still badly swollen but some of the colour was coming back to her face.

"Hi guys" Rob greeted them wanly, the pain in his leg making it difficult for him to sound enthusiastic, but he held out his hand to Justine and she took it and kissed it as she reached his bedside. "How are you this morning" Rob asked.

"A bit battered and bruised, but glad to be alive, thanks to you. More to the point, how are you?" Justine enquired of him.

"Sore this morning, but that's to be expected. I'm going to ask if they can increase the pain relief a bit this morning. They topped up my blood during the night, hence the drip" Rob replied.

"Listen, guys" Joe interjected, "I'm not going to hang about and gate crash this lovers reunion. I just wanted to check that you were both OK so that I can report back to she who must be obeyed with an update on your progress. I also wanted to let you know that your mother and I cancelled the Achravie arrangements and have said that you will get back to everyone when you are fit and healthy again.

We got your car back to the office Rob and it's in a secure area of the car park. Your mother will be in to see you later, she stayed on at the apartment and she'll bring in some of your stuff for you. Andy sends his regards to you both, he called this morning to check on you. I'm going to head for the office now, I feel the need for caffeine coming on. Anything you need from me or the apartment, just shout and I'll get it in to you. OK guys, be good both of you and I'll catch you later."

"Cheers Joe, thanks for popping in. See you later" Rob managed to smile.

"Me too, see you later and thanks for the ride" Justine called after him.

"Happy to be of service" Joe shouted back as he disappeared down the corridor.

"Alone at last!" Rob intoned.

"Rob, what are the police saying about all this? Are they going to arrest you when you get out of here?" Justine asked with a worried expression on her very swollen face.

"What, for? Joe contacted alerted an old mate of ours, who contacted a mate of his, DCI Mark Green, who turned up yesterday, He took control of the police enquiry, and determined that poor Harry broke his neck when he fell over while trying his best to cut my leg off." He smiled dryly. His report to the judiciary will suggest accidental death. He says there will be autopsy because of the circumstances but doesn't think it will even get to court." Rob explained.

"Are you sure, Rob? Did he really break his neck when he fell? Justine frowned.

"Apparently so!" Rob replied looking at the ceiling.

Justine followed Rob's inflection "You killed him, didn't you, you broke his neck" she whispered.

"You may say that, but I couldn't possibly comment" Rob quoted and smiled at Justine.

"Regardless of how he met his end, he is dead, he is a former woman beater and attempted murderer. He will never lay a hand on you again." Rob's eyes hardened and the smile disappeared from his face for a second or so.

A shiver ran down Justine's spine. The professional Rob disappeared as soon as he had appeared but Justine knew that he would always be there, just under the surface. However, Justine was starting to understand her fiancé's psyche and professional Rob no longer frightened her, because twice that person had knowingly put his life in danger to save hers.

"The end justifies the means, you're right Rob" she smiled as she repeated the mantra and squeezed Rob's hand.

"So, the future" Rob changed the subject, "When're you off to Achravie then?" He smiled at Justine.

"You slave driver Rob MacLaine!" Justine laughed "Can we wait till I get rid of the wheelchair, please?" she added.

"I had a thought last night" Rob said, changing the subject again. "You know how we've got that little salmon farm and the trout loch. The estate has just been selling the fish, not really doing anything with it. That makes a small profit but what if we added a bit of value to the fish by smoking and packaging it. We could even produce some other product like smoked salmon pate or smoked trout pate. Create a brand, "Achravie Smokery" or something like that, you're the marketing guru. What do you think?"

"I like the idea, but it would cost a bit to set up and our budgets could be a bit stretched as it is. Let's cost it up though, I do like the idea." Justine considered.

"We might get grants. I could look into that from my sick bed. Sick bed, as in bed I'm sick of already" Rob declared.

"Better get used to it young man" came the voice from the doorway. "We need that leg to be pretty well immobile for a while. The next few days are going to be critical in the healing process longer term" the doctor added.

"So it's my leg that's the problem, that's what is keeping me in bed?" Rob enquired.

"Basically, yes. Although if you did try to stand up, you might just fall over anyway, you'll still be pretty weak from the blood loss, to answer your question. Why do you ask?" Mr MacLaine" the surgeon replied.

"Call me Rob, please. So there's no reason why I can't have my laptop and mobile phone" Rob replied.

"Do you know what" the surgeon said to Justine, "I realised where that was going too late" he smiled. "No Rob, there is no real reason why you can't have these, provided you don't overdo things. I've seen some of the wound scars you have Rob and I dare say you may be a bit blasé about the healing process but trust me, this is probably the most serious wound you have suffered to date and if you disrespect it in any way, you could, no you will, risk the possibility of tearing the stitches holding your leg together at the moment or even more seriously, you will risk an internal bleed. Either way could be "goodbye leg". Do you understand me Rob?"

. . .

"Yes" said Rob quietly taking in the information from the surgeon.

"However and I can see the look on Justine's face, if you do what you are told, you will heal perfectly well. Might even beat me in next years London Marathon, if you are anything like as fit as you look" the surgeon clarified his comments for Justin's benefit.

"If a phone and a laptop will keep you on your best behaviour, then so be it. You're in a private room so you won't bother anyone else, which is always the main concern nowadays. I'll leave you to it for the time being" he added and left with a wave of his hand.

"Please Rob, will you do what he asks? If not for yourself then for me. I'd never forgive myself if you were left disabled because of something I did" Justine pleaded and as Rob started to protest her blame, she added "Rob, you were rescuing me from an ex-boyfriend who might have killed me. If it wasn't for that fact, you wouldn't be in this condition, that's why I couldn't forgive myself. We could never be together if I felt responsible for you losing your leg. I couldn't face you every day."

"OK! Point taken, I'll take it easy, do what I'm told" Rob assured Justine, holding up his hands symbolically.

34

During the next few days, with the aid of his laptop and smartphone Rob was able to do a fair bit of work associated with both Harper MacLaine and Achravie Estate from his hospital room. Joe Harper visited regularly to feed him work and printouts of what he had done and after Justine was discharged a few days later, she visited most afternoons and every evening, often with his mother. Elizabeth had taken to staying with her the odd night to make visiting easier. Rob found the surgeon's regime of rest and more rest for his leg more and more frustrating but after Justine's somewhat impassioned plea, he resolved to do exactly what he was told.

Almost two weeks after the attack, the surgeon suggested that Rob should be able to go home within the next few days if things continued to progress as they had been. Rob took great delight in passing this on to Justine when she visited that afternoon, and Justine almost squealed with delight at the news.

"One thing though Rob" Justine said thoughtfully "I had hoped to get that trip to Achravie with the architect arranged in the next couple of days, if that's OK with you. If you're getting home I need to be there, to watch what you are getting up to, make sure you behave!"

"Fine, I won't be out for a few days yet so, yeah, go for it. It'll let you get on with a few things once the architect has had a look" Rob agreed.

"Good, I've already spoken to Pete Hall and apparently Andy came back from Aruba with a chest infection and he'll be in bed for the next few days, so Pete's still free. He sends his regards, by the way. Let me call him and see what I can arrange, back in a mo'. Do you want anything from the shop by the way?" Justine sounded excited by the prospect of starting to make more progress on her project, which had stalled somewhat as a result of the attack.

"A good rubdown with a hot woman wouldn't go wrong, failing that, a decent Malbec would be good" the reply came.

"No! and no!" was the emphatic and not totally unexpected answer as Justine left the room.

She was back ten minutes later with a wide grin on her face, "All arranged, we're flying up tomorrow. The architect's going to meet me at the Savage building and your mother is coming as well. Pete says there is a small airfield at Popham, quite near Crawley, so Richard is going to drive your mother over and we will pick her up from there."

"I'll tell Fraser" Rob added to the plan.

Justine stayed for a while longer and they recapped on some of the discussion they had had over the past few weeks to fine tune some of the plans they were making and the decisions they had reached. Just before Rob's evening meal was served, she headed back to the apartment to pack for the next day.

"Don't you dare stop off anywhere to pick anything up" Rob shouted after her.

"Oh, I won't" Justine assured him, "In fact, this is probably as good a time as any to tell you. I've had the flat emptied and put it on the market. I couldn't go back there Rob, not after what happened."

"Great, so you're moving in with me permanently? Rob grinned.

"If you'll have me"

"You bet I'll have you."

"ONE THING THOUGH, you need more wardrobe space!" Justine warned. "Must go. I'll call you from Achravie" She kissed Rob and left.

35

THE PHYSIOTHERAPY TEAM WERE WORKING MORE INTENSELY WITH Rob as the internal damage to his leg healed and the surgeons looked to get him ready to be discharged. He was now being encouraged to take regular short walks around the hospital corridors, supporting his still heavily strapped upper leg with the use of a stick. As he limped back from the cafeteria on the second evening of Justine's trip to Achravie, Mars bars in hand, his phone vibrated in his pocket and he stopped to dig it out and as he looked at the screen, saw that the call was from Justine.

"Hello you" he said cheerfully.

"Hello you too" Justine replied "You sound very chirpy!"

"Why not, I'm walking again, I've got Mars bars and I'm coming home in a few days."

"Mars bars? Who brought you in Mars bars?" Justine enquired laughingly.

"Nobody, I went down to the cafeteria and got them, just on my way back now"

"Rob MacLaine, you be careful with that leg!" Justine warned.

"Yeah, yeah, don't worry, walks to the cafeteria are allowed now. They come under the heading of therapy.

"How is the leg?"

"More painful that it's been lately but I'm told that's because I'm exercising it more now and that's bound to have an effect on the pain level. Other than that its fine, doctors and physios are happy with the progress I'm making, so yeah, all positive stuff." Rob responded.

"How about you, how are things in Achravie, how's my mother reacting to being back?"

Achravie's fine. Your mum is really enjoying herself. I'm glad in a way that Pete Hall couldn't pick us up till tomorrow, it's given me a bit more time to get my bearings and your mum a bit more time to catch up with her friends and acquaintances from her time on the island. I've had a few discussions with the architect he's come up with a few ideas that I like and we can go over them when I get back. Your mum's very impressed with our schemes. Fraser was a bit "oh I don't know" at first, but your mum made him see the positive side of the changes."

"He giving you a hard time is he?" Rob laughed.

"No, not a hard time as such. He's just a little frightened that you are putting too much onus on him and that he's going to let you down, which is understandable, he hasn't seen much change on Achravie since he was a young man. I'll tell what, though. He thinks the world of you. Won't hear a bad word said about you. Look after Fraser and you'll get 110% commitment from him in return."

"Yeah, I suppose we really should give some thought to a General Manager, as we talked about. That would probably make him feel a bit more comfortable. It's just finding the right person for the job."

"Well, I just might be able to help you there. Lizzie and I

had dinner last night with Fraser and Lorna joined us, she's lovely Rob. I can see why you two are such good friends. Anyway, we were all chatting and Fraser asked her how things were at the school now. It turns out that since all the trouble and Stella's involvement being uncovered, some of the local parents having been giving her a bit of a hard time over her relationship with Stella and generally making life difficult for her.

SHE HAS ACTUALLY GIVEN THOUGHT to leaving Achravie to look for another job, although she admits, leaving would be a last resort. Lorna's a bright lady, she did Business Management at university, same as me, she loves Achravie, knows the estate, gets on well with Fraser and like Fraser, thinks the world of you…"

"Are you suggesting, what I think you are suggesting?" Rob enquired.

"Offering Lorna the General Manager's position? Yes. I haven't mentioned it to her yet. I wanted to sound you out first, see what you thought about it. I like her Rob, you know her better than I do, but she strikes me as being thoroughly decent and honest and I could certainly work with her. I think we would make a good team, the four of us."

Rob thought for a few seconds, before he replied "If we did offer Lorna the job, it would be because she was the best candidate and you're not just trying to do her a favour as a friend. If you're happy that she is and that's your reason and I have to say, you make a very good case for her, then go for it. Offer her the job. Tell her you've spoken to me and that the offer comes from both of us and is on the best candidate basis."

"OK, good, I'd hoped you would agree. I think it's too good an opportunity to pass up, for all of us."

"I'm standing in the Red Lion car park" Justine added "I'm

meeting Lorna for a drink and she went into the bar a couple of minutes ago, so I'm going to go talk to her now. I'll call you back once we've spoken, if that's OK."

"Sounds good. Good luck, talk soon, love you"

"Mm, love you too. Speak soon, Bye."

Rob got back to his bedside armchair and turned the ringer volume on his phone back up as he was now in the privacy of his room and the ringing of his phone would not disturb anyone. He was reading through a couple of emails from Joe when his phone started playing Eric Clapton's "Layla". Justine, he gave most of the frequent callers their own ringtone and the name on the screen confirmed the call was from Justine's mobile.

"Hi gorgeous" he answered.

"Be careful who you call gorgeous when your girlfriend's sitting next to them" Lorna Cameron laughed "Might get you into trouble one of these days."

"Oops, hey, I need to watch that. How are you, equally gorgeous?"

"Flattery might work for you most of the time Rob MacLaine but I know you too well to fall for your sweet talk."

"Rob, can we be serious for a minute?"

"OK, your minute starts now!"

"Justine has just offered me a job as General Manager at Achravie Estate. She told me that she had spoken to you and that you were in agreement. I'm really flattered by the offer Rob but I'm not convinced you are making it for the right reasons. I don't want a job because you guys feel sorry for me, or feel obliged to..."

"Can I stop you there Lorna?" Rob interrupted. "First of all, this is not Robbie MacLaine the friend that you grew up with that you are speaking to now. This is Rob MacLaine who is putting a lot of money into this regeneration project at Achravie. It cost me £2million just to buy Angus's shares and it's going to cost a lot more than that on top, to fund this project. I don't treat that kind of investment lightly.

I NEED this whole project to work and I need it to make money when it is up and running. I've got other business interests Lorna, you know that, so I can't run the estate on a day to day basis and neither can Justine, although she will be much more involved than I will. Fraser can look after the land side of the estate, just as he always has, but he is not a business manager and that is what Justine and I need. Someone to oversee the day to day management of the company. So think, what do we need in a business manager? We need someone who has the capability to run a business. Someone we can trust. Someone who knows Achravie would be a bonus and someone who would fit into a management team of Justine, Fraser and me.

Secondly, this offer to you is not my idea, its Justine's initiative, all she did was point out to me that, and I quote, Lorna is a bright lady, she did Business Management at university, same as her, she loves Achravie, knows the estate, gets on well with Fraser". She sees you as being a thoroughly decent and honest person she could certainly work with. That's why she wanted to offer you the job Lorna. You fit the profile down to a "T". That's what Justine put to me as a business proposal and that's the business proposal I sanctioned. It's got nothing to do with friendship or sentiment, or feeling sorry for anyone, although the fact that it is you, for me, is a big bonus and I would really look forward to working with you."

"Now do you want the job or not because your minute is just about up?"

"Of course I want the job, but I needed to be sure that I was being offered it for the right reasons and I need to be sure that the job won't affect our friendship Rob, that's too precious to me now that I've got you back in my life."

. . .

"I'm looking Justine in the eye when I say that Rob and she's shaking her head and saying that you think too much of me to let that happen."

"Did she really say all these things about me Rob?" Lorna's voice had a slight quiver in it by now and Rob heard a slight sniff as he answered her "Yes Lorna."

"Rob" Justine's voice was the next one Rob heard "I think we have ourselves a General Manager" she laughed and in the background he heard Lorna say "Yes, you have and I won't let you down, either of you."

36

JUSTINE HAD PHONED THE NEXT MORNING TO TELL ROB THAT SHE had told his mother and Fraser that Lorna was going to be appointed as General Manager of Achravie Estate and while his mother had been pleased by the news, Fraser had been over-joyed. Not only was he getting the support he had so badly craved, but that support would be coming from someone he knew and had treated like a daughter since her own father had left Achravie when she was still at school.

Justine told Rob that Pete Hall was going to be picking them up around midday and that she would see him that later that day, so he was not surprised when Justine and his mother arrived that evening.

Both women kissed Rob and fussed around adjusting cush-ions and glasses on Rob's bedside cabinet before sitting on the bed to talk to Rob in excited tones about their trip to Achravie.

"So, what's happening?" Rob asked impatiently. "Where are we with everything?"

The two women looked at each other, like two excited school girls. It was obvious that they were enjoying each other's company and their involvement with the Achravie project.

"Well", said Justine eventually, we spoke to Lorna again this morning and she has handed in her resignation to the school and was told she had to work her notice period, which is one month. But with the school being on holiday at the moment that's a bit moot, so she can she can start getting involved pretty much right away.

She and Fraser are already sorting out who will do what, lines of responsibility, accountability and so on. We need to agree a role spec and terms and conditions of employment. We talked about some of the hospitality and HSE type training that Lorna is going to need and she is going to look at sourcing all that either in Ayrshire or Glasgow. She is absolutely delighted with the job."

"She's going to be a real asset" his mother chipped in "and Fraser is over the moon, as you might imagine."

After discussing more details and agreeing actions, Justine went to get coffee for them. and Rob's mother leaned over to take his hand.

"Tina's a lovely girl, Rob. She's so open and friendly and she gets on really well with Lorna and Fraser, they've both really taken to her."

Rob smiled, "I wasn't sure how she would interact with Lorna but it was Tina who suggested bringing her on board."

"She understands the different relationships you have with her and Lorna and the two get on extremely well, no jealousy, no resentment. A real friendship blossoming, I would say."

"What about you two" his mother ventured, "You seem close. I know you haven't been together all that long but I sense a real deep bond. She loves you very much Rob, she told me so this morning while we were waiting for Peter Hall."

Rob stared across the room as he determined how to put his feelings into words. "I love her very much, mother. I can't explain the why or wherefore and if you had asked me, I would have told you that I didn't believe in love at first sight. But the minute we met and started to talk, I knew she was going to be someone special in my life."

"Look after her Rob, she's worth her weight in gold and you make a lovely couple" his mother implored him.

AT THAT MOMENT Justine arrived back with two coffees, accompanied by Mr Holmes, Rob's consultant. "Rob, Mrs Reynolds, I found this one doing her best to get some decent coffee out of the cafeteria and she invited me to join you. I hope you don't mind, because I need to talk to you anyway" He said handing Lizzie Reynolds a cup of coffee."

"Justine tells me that's her back home now, so we need to think about getting you back home too" he addressed Rob. "Your latest scan looks really good. The internal injury is healing up probably better than I had envisaged and looks pretty strong now and the physios are more than happy with your progress there. So there's no real reason to keep you here any longer. I think this young lady will keep you in check, make sure you behave and stick with the exercise regime. So please feel free to leave us tomorrow afternoon at whatever time suits. I will arrange a discharge letter and some pain relief for you, to tide you over and you should get that first thing tomorrow morning. You'll get an out-patient appointment to come in and see us in a few weeks just to keep an eye on things"

THE NEXT AFTERNOON, Justine drove Rob home, warning him as they drove that she had added a few personal touches to the apartment since she had moved in and reminding him light-heartedly that he needed more wardrobe space.

"Sounds like a bigger house might be a better idea" Rob laughed as they drove along Chelsea Embankment towards Vauxhall.

. . .

"Mм, in the country with a stream at the bottom of the garden" Justine dreamt out loud.

"Sounds like a plan you've got going there" Rob responded.

"Just a dream. One day, maybe ..." She drove into the underground parking and assisted him to the lift.

In the penthouse apartment, Rob was happily surprised: his mother and Richard were there. "What's this? A welcoming committee? Great to see both of you." He turned to Justine. "Did you know they'd be here?"

"I wasn't sure, Lizzie said that Richard was picking her up this afternoon to take her home but she wasn't sure of timings.

The older couple had been busy in the kitchen when Justine and Rob arrived and seemed to have made up a large plate of sandwiches, which Lizzie Reynolds was now covering with Clingfilm. She turned to Justine, "You mother phoned earlier to say that they were in town and were going to pop in to see Rob at the hospital on the way back home and when I said that you had gone to get him and bring him back here she asked could they would drop by on the way, I said they would be very welcome." Rob she said "They live in Buckinghamshire dear, so it'll be M40 for them. I've done a few sandwiches for you in case you were hungry and in case Tina's parents wanted tea before they set off home."

"Thanks mother, are you not staying for a bit, or have you put something in the sandwiches?" Rob joked.

"No, I have not put something in the sandwiches, cheeky devil!"

"We were just going to go and let you have a bit of time with Mr & Mrs Fellows. They'll be here soon, so we will head off just shortly" Lizzie Reynolds protested.

. . .

"Oh, no, please, my mum and dad would love to say hello again, plus you went to all the trouble with the sandwiches" Justine pleaded, "Richard, you look in need of a cup of tea" she added, taking Richard by the arm and leading him to a chair. Richard, Rob, sit down, I'll make a cup of tea for us."

Justine and Lizzie were arranging cups on a tray when the door buzzer sounded. Justine crossed to the wall phone, answered the call and after a brief exchange, replaced the handset and said that her mother and father were coming up.

When they arrived, they all said their hellos and asked Rob how he was, before going out on to the balcony and sitting round the large glass topped table, talking animatedly about Rob as if he was not there, much to his amusement and both sets of parents were soon chatting happily over the tea and sandwiches.

"Beats afternoon tea at the Ritz" Rob whispered to Justine, nodding to the view of the river and beyond and then at the four parents. Justine nodded and smiled, taking Rob's hand.

"Sorry to say" Richard announced presently, "but we need to head out, I have a Rotary dinner in Winchester tonight, so best beat the traffic on the M25" Rob's mother rose too and they both said their goodbyes to Matt and Ingrid Fellows.

At the door they said goodbye to Justine and Rob. Rob's mother gave him a big hug and said how good it was to see him home and Richard concurred with a firm handshake as opposed to a bear hug.

Rob sat back out on the balcony with Justine's father as the two women gathered the cups and plates and rinsed them and stacked them in the dishwasher.

MATT FELLOWS WALKED over to the glass and stainless steel balustrade and looked out over the Thames. "This is a marvellous view Rob, I can see why Tina was so taken with it the first time she saw it. She loves the sounds of a river, there is a little tributary of the Thames runs along the bottom of our garden at home and she loved to sit there and read when she was young" he said walking back to his chair.

"You've ditched your stick today, Matt" Rob noted.

"Stick? Oh, the walking stick, yes, gone." He laughed "I had these glasses which I hung round my neck with a chain, but Ingrid hated them hanging there. Made me look old she said. So I got talked into these bloody varifocals, first night I wore the dammed things I tripped over my own feet walking down the stairs and twisted my ankle. Hence the walking stick when we visited you in the hospital" Matt shook his head.

"We are looking to move house shortly. Thing's too big for us now. It's getting a bit much for Ingrid and I'm starting to struggle with the garden, so we're going to look for something smaller and more manageable. Tina won't be happy, she loves that house and helped us modernise the interior a couple of years ago, but the exterior and the gardens need a lot of work doing. I think she always saw herself in it after we were gone, but we need something smaller and less work."

"Where abouts in Buckinghamshire are you?" Rob enquired.

"Bourne End, near Marlow."

"OK, I know where you are, I think. Nice area from what I remember, my business partner Joe Harper lives out that direction. We should come out and see you some time, before I go back to work in the office again."

"Why not come out for Sunday lunch this weekend, if you feel up to it?"

"Ingrid" he shouted, "I've just said, why don't the young ones come out for Sunday lunch this weekend."

"Oh, that would be lovely" Ingrid replied.

"OK, consider that a plan" Rob said "Speaking of plans" Rob continued quietly to Matt, "Say nothing to Tina about selling the house for the time being."

37

Sunday afternoon, Justine drove Rob out to her parents' house in Bourne End, it was a beautiful afternoon and the English countryside looked at its best as they drove through Buckinghamshire with the top down on Justine's Mercedes SLK. Justine turned into a narrow country lane as they entered the village and drove past some large secluded houses, before reaching the gravel drive which served the Fellows family home. It was a fairly large traditional house, with white harled walls and red tiled roof. The gardens were extensive and Rob could see why Matt had said the exterior and grounds needed some work doing.

As they parked outside the front entrance, Justine's parents hastened out to meet them. They hugged and kissed their daughter. Ingrid Fellows kissed Rob, albeit more tentatively. Matt shook hands with Rob and ushered him into the house ahead of the women.

The interior of the house belied the traditional exterior. Justine's influence with the interior was abundantly evident in the stylish contemporary décor and furnishings which somehow didn't look at odds with the more traditional aspects of the property. Matt Fellows had said that Justine had helped them modernise the interior and her influence was abundantly evident in the stylish contemporary décor and furnishings which met Rob as they walked through a large reception room, through the dining room into a spacious conservatory.

"You have a beautiful house Matt" Rob commented.

"Thank you Rob. We like it very much. Tina oversaw the refurbishment of the whole house about eighteen months ago. Got an interior designer she was a school with and between them they came up with what you see. Sadly, as I said the other day, we are going to need to look at something smaller now. Ingrid had a slight stroke about nine months ago and although she seems to have made a pretty good recovery, she doesn't have the stamina she had before. Struggles a bit with the house and won't hear of getting some help in. I'm just getting old Rob, plain and simple and I don't have the energy for the gardens now, although I do get a gardener to come in and cut the lawns."

Just at that the two women appeared. "What are you two cooking up?" Justine's mother accused with a smile as they arrived.

"I was hoping you pair were doing the "cooking up" in the kitchen" Matt Fellows laughed, "We were just talking about the refurbishment of the house and..."

"It's a beautiful house Mrs Fellows, I was just admiring the décor. I can see why Tina enjoyed living here when she was younger" Rob interrupted, giving Matt a knowing look.

"Why don't you show Rob around before we sit down for lunch, show him the rest of your handiwork. We'll give you a call when we're ready to eat" Matt suggested.

"Good idea and please, call me Ingrid. Mrs Fellows seems so formal Rob"

Justine helped Rob out of his chair, Rob's leg although healing up well and getting much less painful, still felt very stiff after Rob had been sitting for a while, as he had been in the car, so he was able to walk slowly, taking in details and memorising the layout of the house. Justine showed Rob the family room, kitchen and utility room on the ground floor, the master bedroom with dressing room and en-suite, a further five bedrooms and two additional bathrooms upstairs.

Upon showing him the last bedroom in the northeast corner, Justine opened a door. "Ta-da!" She flourished an arm to indicate a sturdy timber spiral stairway. They descended the stairs with Justine holding Rob's hand for extra balance. At the bottom, Rob found himself in a handsome six-by-six-metre office/study, which boasted a small galley kitchen.

"Wow!" Rob exclaimed "this is one serious study, I love the back stair, makes it almost self-contained."

"That was my idea. That and the galley kitchen. Seemed like a good idea at the time, but I'm not sure it will ever be utilised as I planned it. Justine's folly!" She laughed

"There's a garage with floored attic storage through that wall and there's..."

"Tina, Rob!" Ingrid could be heard shouting to them "lunch is on the table."

"Coming mum" Justine called in reply.

"I was about to say that there is another garage and a gym which we passed on the way in and a heated eight metre pool behind them. We better go through to lunch now, but I'll show you those after lunch."

Lunch was a slow cooked leg of lamb, cooked with garlic, rosemary and red wine followed by a red berry Pavlova. The four talked easily all through the meal Justin's parents and Rob got to know a bit more about each other. Justine and Rob told them some of the detail of the regeneration project on Achravie Estate and Matt Fellows fetched his IPad to find out exactly where the island was.

After lunch, Justine showed Rob the garage, the gym and

the swimming pool. They soon found themselves standing on the river bank, watching the water rattling over the stones and pebbles in the shallows and flowing gently round the larger rocks and boulders in the main channel. Rob could feel any tension in his body ease as he watched and listened to the water. It was almost hypnotic in its effect. A feeling heightened by the warmth of the late afternoon sun on his back.

"Mum kind of hinted to me before lunch that she and dad are thinking of selling up here and looking for something smaller. I know it's selfish of me but I would be really sorry to see it go. I love it here" Justine said, as she stared out at the river.

A smile tugged at Rob's lips. "That study ... I was thinking about it. We could knock through to the garage and form a reception area, and a separate outside entrance. We wouldn't need six bedrooms, so we could use the bedroom at the top of the stairs as a conference/meeting room. That would give us more office space than Harper MacLaine has at the moment. Joe lives in Beaconsfield, which would be closer to here than the office." He hooked an arm around her waist. "It could work."

Justine, turned slowly to stare at Rob. "What!"

"I said.."

"I know what you said! I meant "what", as in "what are you talking about"? Justine stared at Rob, a look of disbelief on her face.

"If we bought the house!" Rob shrugged.

"If we bought the house! What do you mean, if we bought the house?"

"Just that, "If we bought the house!" Your parents are looking to down size, you love the place, and you've just said that you would be really sorry to see it go. I really like it and it has the potential to incorporate a good office for Harper MacLaine if we converted the garage. It sounds to me like a perfect solution all round. What do you think? Are you not keen on the idea?"

"Are you serious?"

"Yeah, do I not sound serious?"

"I never know with you Rob MacLaine, whether you are serious or winding me up."

"I wouldn't wind you up about something like this. I know how you feel about this house."

"You're serious, aren't you, you would actually buy this house, because of me and how I feel about it?"

"Yes!"

"But, what.. how... I don't know what to say Rob. Of course I'd love to be able to buy the house. But, what... I'd want it in both of our names. I'd want us to buy it together, use the money from my flat as part payment. Oh God Rob, we could actually do this. We could buy mum and dad's house and make it our own" A tear ran down Justine's cheek as she spoke. Justine was not prone to bouts of emotion, but the thought of living in the house where she was brought up was so overwhelming that she almost cried with joy.

"Wouldn't it be nice if we were to move into the house as husband and wife?" Rob ventured.

"What? Are asking me to marry you?" For the second time that afternoon, Justine was stunned.

"Can you think of one good reason why we shouldn't get married?

"Are you really asking me to marry you Rob?" Justine repeated.

"OK to avoid any confusion" Rob said taking Justine's hand and painfully kneeling in front of her "Justine Fellows, will you do me the honour of becoming my wife?" he asked looking up at Justine with a smile."

"Oh Rob! Yes, of course I will. I love you so much."

"I heard that!" said an excited Ingrid Fellows, who unbeknown to the young couple had been coming to offer them coffee in the conservatory and was standing just off to their right by a large willow tree.

She rushed forward to hug Justine, "Oh darling I'm so pleased for you" she said with a voice full of emotion.

"I'm delighted your pleased Ingrid, now if you could help my future wife to get me standing up again I would be much obliged. Getting down on one knee may be the done thing when proposing marriage, but it's not such a good idea when you've got a gammy leg" Rob laughed through the pain in his leg.

The two women carefully helped Rob to his feet and both hugged and kissed him. Justine threw her arms around him and held him tight, her tears of happiness soaking into the collar of his shirt. The two women took an arm each of Rob's as they walked back to the conservatory for coffee. As they walked inside Matt Fellows looked up from pouring coffee.

"Thought you had got lost out there" he joked, but stopped when he saw the expressions on the threesome's faces "Am I missing something here" he enquired.

"You better tell him before I do Justine" said an excited Ingrid Fellows.

"Tell me what?"

"Tell you that Rob has asked me to marry him Dad" Justine announced.

"Ah, that's wonderful, darling. Congratulations, to both of you" Matt enthused, hugging and kissing his daughter and shaking hands with his now future son-in-law.

"And, that's not all" Justine went on "If you *are* looking to sell the house as you have hinted at, we would like to buy it. That's what we were talking about out there."

"Well funnily enough, I got a feeling that Rob was thinking along these lines when I spoke to him at his apartment the night he came home from hospital" Matt began "so your mum and I have had a bit of a pow-wow about things as well. This house would have been yours one day anyway, you know that, but if we leave here now, as we have talked about, we need somewhere to live. We had the house valued a few weeks ago and the surveyor suggested we market it at around £1.8 Million. Now we think we would need to spend about half of that to get what we want, where we want it.

We have actually looked at a rather nice 3 bedroom terraced house in a beautiful development for over 55s in Beaconsfield, which would fit the bill nicely. Basically we would need about £900,000. Bearing in mind what I said earlier, if you could give us £900,000 for this house, you can have it now instead of later, we can buy something like that and you can look forward to inheriting a terraced house for over 55s."

"We talked it over Tina and we think it is stupidity for you buy a house that you are going to inherit anyway" Ingrid said "But as dad says we need to live somewhere so we thought this was the best way to do it, everybody wins."

"Wow, I don't know what to say" said a somewhat surprised Justine.

"Just agree and save us all a bit of time" Matt urged.

"ROB?" Justine looked at him for guidance

"From a purely practical point of view, it's an excellent solution. I can see where you are both coming from, but if you change your mind we will give you full market price for the house."

"We've thought it all out Rob, it makes perfect sense. We've no reason to change our minds" Matt replied.

"OK" Rob nodded to Justine.

"Thank you Dad, Mum" Justine hugged her parents "With me selling my flat we can move on your timetable. Just let us know when you want to move things along"

38

JUSTINE DROVE BACK TO LONDON SAYING VERY LITTLE AND answering Rob's conversation with one word answers mostly and eventually Rob left her to her thoughts. When they arrived back in Rob's apartment. Justine dropped her things and opened up the terrace doors.

She walked out and stood on the terrace looking out over the river, the breeze blowing her long blond hair about her face. Rob left her alone as it was clear that was what she wanted and was hanging up his jacket in the wardrobe when he became aware of Justine standing in the bedroom doorway.

"You OK?" he asked.

"Yes, just thinking how my life has changed so much in so short a time."

"You having second thoughts?"

"Oh, absolutely not, I've never been so happy, or so busy. I've got Achravie to organise and now mum and dad's house."

"And a wedding" Rob interrupted

"And a wedding" Justine confirmed. "You're mother and I saw the loveliest little church on Achravie, just outside the village. Can we get married there, Rob, please?"

"Get married on Achravie? Sure, if that's what you want" Rob agreed with a laugh.

"Do you really want to move into our new home as husband and wife?" Justine asked.

"That was just my way of broaching the subject. It probably wouldn't work timescale wise unless we really want it to. I think you're mum and dad will move quickly, they seemed to be quite keen on that house they looked at in Beaconsfield. We can use some of the Achravie funds, if need be, 'till we sell this place and then replace it."

"You're going to sell this apartment?"

"Why would we keep it Tina? It's a brilliant bachelor pad but even now it's kind of short on space. There's the parking as well. We only have two parking spaces allocated and we have your car, my car and the Beamer for work. Anyway, we won't need this place plus your mum and dad's house."

"Mm, I suppose, if you're sure"

39

THE DOOR BUZZER SOUNDED THE NEXT MORNING AND ROB buzzed Joe up for a prearranged meeting to discuss two contract renewals. Justine stopped drying her hair to come and greet him and to allow both of them to break the good news of their wedding.

"That's brilliant, guys, I'm so pleased for you and Suzy will be delighted too. So when's the big day going to be?" enthused Joe.

"Well that's still up for discussion but Tina wants us to get married in the little church on Achravie and with everything else that's going on it'll take a month or two to make all the arrangements" Rob explained.

"What about a Hogmawhat wedding, New Year's Eve, big celebration in your part of the world?"

"Hey, now that's not a bad idea" Rob answered.

"Hogmawhat?" interrupted a very confused Justine.

"He means Hogmanay."

"That's the one! New Year's Eve to southern softies like us" Joe said with a cheery smile.

"New Year, new marriage, how does that sound Tina. We

could have a combined wedding, New Year celebration at Hill-crest. Pipers, ceilidh band, fireworks at midnight!"

"That sounds amazing Rob, let's do it. You're not just a pretty face Joe" Justine enthused.

"Face isn't that pretty either, when you look at it. Still if it's well enough scrubbed on the day it would do for a best man and that's not me asking, it's me telling. If you and that interfering woman you married hadn't sent this young lady to Corfu to look for me, this wouldn't be happening" Rob laughed.

"Of course I'll be your best man, let's face it who else would take on the responsibility of looking after you for a day, with your track record."

The couple went on to tell Joe that they had agreed to buy Justine's parents' house in Bourne End and Rob floated the idea of using part of the house as an office for Harper MacLaine instead of having to make the daily commute to a rented office in London.

Rob showed Joe the floorplan of the property which Matt Fellows had had prepared, to give to an estate agent and the two worked out how the area could be utilised to form a reception area, office accommodation for both Rob and Joe, plus office space for Justine and Achravie Estate as well as a board/meeting room on the first floor.

Joe liked the idea very much as it would cut down his commute by over two hours a day and save on overheads at the same time. There was still more than enough space for a bit of future expansion if need be and he gave his approval to go ahead.

40

AFTER JOE LEFT, ROB CALLED HIS MOTHER TO TELL HER THAT HE and Justine were getting married and had decided to have the ceremony on Achravie on New Year's Eve. Elisabeth was delighted and promised that both she and Richard would be there on the day.

Time passed quickly. Angus said during one of their now regular Skype calls, that he would break a promise he had made to himself after their Father's funeral by returning to Achravie for the wedding.

Three months after agreeing to buy the house in Bourne End, Justine and Rob signed contracts and the house became theirs, Justine's parents, in the interim, bought their house in Beaconsfield.

Having received planning permission for the developments on Achravie, Justine had the final plans from the architect and agreed them with Rob. By a process of tender, she had appointed contractors to carry out the work on both sites to erect the luxury log cabins, build the necessary service buildings, form access roads and landscape the sites.

She had even managed to negotiate grants from the Scottish Government for diversification, which cut down the overall cost and left funds to buy smoking equipment from a small smokehouse in Cornwall which was closing down. Justine's father, a Cornishman by origin knew the owners and alerted Justine and Rob, having been told by Justine about the "smokehouse" conversation in the hospital.

Rob's leg healed well, because he had taken the advice of the surgeons rather than incur Justine's wrath and as the Achravie project progressed he got back to the gym and started running again. Short runs to begin with and slowly progressing to his normal route.

As October passed and November arrived, Justine suggested that they both make a trip to Achravie to inspect the sites and see the progress in case they wanted to make any last minute adjustments to the plans.

They caught a BA flight from Heathrow to Glasgow, picked up a rental car at Glasgow Airport and drove down to Ardrossan. From there it was a ferry to Brodick, a drive to Blackwaterfoot and another ferry to Achravie, arriving at Hillcrest House on Achravie Estate, early evening. They had told Lorna Cameron that they would eat at the Red Lion that evening, but on arrival, discovered that Lorna had cooked a meal for them at Hillcrest. Rob and Justine capitulated on the basis that Lorna joined them for dinner, which she reluctantly agreed to, suggesting that they must be tired after the journey from London.

As the three sat down in the library after enjoying Lorna's cooking and indulging in mostly small talk over the meal, Justine turned to Rob and smiled at him.

"Well, are you going to tell Lorna or am I going to have to tell her?" She asked mischievously.

"Mm, I was going to tell her, but if you want to, that's fine."

"No it would probably be better if you told her Rob."

"You sure, I mean.."

"Tell me what for God sake?" Lorna interrupted, her curiosity getting better of her.

"Don't make any plans for Hogmanay, Lorna."

"What, why?" Lorna exclaimed.

"Because you're going to a wedding" Rob explained.

"A wedding, who's wedding? No! You're not? You are! You're getting married!" Lorna suddenly realised.

"Mm, Hogmanay, here in Achravie church, then back here for a bit of a do" Rob managed before Lorna jumped onto his lap and hugged him tightly.

"Oh Rob, I'm so pleased for you, both of you" she laughed and she ran over to the settee, sat beside Justine and hugged her too.

The two girls laughed and hugged excitedly, then Justine asked, "Pleased enough to be my bridesmaid?"

"Your bridesmaid?"

"Yes."

"Oh Tina, I'd love to, if that's what you want."

"I'd really like you to Lorna, we've got really close over the last few months and I can't think of anyone I would rather have with me when I get married."

"Oh guys, I would love to. I'm so pleased for you. The first time I saw you both together, I just thought how perfect you were for each other." Lorna enthused.

"I think you've got yourself a bridesmaid, Tina" Rob smiled "All we need now is a minister.

The next morning Rob and Justine's news got a similar response from Fraser. He could hardly contain himself at the news and uncharacteristically, hugged Rob and then Justine, before returning to his normal reserved self.

Rob, Justine and Lorna then drove up to the north east of the island to inspect the work being done at the first of the sites. This would be a family site with a younger children's play area and an adventure playground for older children. There was also a café, a small shop and a site office to support the twenty family sized log cabins.

Having spent time with the contractors and made a few minor adjustments to the landscaping, they drove to the other site in the south west of the island. This was an adults only site and had ten two bedroom and two three bedroom cabins, with Hot-Tub Jacuzzis on the verandas. An eighteen hole par three golf course also under construction.

It was close to the village and was within easy reach of the Red Lion's restaurant, local cafes and shops so Rob had stipulated that he did not want to introduce competition to these local businesses. Again they spent some time with the contractors and as with the family site, made a few minor changes to the layout and landscaping of the site. The contractor also suggested some alterations to the site to aid drainage and these were agreed.

They then returned to Hillcrest House for a light sandwich lunch and to discuss other matters concerning the Estate with both Lorna and Fraser. Rob and Justine then had a conference call with the minister who was based in the church in Blackwaterfoot and he agreed to marry the couple at five o'clock on the evening of the 31st December.

This was agreed partly because the minister already had a wedding ceremony to conduct at three o'clock that afternoon and partly because it would allow the minister and his wife to attend the Hogmanay ceilidh at Hillcrest after the wedding. As the couple were talking to the minister, Lorna booked a table for dinner at the Red Lion.

The bar in the Red Lion was busy when the management team of Achravie Estate walked in. Word of Rob's and Justine's impending marriage had spread quickly and a loud cheer went up as they entered the bar. Hamish and Lizzie were behind the bar wearing broad grins as the party approached.

"Ah, it's the new Laird of Achravie an' his intended Lady

Laird, come to grace us wi' his presence the night." Hamish greeted them, "A ha'nae got a forelock that I could touch any mair son but Lizzie here has been practicin' her curtsey awe day. Curtsey to the new Laird, Lizzie."

"Don't you dare, Lizzie Allan" Rob laughed "And you behave yourself Hamish."

"Am no gone tae change the habit o' a lifetime at ma age young Robbie, no even fur the new Laird" Hamish protested "But a will crack a bottle of Champagne tae celebrate wi ye son" he added producing a chilled bottle of Moet from under the bar and popping the cork in theatrical style.

As Hamish poured the fizzing Champagne, Lizzie handed Rob, Justine, Lorna and Fraser a glass each. A second bottle was opened and a few more glasses were poured.

"Quite everyone, quite, please. Ave a few words tae say here. Thank you" Hamish shouted above the noise of the bar.

A hush settled over the bar and all eyes turned to Hamish, who had walked round the bar with Lizzie.

"A knew this man when he was a bairn, then a big gangly boy. Then he left us fur a while, no through ony fault o' his. Then he came back as a grown man and at that time proved the man he was. He rid this island of evil, make no mistake. Now he's back again. No jist as a grown man but as the new Laird of Achravie and he's brought wae him a lady who's to be the new Lady Laird and what a lady, if I may be so bold. The fact that ave opened *two* bottles of *real* Champagne should tell you how much regard I hae fur ye Robbie, *Two* bottles!" Hamish said shaking his head and raising a laugh from the bar patrons.

"The fact that I got them as free samples in the first place, is beside the point," he added with an exaggerated wink, to another burst of laughter.

"But seriously Robbie, I would like on behalf of everyone here to congratulate you and Justine and to wish you every future happiness as the Laird and Lady Laird of Achravie."

"Robbie and Justine, I wish you health and happiness!" Hamish finished as he raised his glass.

"Health and happiness!" the bar patrons echoed.

Rob was visibly taken aback by this and stood silent for a moment, before becoming aware of all eyes in the room on him.

"Eh, thank you, all of you. This is somewhat unexpected. I'm not sure what to say at this point. As you all know we are making a lot of changes at the estate, changes which I hope will benefit the whole island, not just the estate. I've not thought of myself as the Laird of Achravie until tonight, but I am aware of the responsibilities that title brings with it and will do my best to discharge these responsibly. I hope you will all work with me on this and help to make Achravie a better place. Thank you all again for your welcome and your wishes. Let's lift a glass to Achravie and the future."

"Achravie and the future" came the chorus of reply.

"Let's eat" Rob suggested to his companions.

Early the next afternoon, Rob and Justine set off for London again, having had a memorable evening in the Red Lion. Justine was very taken with her future title of Lady Laird and had determined to take the responsibility seriously as Lizzie Reynolds had during her time on Achravie, She had made a mental note to talk to Lizzie when they were back in London.

41

"Remember we talked about moving in as husband and wife" Justine said looking over at the new entrance to the Harper MacLaine offices which was now replacing the double width, up-and-over garage door on her parents' former house.

"Yeah, we still can if you want. The work on the offices won't be finished for a couple weeks yet and it's going to need a tidy up when all the tradesmen have finished. Being as this is us into the last week in November already, why rush it." Rob suggested in reply.

"I've got this thing in my head about us getting married and then coming back here afterwards and you carrying me over the threshold of our new home" Justine added, taking hold of Rob's arm.

"Mm, sounds good to me. What happens then?"

"Well we could go through to the office and check e-mails or we could go upstairs and eh, check out a few other things" Justine laughed coyly.

"OK, you've talked me into it. We should get stuff delivered before we head up to Achravie, get our clothes and the rest of what we are bringing from the apartment brought over too.

That way, we just come back here in January after the wedding celebrations and that's that."

Justine had talked Rob into keeping the river-view penthouse and renting it out, rather than selling. She'd never forget the first night they met and standing on the terrace, looking over the Thames, sipping champagne. That night had changed her life; and as such, she wanted to keep the apartment.

Because of that, they had agreed to buy most of the furniture for the house from Justine's parents; as they'd be furnishing the Vauxhall apartment with the existing furniture and a few bits and pieces from Justine's apartment. The furniture in the house, Justine had argued, was just over a year old, she had chosen most of it and it was chosen to fit the house. She doubted if it would look right in her parents' new townhouse and they saw the logic in Justine's proposal.

"How are we getting up to Achravie? We really should get things booked up, being as Scotland gets a bit busy at New Year I believe" Justine adding a more serious note to the conversation.

"All sorted, I meant to say to you. I had a meeting with Andy Savage last week, as you know. We talked about some upcoming work, something to do with a new product he has been working on. Anyway, we got round to talking about transport and logistics and the upshot of it all is that I have agreed to hire his Agusta complete with Pete Hall for 50 days a year. Achravie Estate will have it for a nominal 35 and Harper MacLaine the other 15 and we can adjust that for invoicing purposes if it works out differently.

Anyway, I've arranged to have it over the New Year period to take us and some of our guests, parents and the like up to Achravie before the wedding and back down afterwards. I've invited Andy and his wife to the wedding as well, by the way. We said we would." Rob looked at Justine for her approval.

"That's brilliant, you don't hang about, do you?" Justine laughed again.

"Well, we're both going to want to get up and down to Achravie pretty regularly and if you saw my day rate to Harper MacLaine clients, you would see that it is more that the cost of Andy's Agusta for a day. It's more cost effective to spend a couple of hours in a chopper and have a billable day, than spend a whole day travelling. It gets us up there in our time, not dependant on when we can get flights and it takes five or six passengers.

Joe wanted to drive up as he and Suzy will either have a new baby with them or Suzy will be in danger of giving birth at any time. Either way they weren't keen on flying, but I managed to persuade them that it was a two and a bit hour ride in comfort in a chopper that could get them to most hospitals on the way up and dammed site quicker than Joe's Audi, if need be." Rob explained with a shrug.

"So Laird, are you going to buy the future Lady Laird of Achravie Sunday lunch or not?" Justine enquired and got a positive response.

42

JUSTINE HAD NOT WANTED A BIG FORMAL WEDDING WITH A profusion of guests that she hardly knew and this had gone down well with Rob who was like minded on the subject. The church in Achravie was small, as most village churches in Scotland are so it made for a reasonable excuse to keep the numbers down.

Rob and Justine flew up to Achravie four days before the end of December, they checked the contractors' progress. Satisfied that all was well there, Justine and Lorna started to finalise the last minute arrangements and details ahead of the big day.

Angus and his family arrived at Heathrow from New Zealand, early on the morning of the second day and were met by their mother and Richard, who Angus had not met till that morning. They in turn, met up with Pete Hall at the Savage building in Chiswick. The four adults and two boys, aged six and three years, squeezed into the Agusta and flew north to Achravie, arriving there just in time for lunch. Rob was straining to meet his brother, who had not seen in over twenty years. Like his mother, he had never met Angus's wife and his nephews, so it was a big day for all the family. Fraser had prepared a temporary helicopter landing area close to the front lawns of Hillcrest and as the Agusta settled, Rob, Justine and Lorna moved forward to meet the rest of Rob's family. Angus had been sitting up front with Pete and he got out first and helped the others out before turning to Rob.

"Hey, baby brother, if I look that good when I've been dead for years I'll be pretty happy!" Angus exclaimed as he appraised the brother he thought was dead and had not seen since he was eighteen years old. The two brothers embraced and slapped each other's backs laughingly. "I couldn't believe mother when she told me you weren't dead, why would Bruce do that. Sure he was an evil bastard, but to tell us you were dead like that, that's crazy Robbie." He turned to Justine who was standing just behind Rob.

"And you are definitely Tina. My mother has talked so much about you, I feel that I know you already. Come and give your new brother-in-law in hug" Angus invited Justine with open arms and gave her a big hug.

"Guys, meet the family" Angus added turning to the others "This is Val, my wife and these two tearaways are Robert and Jaimie" he explained. Val MacLaine stood almost as tall as Angus, slim, with short fair hair and a ready smile. She stepped forward and embraced first Rob then Justine.

"This is amazing" she enthused, "The boys were so excited about the helicopter ride and meeting everyone, now they've gone a bit shy" she added looking down at the two boys who were doing their best to hide behind their mothers legs while appraising these strange new people.

Lizzie and Richard came forward to join in the family reunion. Having introduced each other and started to get to know a bit about each other, they all started off to walk up to the house to catch up on the past twenty or so years and eat the lunch that had been prepared for them, while Pete Hall supervised the offloading of the luggage into two white Achravie Land cruisers.

As the MacLaine family and their close friends talked and ate the buffet lunch, Rob and Angus slowly wandered off to one of the big bay windows and sat on the window seat.

"So, who'd have believed it then, my baby brother, the new Laird of Achravie?" Angus laughed, shaking his head. "What have you been doing with yourself these past twenty years or so?"

Rob smiled, "Mostly military, Black Watch, then Special Forces in Iran, Afghanistan and other places I'm not allowed to talk about 'cause it was all a bit secret squirrel. Left the military, set up Harper MacLaine with Joe Harper, met Justine and we're here to get married. That just about covers it"

"Aye right, as they say in certain parts of New Zealand!" Angus joked.

The brothers laughed and over the next two hours or so, with questions and answers from both sides, filled in the gaps and their relative life stories of the previous twenty years since they had last set eyes on each other. Rob outlined the plans he and Justine had for Achravie Estate and promised to take the family out to see the progress the next day, before the other guests arrived.

They spent the rest of the afternoon and early evening with their new extended families, getting to know them and exchanging stories and anecdotes with them as well as catching up with friends they had not seen for years. They had dinner, a few drinks and then the travel weary group went to bed reasonably early.

The next day Rob and Justine commandeered two of the estate Land Cruisers and took their guests on a tour of the new developments on Achravie, stopping off at the Red Lion for lunch before greeting their next guests brought in by Pete Hall mid-afternoon. His full complement of passengers was made up of Joe and Suzi Harper, Matt and Ingrid Fellows as well as Sir Andrew Savage and his wife Sharon. On their arrival there began a final round of introductions and familiarisations transpired.

They all enjoyed drinks before a lavish dinner prepared by the Red Lion chef and Lizzie Allen in the kitchen in Hillcrest House. After dinner, drinks and coffee were served in the library where more conversation and reminiscence could be heard. Slowly but surely the party retired, in preparation for the wedding and the night of celebration to follow, as was Scottish tradition at the end of one year and the start of a new one.

Rob and Justine stood on the steps of Hillcrest House, their arms wrapped around each other against the cold winter breeze. In line with tradition, Justine and Rob had agreed not to stay under the same roof on the eve of their wedding and Lorna was sitting in her car, engine running, waiting to take Justine back to stay with her till the wedding.

"So, Miss Fellows, this time tomorrow you'll be Mrs MacLaine, Lady Laird of Achravie, you still OK with that?" Rod teased.

"Oh I think I can live with that. It would be nice if Achravie was to be our full time home, wouldn't it?"

"Maybe one day, Tina"

"Maybe sooner that you think, Laird" Justine teased in return, kissed Rob, turned on her heel and walked down to Lorna's car. "Maybe sooner than you think. See you in church!"

Lorna waved as they drove off and Rob stood bemused on the steps of Hillcrest as they drove off. "What, you on about woman?" he mused.

43

THE NEXT MORNING ROB WOKE LATE AND STUCK HIS HEAD OUT OF the curtains of his first floor bedroom.

"Bloody hell!" he exclaimed,

Snow covered the landscape, a rarity in southwest Scotland —but there it was, six inches or so, by the looks of it. Fresh pristine snow as far as he could see. It had been years since he'd seen snow like that.

After a quick shower, he dressed in jeans and a heavy wool sweater, and went downstairs. Most of the others were already sitting at breakfast and he said his good mornings before donning a pair of Wellington boots kept at the back door.

He strolled into the snow-covered courtyard at the rear, and stood and inhaled the sharp morning air. The sky was now clear and the sun was shone brightly; it felt surprisingly warm on his face as he walked up steep hill behind the house.

He gazed across Achravie, towards the Isle of Arran and the Scottish mainland beyond. Rob remembered his boyhood; the visibility and vibrancy had never existed in the hot and dusty warzones of Iran and Afghanistan. This was home—the home of his ancestors, from which he'd been removed by his father as a result of his brother's lies and deceit.

Now, nearly two decades later, Achravie was again his home ... and tonight it would be his and Justine's. While he couldn't live there full-time, it would always be his home and he hoped Justine would grow to share his love of the island in the years to come.

IN THE PAST Rob had always worn the regimental tartan when wearing a kilt, but today for the first time Rob would wear the Modern MacLaine tartan, as would all the men in the wedding party. Angus's two boys would follow suit and they were excited by the prospect of wearing a kilt for the first time.

It was all shaping up to be a day to remember as Rob slithered and slid back down the hill to the warmth of the house and lure of a full Scottish breakfast.

The wedding ceremony was arranged for 15.00hr which gave the family and friends some time to relax and enjoy each other's company and allow the children, large and small to play in the snow and build a snowman in the rear courtyard. Rob and Joe even talked a little business with Sir Andrew and heard of a new product development he was working on, in collaboration with an overseas partner. After lunch, the party went back to their respective rooms and began to prepare themselves for the wedding.

Rob stood looking out of the large bay window which gave a view over the estate towards the village and beyond to the Firth of Clyde. The sky was unseasonably clear and blue and the winter sun was low in the sky, but shining brightly. Looking out, the uninitiated could be forgiven for thinking that the air would be warmed by the sunshine, but as Rob had discovered this morning, nothing could be further than the truth. The still unbroken covering of snow gave a clue as to the outside temperature.

Rob picked up his mobile and called Lorna's number, she answered on the third ring sounding more than a little distracted.

"Just wanted to check if my future wife was still up for this, or whether she had gotten cold feet without walking on the snow" Rob said into the phone.

"WILD HORSES COULDN'T STOP her from becoming your wife today. I had to stop her going to the church an hour ago and waiting for you" Lorna laughed.

"Do you not know its bad luck to talk to the bride on the day of the wedding? She added.

"Is it not, bad luck to *see* the bride before the wedding? Anyway, I'm speaking to you, not the bride to be, so that's allowed. I just wanted to check before I put on this brand new kilt."

"And will anything be worn under this brand new kilt sir?" Lorna teased, looking over at Justine.

"No" came the reply, "Everything will be in perfect working order"

"Too much information Rob!"

"You did ask!"

"Go and put your kilt on and don't you dare be late" Lorna chided Rob.

"Yeah, OK. See you in church"

AT TEN MINUTES TO THREE, with the wedding guests seated in the cosy little church, Rob and Joe, both looking resplendent in their Modern MacLaine kilts and Prince Charlie jackets, stepped from an Achravie Estate Land Cruiser and made the short walk into the church.

They stopped to greet some of their guests and the families as they made their way to the front of the church to await the arrival of the bride.

At twenty minutes past three, the wedding guests, and best man were getting restless, the groom was beginning to fret.

"Where are they, they should be here by now" Rob frowned, worry starting to creep into his voice.

"Bride's prerogative to be late" Joe responded, trying to hide a slight concern he was starting to feel.

At thirty two minutes past three, there was major concern starting to show throughout the church. Something was not right. Rob decided to phone Lorna and with his heart in his mouth pressed the buttons on his phone and waited for a reply.

"No answer" Rob said eventually, "Somethings wrong" he added and started towards the exit.

He got half way down the aisle before he heard someone shout "They're here, they're here!"

Rob turned back to Joe with a smile, "They had me worried for a minute!"

"Excuse me, you've been worried for the last forty minutes" Joe smiled.

The organist started to play the bridal march and Justine, her father and Lorna appeared at the far end of the aisle. Rob looked at Justine. She looked breathtakingly beautiful as she stood smiling at Rob. Her father, like the other males in the wedding party was dressed in kilt and Prince Charlie. Lorna, standing just behind them looked beautiful in a dress of duck egg blue which matched the colour in the MacLaine tartan sash which she wore over the dress that she and Justine had picked in London.

Slowly, it seemed to Rob his bride and her party made their way to join him at the altar.

"The bridal Rolls Royce that you laid on for us is still stuck at the bottom of the hill at Lorna's house" Justine whispered to Rob as they stopped beside him. "She had to call the house to send one of the Land Cruisers to our rescue." she explained quietly.

Rob smiled and shook his head. "I thought you had changed your mind after all"

"On no, you don't get away that easily Rob MacLaine" and with that the minister held up his hands.

"Ladies and Gentlemen, we are gathered here together....."

The ceremony was a simple, informal one as had been requested by both the bride and groom with both parties agreeing to "love, honour and respect" until death did them part. Afterwards the wedding party gathered outside the church for photographs, the bright winter sun reflecting off the snow.

The ceremony was simple and informal with bride and groom happily agreeing to "love, honour and respect" until death did them part. The wedding party gathered outside for photographs with the bright winter sun reflecting off the snow. The photographer, aware that guests were becoming increasingly uncomfortable in the chilly late afternoon air, worked quickly; the rest of the photographs would be taken in the warmth of Hillcrest House.

The evening seemed like a blur to Rob—with more photographs, a welcome line-up, many-course dinner, countless toasts, music and dancing. It was beyond anything he'd dreamed of. He and Justine chatted with guests, danced for hours it seemed, laughed heartily and revelled in the unique mix of wedding celebration and New Year festivities. In the wee sma' hours they collapsed into bed, wrapped their arms around each other, and fell sound asleep.

44

Rob woke with a start, his ultra-sensitive inbuilt alarm system telling him that a phone was ringing. He sat up quickly, his mind focussing instantly, and he gazed at the blond goddess lying beside him.

"I've been here before," he thought as the phone continued ringing, remembering the first night with Justine.

He answered and was met by a panicking Joe Harper. "It's Suzy, Rob! She's in labour. We need to get her to the hospital".

"Be right there," he said, already on his feet and pulling on jeans and a sweater.

"What's wrong?" Justine mumbled, not fully awake.

"Suzy's in labour. We need to get her to hospital."

"What!" Justine jumped to her feet and quickly began dressing.

They ran down the hall to the room Joe and Suzy were in, knocked and entered. Sure enough, Suzy's water had broken and she was experiencing contractions.

"You sober?" Rob asked Joe, scanning his pale face.

"I didn't drink much, just in case."

"Good, you're driving. We'll grab a Land Cruiser. Justine, wrap a blanket round Suzy and help me get her downstairs."

They helped her into the Land Cruiser and drove as quickly as the snow covered roads would allow. The Cottage Hospital was less than ten minutes away from Hillcrest House. Suzy was wheeled into a delivery room.

AT 4.57 ON the first of January, baby James Harper came into the world, a healthy lad with a good set of lungs by all accounts.

Justine, Joe and Rob sat in the waiting room to let the staff do what they had to do and drank watery coffee from a vending machine.

"You do realise that your son is Scottish" Rob said eventually

"No!"

"Yes. Did you not hear his accent when he was crying earlier?"

"No. Oh God we'll never understand a word he says" Joe help his head in his hands

"I'll translate for you, it'll be OK. He'll need a kilt and a Scotland top"

"Rubbish he'll get a cricket bat and an England rugby shirt, like any other child" Rob protested.

Rob noticed Justine sitting quietly through the banter, and smiled over to her.

"Listen Joe, all joking aside, we're going to head back up to Hillcrest, leave you to get on with the "need to does" that new babies bring with them.

Rob and Justine left Joe, Suzi and their new baby and drove back up to the house. The journey was fairly quiet apart from comments from both about the snow and not expecting to be wakened so early on their first night as husband and wife.

Justine and Rob were alone in their bedroom "Before we got

married yesterday, did you give any more thought to the fact that I can't give you a child Rob?" Justine asked with a frown creasing her forehead.

"What?" Rob looked startled

"Before the wedding yesterday, did you give any more thought to the fact that I can't give you a child? Now that you are the Laird of Achravie, having an heir takes on a different dimension. What happens to all this when you die?

Rob sat on the edge of the bed and looked over at Justine who was leaning against the bathroom door, holding her robe tightly around herself.

"No!" Rob responded without a moment's hesitation

"It didn't cross my mind. The only wobble I had yesterday was that maybe you would change your mind. That's why I phoned Lorna yesterday and when you didn't turn up till after half three, I was convinced you weren't going to come. I've never taken it for granted that you would go through with this marriage. I know how you feel about my background and have never been convinced that you had fully come to terms with what I do.

But children? No, never crossed my mind. For me yesterday was all about you becoming Mrs MacLaine and me becoming your husband. Being Laird of Achravie will always be important to me, it's a big responsibility, for both of us now, but it will never take priority over what I feel for you"

"But what about an heir?"

"Would you want kids if you were able to?" Rob ventured

"Yes, I'd always seen myself as a mother until...."

"Then maybe we can look at adopting if and when we feel we are ready. There are a lot of kids out there needing good homes and adopted kids can be a real part of the family. I told you once before, kids are not an issue for me and that's still the case."

. . .

Rob stepped over to Justine and held her tightly to him. "You're what's important to me and I think I can prove that," he said, lifted her up and carried her over to the king-sized bed.

Later that morning, having risen late, Rob & Justine met with Joe at breakfast. He'd phoned the hospital to get an update on Suzi and James, and late morning all three went to Cottage Hospital to bring Suzy and baby back.

Guests started leaving. Angus and his family, Elizabeth and Richard, returned to London. Rob's parents would meet up with him and Justine later in the week.

The remnants of the celebrations the previous evening were cleared away and Hillcrest House returned to normality. Justine met up with Lorna and Fraser to discuss issues wth the development work.

Justine was keen to see the lodges finished so they could be photographed for marketing materials, including a website. Rob was intrigued with the progress with Achravie Smokery, which he treated as his pet project.

In the evening, Joe and Rob went to the Red Lion in the evening, to "wet the baby's head" and returned to Hillcrest at ten o'clock so that Joe could "help" Suzi feed young James.

Just after eleven, Rob and Justine were finally alone in their bedroom. Justine stood beside Rob, looking out the window to the snowy landscape. There was a mostly clear sky and the bright moonlight reflected on the landscape.

She slipped her arms round his waist. "Thank you for what you said last night – about not being able to have children of our own."

"I meant it Tina, this – our marriage, Achravie, our future together – it's all about us – you and me. You were totally honest with me about not being able to have children. It's not an issue for me, it's *you* I love. Owning Achravie doesn't change that. If anything happens to me then Angus's boys can inherit and fight over it."

"Let's go to bed" Justine said quietly, with a coy smile.

45

The next morning, Pete Hall ferried more of the guests, including Joe, Suzy and young James, back to London. With instructions to return for Andrew Savage, his wife and Rob & Justine around mid-afternoon.

Rob and Justine had some more discussions with Lorna and Fraser to make sure everyone was up to speed with the changes, alterations and progress with the redevelopment. After the meeting they all went down to the Red Lion for lunch, which gave Rob and Justine the opportunity to thank Hamish Allen and his daughter Lizzie who had provided the catering for the festivities.

The journey south in the Agusta that afternoon, was pleasant and uneventful, the109 E Grand was a comfortable machine. The two women discussed a variety of topics with Sir Andrew and Rob talking a bit of business and Sir Andrew giving Rob a heads–up on a new project his company was working on with a UK based drone manufacturer and a small munitions manufacturer, which was already attracting a great deal of interest with a select number of clients they had briefed on the project, including the UK and US military.

Sir Andrew said that a very hush-hush demo was being arranged for these select few and suggested that he might want Rob along in his professional capacity. Rob said he would be happy to be there if he was free and Sir Andrew promised to email him the dates once the final arrangements had been made.

The two couples parted company when the Agusta dropped Rob & Justine off at Wycombe Air Park also known as Booker Airfield in South Buckinghamshire, where Rob had parked the black Harper MacLaine BMW X5 M5 before their journey north to Achravie. It was dark as they drove through Bourne End and up the narrow lane to their new home.

Rob had had new electric gates and a secure entry system installed while they were away and as he reached for the remote button to open them, his eyes were drawn to an equally new illuminated slate name plate on the stone pillar. He stopped the car and stared at it. The white lettering on the sign read "Achravie".

"Post Office weren't too pleased about the change of name, but hey-ho, I thought you might like to live at Achravie full time" Justine explained.

"You did this? I had no idea. Is this what you meant when you said "Maybe sooner than you think" Justine just nodded, "That's brilliant Tina" Rob was flabbergasted.

"Welcome home Laird, you just need to carry the Lady Laird over the threshold now" Justine said with a smile, patting Rob's knee.

Dear reader,

We hope you enjoyed reading *The Prodigal Son*. Please take a moment to leave a review in Amazon, even if it's a short one. Your opinion is important to us.

Discover more books by Les Haswell at https://www.nextchapter.pub/authors/les-haswell

Want to know when one of our books is free or discounted for Kindle? Join the newsletter at http://eepurl.com/bqqB3H

Best regards,
Les Haswell and the Next Chapter Team

The Prodigal Son
ISBN: 978-4-86750-757-5

Published by
Next Chapter
1-60-20 Minami-Otsuka
170-0005 Toshima-Ku, Tokyo
+818035793528

9th June 2021